The Lady's Protector

Books by Emma Prince

Highland Bodyguards Series:
The Lady's Protector (Book 1)
Book 2 coming summer 2016!

The Sinclair Brothers Trilogy:
Highlander's Ransom (Book 1)
Highlander's Redemption (Book 2)
Highlander's Return (Bonus Novella, Book 2.5)
Highlander's Reckoning (Book 3)

Viking Lore Series:
Enthralled (Viking Lore, Book 1)
Shieldmaiden's Revenge (Viking Lore, Book 2)
The Bride Prize (Viking Lore, Book 2.5)
Desire's Hostage (Viking Lore, Book 3)

Other Books:
Wish upon a Winter Solstice
(A Highland Holiday Novella)

The Lady's Protector

Highland Bodyguards

Book One

By

Emma Prince

The Lady's Protector
(Highland Bodyguards, Book 1)

Copyright © 2016 by Emma Prince
Print Edition

All rights reserved. No part of this publication may be reproduced, distributed, or transmitted in any form or by any means, or stored in a database or retrieval system, without the prior written permission of the author except in the case of brief quotations embodied in critical articles and reviews. For more information, contact emmaprincebooks@gmail.com.

This is a work of fiction. Names, characters, organizations, places, events, and incidents are the products of the author's imagination or are used fictitiously. Any resemblance to actual events or persons, living or dead, is entirely coincidental. V 1

For Scott. Always.

Chapter One

Dunrobin Castle, Scottish Highlands
Late September, 1314

"A Sinclair approaches!"

Ansel Sutherland froze in mid-attack. His sword hung in the air between himself and his opponent, flashing in the late-afternoon sun.

With a flick of his wrist, he spun the sword around and tossed it hilt-first to the young Sutherland lad he'd been sparring with. The lad, Peter, fumbled with his own blade as Ansel's sailed toward him. He dropped his sword just in time to catch Ansel's weapon.

"What did I tell ye about respecting yer blade, Peter?" Ansel said over his shoulder as he strode toward Dunrobin's thick stone wall.

The lad stammered in an attempt to form an answer, his tongue as clumsy as his hands. Perhaps Ansel would have to go back to the wooden practice sword with the boy.

As he mounted the stairs that rose from the yard up the inside of the wall, Ansel shoved all thoughts of Peter and his awkwardness aside.

"Show me," he said tersely to the guard who stood atop the wall's parapet.

The guard pointed off to the south, where the forest sheared away to provide long sightlines from the walls of the Sutherland clan's defensive stronghold.

Ansel raised a hand to shield his eyes from the slanting afternoon sun. Sure enough, a rider approached—and he was cutting a resolute path directly toward Dunrobin Castle.

"Shall I call for the archers, my lord?" the guard asked, his voice tight.

Ansel squinted in the bright light. The lone rider did indeed bear the Sinclairs' distinctive red and green patterned plaid over his shoulder. It made the man stand out like a sore thumb in Sutherland territory, where they wore their blue and green plaid with pride.

But the Sinclairs resided to the north of Dunrobin. Unease slid up his spine. Why would this man be riding with such determination from the south?

"Nay, no' just yet," Ansel said to the guard, never taking his gaze from the rider. There was something familiar about the dark-headed figure riding hard for Dunrobin's gates.

Though the guard remained tense at his side, Ansel felt his apprehension dissipate with each stride of the warhorse beneath the Sinclair rider. By the time the abnormally curved bow over the rider's shoulder came clearly into view, Ansel had called for the gates to be opened.

"Garrick Sinclair!" Ansel barked when the rider reined his warhorse within Dunrobin's yard. He bounded down the stairs from the wall and strode toward Garrick.

The two embraced heartily, exchanging hard thumps on the back. But then Garrick tensed, his gaze locking on the wall behind Ansel.

Ansel glanced over his shoulder to find the guard who'd spotted Garrick, along with several others, watching their exchange warily, their hands resting on their weapons.

"Stand down, men," Ansel snapped. "This is one of King Robert the Bruce's most trusted warriors. He is an ally to Laird Sutherland and all within the clan." Ansel turned back to Garrick and lifted a skeptical brow at the red plaid. "Sinclair or nay," he added wryly.

The guards on the wall's parapet relaxed somewhat, dropping their hands to their sides, but several still looked warily at Garrick's Sinclair plaid.

"It's no' every day that we see the Sinclair colors tearing across our land, let alone flapping in the middle of Dunrobin's yard," Ansel said, eyeing his travel-worn friend.

Garrick snorted, though his steel-gray eyes flickered with merriment. "Trust me, I didnae come to this viper's den willingly."

Icy trepidation slid into Ansel's veins. "What brings ye away from the King's side? Is all well?"

"Aye," Garrick said quickly. "Though there is a

matter of some urgency I wished to discuss with ye."

"Laird Sutherland isnae here, if that is who ye need."

"Nay, it's ye I came to see," Garrick said.

That same cold unease pulsed stronger. What could possibly draw Garrick away from the Bruce and send him into Sutherland territory? And what did it have to do with Ansel?

With a curt wave, Ansel motioned Peter over. The lad had retrieved his blade from the ground and now held both his and Ansel's swords in his hands. Though he was trying valiantly to stand up straight in the face of a Sinclair, Peter stared at Garrick with rounded eyes.

Although the Sinclairs and the Sutherlands had been united under Robert the Bruce and the fight for Scottish independence for nigh a decade, the centuries-old tension between the two clans wouldn't fade so quickly. Peter's face, along with the wary guards perched on the wall, told Ansel as much.

"See to Garrick's horse, lad," Ansel said sternly as he took his sword from Peter's hand and re-sheathed it.

Peter could only manage a nod and another darting glance at Garrick before taking hold of the warhorse's reins and leading the animal toward the stables.

"Come, friend," Ansel said, motioning toward the stone keep at the far end of the yard. "Ye could likely do with some refreshment."

As Ansel led Garrick into the keep, he called to one of the serving maids for ale.

"Aye, my lord," the maid said, her wide-eyed stare at Garrick matching Peter's.

They crossed through the great hall, but Ansel didn't stop at the high table atop the raised dais where guests were normally entertained. Instead, he continued on to a small chamber that he and the Laird often used to discuss more delicate matters of strategy.

"So yer cousin isnae here?" Garrick asked as he stepped into the cramped chamber. He removed the unusually curved bow from his back and propped it against one of the few chairs that furnished the small space, then sat.

"Aye, Kenneth is with the McKays discussing our northwest border. Apparently the sheep stealing has started up again."

Garrick snorted again, but this time there was no mirth in it. "Just a few bloody months after Bannockburn, and we Highlanders are nipping at each other once more. So much for a country united behind the Bruce."

Ansel sat down across from Garrick. "It's no' so bad as that. Aye, we bicker amongst ourselves, but now that the English have their tails between their legs—"

Just then, the door opened and the serving maid ducked in with two pewter mugs of ale. Once she'd handed them to Ansel and Garrick, she scurried away, closing the door swiftly behind her.

"Ye were saying?" Garrick said dryly, setting the mug on a small table next to him. "I see the way ye

Sutherlands look at me. We'll be lucky if we can sustain the victory of Bannockburn another year before we turn on each other like we always do."

Garrick's words struck deep. Aye, the Battle of Bannockburn had only taken place this past June. Ansel had been at Garrick's side, fighting under the Bruce for freedom. And yet now that he was back at Dunrobin, far from the battlefield and the Bruce's camp, the petty squabbles between the clans were sprouting like weeds.

"Bloody hell," Ansel said, suddenly weary. "I wonder at times if we will ever truly know peace."

Garrick leaned back in his chair and considered Ansel for a long moment. "The news I bring may no' be welcome, then."

"Ye say all is well with the Bruce and the cause," Ansel replied. "Yet I ken ye wouldnae ride across Sutherland territory simply for the view and the fresh air. Out with it, man."

Garrick's gray eyes filled with hard assessment as he continued to study Ansel for another moment. Ansel waited, unease knotting in the pit of his stomach. What in bloody hell did Garrick have to say that gave the man such pause?

At last Garrick spoke, seeming to choose his words carefully.

"A little over a sennight ago, the Bruce received a missive with a request for help. Someone may be in danger—someone of great import. The man who contacted the Bruce wished for one of the King's best warriors to provide the protection and skill necessary to keep that someone safe."

Ansel slowly leaned his elbows on the wooden arms of his chair. "And why does this request bring ye to Dunrobin?"

"The Bruce initially thought to put me on the mission, but he requires me at his side for the time being."

"Ye are still in the Borderlands with him and his army, are ye no'?"

"Aye. With the English still off-kilter after Bannockburn, we are reclaiming much of what they have taken from us," Garrick replied. His gray eyes flickered with a wolfish determination for a moment. "Though we are making great strides, the Bruce still needs my skills at his disposal."

Garrick was known throughout the Highlands—and perhaps the Lowlands and England as well—as one of the deadliest archers to ever draw an arrow. He'd been serving the Bruce and the cause for Scottish freedom almost since the beginning of the Bruce's quest for the crown. Ansel had fought alongside Garrick enough times to know just how valuable a warrior he was to their King.

"And so ye sought me, with the Bruce's blessing?"

"Aye."

"Why?"

Garrick's mouth quirked in a lopsided smile. "Fishing for compliments?"

Ansel snorted. "If I were, ye'd be the last man I'd seek. I might as well be talking to Dunrobin's curtain wall for all the information I've gotten out of ye since ye crossed into the keep."

Garrick arched a dark brow for a moment, but then his hard features grew serious. "I'll be honest with ye, then. Ye have been one of the Bruce's most prized warriors since ye joined the cause all those years ago. Ye earned yer spot in his inner circle when ye helped him secure his ancestral home from Raef Warren and the English."

Ansel felt pride curve his lips at the memory. Six years ago, he'd been called from Dunrobin in the Highlands to Loch Doon Castle in the southwest, the keep Robert the Bruce had built with his own two hands. Loch Doon had been dangerously close to falling into the hands of the English, yet they'd driven back their enemies and secured the castle. It had been Ansel's first taste of victory in the Scottish battle for freedom—the sweetness of that success had seen him through many hard years since.

"No' that ye needed to, but ye proved yerself yet again at Bannockburn. The Bruce is proud to call ye one of the finest warriors he's ever known. Since I cannae offer the help requested of the King, the only other man I'd consider for the job was ye."

"I thank ye for yer honeyed words, Garrick," Ansel said wryly. "I know they dinnae come easily to ye. I still dinnae ken how Jossalyn puts up with ye."

Garrick rolled his eyes at the mention of his wife, who worked as a healer in the Bruce's camp. Though he enjoyed teasing Garrick, Ansel had spent enough time in the Bruce's army to know just how deep Jossalyn and Garrick's love ran.

He swiftly thrust aside such soft thoughts. Like Garrick, Ansel had dedicated his life to serving men more important than he was. They both worked under their respective Lairds—Laird Sinclair was Garrick's older brother, and Laird Sutherland was Ansel's cousin—and both had pledged themselves to Robert the Bruce, King of Scotland. Yet unlike Garrick, Ansel found little room for love or marriage in the midst of his duties to clan, King, and country.

"Who is this crucial person in need of protection?" Ansel asked, growing serious once more.

Garrick hesitated for one beat before answering.

"He is the bastard son of the Earl of Lancaster."

The low level of unease that had been simmering in Ansel's stomach flared suddenly. "Lancaster's son? And who requested yer help in protecting him?" He feared he already knew the answer, but he had to hear it from Garrick's mouth.

"Lancaster himself."

Bloody hell.

Ansel stood so swiftly that his chair tipped back and clattered to the floor. Outrage ignited within him like a flame in dry kindling.

"Ye are saying," he began, pinning Garrick with a

hard stare, "that the Earl of Lancaster sent King Robert the Bruce a missive requesting that *ye*, a Scottish rebel, help *him*, a scheming English nobleman—and King Edward's cousin, no less—by protecting his son?"

"Aye."

"And ye are asking *me* to take yer place and watch over the man's son—at Lancaster's request?"

"Aye."

"And why in bloody hell would I help some English noble do aught other than warm my blade with his blood? Last I checked, the English are still our enemies."

Garrick actually had the nerve to throw back his dark head and laugh. And laugh. And laugh.

Ansel righted his chair but found he wasn't ready to sit just yet, even though it took Garrick several long moments to regain control of himself.

"That is just what I said when the Bruce proposed this mission to me a sennight ago," Garrick crowed when he was finally able to speak again.

"And what did the Bruce say to convince ye to ride to Dunrobin with such a preposterous task?" Ansel ground out through clenched teeth.

All mirth fell completely away from Garrick then. He leaned forward in his chair, pinning Ansel with stormy gray eyes.

"He reminded me that the enemy of my enemy is my friend. Lancaster has been a thorn in King Edward's side for years. But now with Edward's defeat at Bannockburn, Lancaster stands to bring down Edward once and for all—and perhaps even become King of England himself."

Though Ansel prided himself on his normally unflappable nature, he did nothing to attempt to hide his stunned confusion from Garrick.

"I knew Lancaster has been giving Edward trouble for some time, but are ye jesting, man? Ye're speaking of civil war in England. Ye truly think Lancaster will make a play for the throne?"

"Aye, so our sources say," Garrick replied soberly. "From the moment Edward replaced Longshanks as King, Lancaster has been working against him. Now Lancaster has come out publicly to oppose his cousin's reign. Bannockburn only proved what Lancaster has been saying all along about Edward—that he is a weak and ineffectual ruler."

Ansel shook his head in astonishment, the wheels of understanding grinding slowly. Before he could form his next question, Garrick went on.

"Which brings us back to why I'm here. Lancaster fears that his bastard son will be used as a weapon against him. Edward's allies may come after him, either to ransom him back to Lancaster, or more likely to simply kill him and end Lancaster's bloodline if he is successful in gaining the throne."

"Lancaster doesnae have any legitimate heirs?"

"Nay," Garrick said. "He has been bound in an unproductive marriage since he was fourteen. He has only sired the one bastard. If he somehow managed to ascend to power, his son will be in serious danger—hell, he likely already is."

Ansel released a slow breath through his teeth. At last, he lowered himself into his chair once more, though he had to grip the wooden arms to give his hands something to do.

"And ye think that having Lancaster ruling England is better than Edward?"

"One of Lancaster's main qualms with his cousin's rule is that Edward has wasted countless men, time, and coin fighting against the Bruce," Garrick said with a shrug. "Lancaster has vowed that he will see an end to these fruitless wars once and for all—either by blocking Edward from taking action or by wresting the throne from his cousin and halting the wars himself."

Finally, Ansel's initial shock was ebbing and he could see the threads of strategy weaving together in his mind.

"So the Bruce considers Lancaster the enemy of his enemy—King Edward. He thinks that if the Scots offer to aid Lancaster, when Lancaster comes to power, he'll leave us be."

"Aye."

"Answer me this, then. Lancaster wishes to end England's conflict with Scotland. But isnae that exactly what we already accomplished with Bannockburn?" Ansel asked. "Granted, ye and the Bruce's army are still finishing the work that must be done—taking back what was ours. But the war is over, Garrick. The English are whipped and on the run. All has been quiet since June, thank God. We dinnae need Lancaster at all."

"That is where ye're wrong, Ansel," Garrick said, his mouth drawing tight. "The battles may have stopped for the time being, but the war is far from over. The English arenae going to hand us our freedom so easily."

Ansel crossed his arms over his chest against a fresh surge of unease. "What are ye saying?"

"Remember the days when the Bruce's army tried to play by English rules on the battlefield? We met them in open combat, face to face, just as they wished?"

"Aye," Ansel replied. "And we had our arses handed to us many a time until ye encouraged the Bruce to fight differently."

"We learned how to use the land we know and love so well to conceal us," Garrick said, leaning forward intently. "We struck swiftly and silently, then dissolved away so that they couldnae strike back. It changed the course of the war."

At Ansel's cautious nod, Garrick exhaled and sat back once more. "And now the English are changing the nature of war themselves. They willnae meet us in open combat after the mess they made of Bannockburn. But that doesnae mean that they have given up trying to undermine our efforts for freedom."

A dagger of dread slashed through Ansel's gut. "What has happened?"

"Sir William of Airth was found murdered. And no' cleanly, either."

The slice of dread turned into a hot knot of anger. William of Airth controlled a small region in the Lowlands. Though Ansel hadn't spent much time with him, he'd met the man at Bannockburn and had fought by his side.

"What did they do to him?" he ground out.

"He was tortured first, from what we could gather. There wasnae much of him left, to be honest. Whoever it was, they tried to get answers out of him, though he never was privy to the Bruce's plans. Like as no', the bastards hoped to send a message—even lords arenae safe in Scotland. That's the third one to be murdered in as many months since Bannockburn."

Ansel let out a long breath. "War used to be men with swords facing off. And now this. Is this war, or is this what peace looks like?" he muttered, suddenly heartsick and weary.

"I dinnae relish this any more than ye, Ansel," Garrick said lowly. "But yer King is calling on ye. He needs ye for this mission. Protect Lancaster's bastard-born son."

Honor tugged hard in Ansel's chest, yet the thought of working for an English nobleman sent sour bile rising in his throat.

"Why does Lancaster want a Scot? Why no' send

one of the many English lackeys I'm sure he keeps at his heels to protect his son?"

Garrick's mouth twisted, but he managed to refrain from laughing this time.

"The Bruce thinks it is Lancaster's attempt to strengthen ties between himself and the Scottish freedom fighters, but I'm no' so generous. I trust Lancaster about as far as I can throw him. I'd place coin on Lancaster thinking strategically in calling on a Scottish warrior to guard his son. If word gets back to Edward that Lancaster is working with us, or if things go south for his son, a Scot is a lot easier to disavow or stow away somewhere—or get rid of, if need be. Lancaster is counting on discretion—that's why he approached the Bruce in the first place."

"So I am to be the sacrificial lamb," Ansel bit out. "I am to be Lancaster's pawn in his little game of playing allies with the Bruce."

Garrick's lips twitched, but it looked more like a wince than a smile. "I said the Bruce hopes for Lancaster to leave us alone, no' that the man would be our ally. That is also why the Bruce wished for me to send for ye. He trusts in yer sense of honor and responsibility, and yer skill to protect the bastard son, but also yer cautiousness. The Bruce is counting on ye to remember that yer mission is to protect the son, no' serve Lancaster. In protecting the Earl's bastard, ye are serving *our* King, no' the English."

A stone of resignation sank in Ansel's stomach.

There was clearly no way he was going to talk his way out of this task, no matter how much it repulsed him to do an English nobleman's bidding. He'd placed his faith, his trust, and his life in Robert the Bruce's hands when he pledged loyalty to him all those years ago during the darkest days of Scotland's fight for independence. He could not simply shirk his duty now that the fight had slipped into this dank underworld of secret alliances and stealth attacks.

But nor would he accept this distasteful mission without trying every angle to escape it.

"Kenneth placed me in charge of Dunrobin while he is away with the McKays. I cannae simply leave the castle and the clan without a leader," he said, but the appeal sounded feeble even to his ears.

A slow smile began to spread across Garrick's hard face.

Shite.

Ansel had lost, and they both knew it now.

"That is why the Bruce instructed me to stay on in yer stead until yer cousin returns."

"What?" This time Ansel stopped his chair from tumbling backward, but he still jerked to his feet swiftly enough to send it wobbling. "A Sinclair watching over Laird Sutherland's stronghold? Bloody—"

"Dinnae get yer bollocks in a twist," Garrick said, that wolfish grin still on his face. "I am to send a missive to Kenneth letting him know what has transpired and urging him to return to Dunrobin with all haste.

That is, unless I find that having yer clan under my thumb is just too much fun."

In the back of his mind, Ansel knew that Garrick was jesting, trying to get a rise out of him. Yet his fist wasn't connected to his mind at the moment.

He acted on instinct. His hand darted at Garrick's smug face. At the last possible moment, he pulled back slightly so as not to damage his friend overmuch. Still, Garrick's head snapped back when Ansel's fist made impact with his jaw, and his chair rocked backward precariously.

In a flash, Garrick was on his feet. Yet instead of the blow wiping the grin from his face, as Ansel intended, Garrick only smiled broader.

"Aye, there's the fighting spirit I came here seeking!" He playfully pounded Ansel on the shoulder with enough force to send him staggering.

Garrick took his seat once more, his body relaxed with his victory. Ansel smoothed back his hair with one hand. His mind swirled as he contemplated this new mission. Though he resented doing anything to aid a bloody Englishman, he felt the familiar stirrings of honor-bound purpose in his chest.

"What can ye tell me about Lancaster's son? How old is he? What does he know of the threat to his life?"

"Unfortunately, I dinnae ken much," Garrick said. "I've told ye all that the Bruce shared with me. He did give me this missive though."

Garrick removed a piece of folded parchment from

the sporran pouch on his hip and extended it toward Ansel. A broken blot of red wax stood out in the dim light of the small chamber, but there was no distinguishing seal on it.

He quickly scanned the missive, but as Garrick had said, it contained little detail, likely to safeguard against the danger of the message falling into the wrong hands. Yet the mission it laid out was clear enough.

Protect my son from the forces that work against us.

The missive was signed "King Arthur." At Ansel's snort, Garrick spoke.

"It is the code name he gave himself. He fancies himself the future King of some mystical kingdom."

"Christ," Ansel muttered.

Garrick stood, his gray eyes dancing. "It's settled then. Lancaster has stashed his son in some stronghold he controls in the Borderlands—Dunstanburgh, the Bruce said. Ye'll travel there with all haste and ensure that no harm comes to Lancaster's son. The fate of our cause may rest on whether this bastard lives or dies."

"Ye dinnae need to remind me," Ansel muttered.

Garrick slapped him on the back once more, but this time, his face bore no trace of a smile.

"Ye'd best be away, then."

Bloody hell.

What had Ansel gotten himself into?

Chapter Two

Isolda picked her way carefully across the Rumble Churn. It was a fitting name for a haunting place—the expanse of beach stretched just below Gull Crag, where chunks of the cliff's black rock had fallen and lay partially submerged in the lapping sea.

The rocks beneath her feet were slick with a combination of ocean water and the low mist that almost always clung to the ground here.

Though even at the height of summer the days remained cool and pleasant thanks to the salty breeze wafting from the North Sea, fall now stung the air with a sharp cold. She pulled her shawl tighter around her shoulders. Soon enough she'd have to start wearing her thicker woolen cloak.

The old, dull ache flared hot in her chest at the realization. Fall was upon her—the first fall without John.

Tears burned her eyes, their brine mixing with that of the North Sea wind. She swallowed hard and inhaled a fortifying breath, despite the fact that no one was nearby to witness her sudden surge of emotion. But *she* would know if she lost control. And she could never do that, for if she succumbed to the pain, she might never be able to drag herself back to sanity.

Isolda carefully lifted her skirts to keep them from tripping her on the black, sea-rounded rocks. She'd already reluctantly turned around where the walls of Gull Crag grew too steep and the ocean swallowed the Rumble Churn.

In the mornings, when the newly born sun illuminated the mist shrouding the rocks, Isolda let herself imagine that she was in some fairy land as she picked her way across the expanse.

But she only allowed herself to walk the length of the Rumble Churn once each day, lest she come to rely too heavily on the escape from the real world. This morning had been squally and temperamental, so she'd been forced to wait until late afternoon to indulge in her daily walk.

She made her way across the last of the rounded black rocks and began her scramble back up Gull Crag. Though the cliffs stood nigh one hundred feet tall in some places, she'd discovered a narrow but less steep path where the northeast corner of Dunstanburgh Castle clung to the top of the Crag. Soon enough, this path down from the cliffs to the sea would be sealed in by the curtain wall, but for now, with construction only partially complete, she treasured her secret route.

Once she crested the narrow trail, her stomach reknitted into its normal pinch. Though the curtain wall was still only a few feet high in many places, the stones did their work well enough. This was her prison. Only the North Sea at her back wasn't walled off, but the ocean was its own barrier, pinning her within the confines of Dunstanburgh.

The Earl of Lancaster had chosen this site for his newest castle well. And he'd chosen her prison well.

Though she normally kept a tight rein on her emotions, she suddenly felt choked by her surroundings. Her gaze ran along the partially built wall in search of relief.

With the afternoon advancing toward evening and the accompanying waning of daylight upon them, the workers were busy at their tasks. Some were lifting enormous stones with pulleys and guiding them into place on the wall, while others slathered plaster onto the stones that had already been set.

None of the two dozen or so workers raised an eye to her. They were used to her routine of walking along the Rumble Churn every day, and also her occasional appearances in the yard as they worked. She imagined they thought of her as little more than a ghost, slipping silently around the unfinished castle in the fine gowns Lancaster had bought for her.

Her gaze landed on the partially finished gatehouse that stood at the southwestern edge of the wall. It was the tallest structure by far, and when it was complete, it would provide a dominant lookout over both land and sea. Perhaps if she climbed to the top, she'd be able to see even more of the North Sea and have one last taste of freedom for the day. None of the laborers worked nearby, which would afford her some privacy as well.

Straightening her spine, she glided as calmly as possible across the grassy yard and toward the gatehouse. Blessedly, her movement still didn't draw any attention among the workers. Though her fine garb said otherwise, she preferred not to be noticed. Such was the case ever since—

Nay. She pushed the thought aside harshly. She would climb the gatehouse tower and look at the sea for a while. That was all. Then she would return to her chamber in the squat tower against the northern wall and busy herself with work on her fine garments, as she always did.

Gripping her brocade silk skirts, she walked into the stone gatehouse, which still didn't have a door yet. She crossed to the spiral staircase and began winding her way upward. She passed the landing that opened into an enormous room that would eventually be the keep's great hall, then climbed higher still past the chambers above that were meant for Lancaster and his family. Her chest pinched, but with practiced willpower she ignored it.

At last, she reached the top of the gatehouse. Though one day there would be a crenelated parapet atop which guards could keep watch, it had yet to be finished. Instead, the stairs ended abruptly on a smooth stone roof several dozen feet above the yard.

As she stepped onto the flat roof, the wind whipped

her skirts and threatened to unplait her hair. Her eyes landed on the sea, its seemingly endless expanse spreading before her. A jolt of energy surged through her veins. How long had it been since she'd felt so alive, even briefly? *Not since John left.*

The pain mingled with the swell of fleeting freedom as she stood atop the gatehouse. Just then, a beam of sun broke through the clouds behind her and fell on her back. The sun held no warmth, but she let its light bathe her. The wind stung her cheeks, cleansing as prayer.

The rumbling thump of a stone being dropped into place on the wall snapped her attention back to reality once more. The men swarmed at their tasks in the yard below like dutiful insects.

Her gaze swept beyond the castle walls to the east where the ray of sun had struggled to break through the clouds and fall on her. With another lash of wind, the gap in the clouds closed and the beam of sun winked away.

A flicker of movement drew her eye to the rolling green hills beneath the gray-purple clouds.

A rider approached.

Isolda's stomach leapt to her throat in an instant, nigh choking her with panic. Could it be another attack? Her fingernails bit into her palms as she clenched her fists.

The rider drew closer. He bore a sword on his hip, but no armor. So he wasn't a knight. She squinted, quickly assessing his attire. He wore the simple breeches and tunic of a commoner, yet commoners did not bear swords.

She took a steadying breath. The last attack had occurred at night, done by a drunken madman. The one before that hadn't been an attack at all, but merely an accident, or so it had seemed.

No one would dare attack the Earl of Lancaster's castle in broad daylight, and especially not with only one man armed with naught but a sword. He was likely just a messenger, or a new laborer brought by the Master Mason. The logic of this realization set her somewhat more at ease, though she still trained her gaze on the lone rider.

He slowed his bay horse as he approached and guided the animal down the length of the three manmade ponds that ran along the front of the castle. The ponds served as moats of sorts, and when they were complete, the bridges across them could be tightly controlled.

With no bridges built yet, the rider found the narrow dirt entrance between two of the ponds that the laborers used to cart in supplies. He spurred his steed toward the gate.

The rider crossed through the gate and reappeared a second later in the yard. With practiced ease, he swung from the saddle. He turned a slow circle, seeming to take in the construction and the unfinished nature of the castle.

This close, she could now see that he was soaked to

the bone. His simple clothes clung to him, his dark, uncovered hair dripping down his back. He was far larger than she had realized from a distance. He would likely tower over most of the laborers, though his wide shoulders spoke of a familiarity with hard work.

"Who is in charge here?" he barked to no one in particular.

Isolda felt her brows collide. Did she detect a Scottish burr in the man's deep voice? A new rush of unease thrummed in her veins. A Scottish accent was not so unusual to hear in the Borderlands. Yet the man who'd just barreled into the yard didn't look like a simple Lowland laborer. His movements were too fluid, too…lethal. Like a warrior's.

Disquiet coiling tighter in her belly, she lifted her skirts and hurried toward the spiral stairs leading back down to the yard. When she was almost all the way down the gatehouse stairs, she heard the stranger's booming voice demand once more who was in charge.

Where was Bertram? She couldn't hide like a coward and wait for her guard to arrive. Nay, she was the lady of this keep.

She stepped through the open doorway and into the yard, dropping her skirts with a swish of silken fabric. The rider spun on his heels and pinned her with a hard stare, his dark eyes sharp and penetrating.

Shoving down the quake of fear that jolted through her, she lifted her head in an imitation of the most regal of ladies.

"I am."

Chapter Three

Ansel narrowed his eyes on the woman who stepped from the stone tower with the air of a queen, her red gown swishing softly.

"What do ye mean, ye are in charge?"

Whatever Ansel had been expecting, it wasn't this. Granted, he hadn't had much information to go on, but a castle in shambles housing an English noblewoman who claimed to be in charge was a stretch.

He'd ridden hard for nigh a sennight to get here as fast as possible, imagining that Lancaster's bastard son could be set upon by Edward's lackeys at any moment. Though he'd been caught in squall after squall, with the latest rainstorm lasting all through last night and into this morning as he'd approached the castle, he'd pushed onward, determined to take on this mission.

From a distance, Dunstanburgh Castle had been the imposing stronghold he'd been led to believe it was. But as he'd drawn closer, he made out the rough, unfinished lines of the curtain wall and the jagged protrusion of several incomplete towers. What kind of God-awful place had Lancaster stowed this son whom he claimed needed protection?

And when he'd ridden right through the open—nay, nonexistent—gates as if he owned the damn keep without so much as a guard to greet him or a question leveled at him about what his business was, he felt as if he'd been kicked in the ribs. Could this assignment be even more absurd and ill-conceived than he'd let himself suspect?

Now, the Englishwoman before him was looking at him as if he were a clump of shite stuck to a horse's hoof. Though he would tower over her if she stood closer, her pale chin was tilted in such a way that she managed to appear as though she looked down on him.

"What do I mean? I mean that I am the lady of this keep," she responded tersely. "What business do you have here?"

Ansel's mood turned a shade darker. No one had mentioned anything about an English noblewoman running Dunstanburgh in Lancaster's stead. What else didn't he know about this cursed mission?

"I am here to collect the Earl of Lancaster's bastard son," he ground out.

Perhaps if he hadn't been operating with only a few hours' sleep each night for nigh a sennight, he would have modified his tone. Perhaps if he weren't soaking wet and saddle-weary, he would have chosen his words more carefully. And perhaps if every sign didn't indicate that this was a fool's errand, he would have observed more decorum. As it was, he didn't much care.

The Englishwoman's lips tightened ever so slightly. Her gaze swept over him, but he detected more than just disdain in her eyes. Was that…fear?

As her gaze traveled back up his length, her eyes flickered ever so slightly over his left shoulder. It was all the warning he had.

He spun instinctively, yanking his sword free of its scabbard. The blade whirred through the air, flashing against the overcast sky. Just before his sword made contact with the person who'd snuck up behind him, Ansel snapped his arm to a halt. The blade vibrated an inch away from the neck of an aging man.

The man's dark blue eyes rounded as he took in the sword at his neck. Ansel held the blade steady, his body nevertheless tense and ready to strike. Slowly, the man raised his hands to indicate that he hadn't drawn a weapon.

With a quick glance, Ansel took in the sword on the man's waist. Though the weapon looked to be in good condition, the man's middle was thick from advanced years and inactivity. His coppery head, which was dashed liberally with white streaks, was held proudly aloft, like his lady's was.

The Englishwoman's gasp behind him broke through his battle-taut mind.

"Nay, do not harm him!"

Ansel lowered his blade slowly, keeping his gaze trained on the older man.

"Who the bloody hell are ye?" Ansel snapped.

"I am Bertram, Lady Isolda's personal guard," the man said, blinking at Ansel.

So the Englishwoman had a name. Ansel pivoted and took several steps backward so that he could bring both the woman and her guard into his line of sight.

"I dinnae ken what yer role is in all this, Lady Isolda," Ansel said, re-sheathing his sword. "But I suggest ye keep yer man from attempting to attack me from behind again. I'm no' always so eager to let my blade go unused."

He shifted his gaze to Lady Isolda. Confusion now mingled with fear in her eyes as she watched his sword slide back into its sheath. Then as if consciously fortifying herself, she drew her chin up and straightened her spine. She met his gaze, and he realized suddenly that her eyes were the palest green imaginable.

"Who are you?" she demanded, taking another step toward him.

Ansel let himself truly look at her for the first time.

Though she carried herself with an air of regality, she was a petite woman. If she stood directly in front of him, the top of her head likely wouldn't clear his chin. Her chestnut hair was pulled back into a braid, though wild wisps had come loose around her face.

Those pale green eyes were framed by dark lashes and gently arching eyebrows the same rich color as her hair. Though the skin of her neck and hands was creamy, her cheeks were rosy, either from the salty breeze rushing through the yard or from the intensity of his scrutiny, he knew not which.

Under the plain shawl around her shoulders, she was clad in a dark crimson surcoat with intricate designs of flowers and leaves stitched onto it. The surcoat fit snugly over the soft curve of her breasts and tapered around her narrow waist. Now that she stood closer, he noticed that the surcoat ended at her elbows, revealing a gown underneath of a similar dark red. The gown's sleeves stopped just above her wrists, where a creamy chemise showed.

Though Ansel didn't bother to follow English fashion, he knew what her garb was meant to convey—wealth. No commoner ever wore a surcoat, for fabric of the kind Lady Isolda wore was far too expensive. To show three layers of such rich material spoke of coin, and a great deal of it.

Bloody hell.

A rich English noblewoman with her chin raised to the heavens was the last thing Ansel needed.

Under his perusal, her eyes slowly widened, their pale depths disbelieving. Aye, he was being rude by not answering her question and staring so openly. He repressed a sigh. He still had a mission, and he wasn't going to fail his King by getting on the bad side of some uppity English lady.

"I am Ansel Sutherland," he replied at last.

She waited a beat, but when he said no more, her rosy lips thinned slightly.

"And what business do you have here, Ansel Sutherland?" she asked again.

"As I said, I am here to collect Lancaster's bastard son."

"To the Devil with you, you Scottish barbari—" Bertram, the aging guard, blurted.

Lady Isolda held up her hand, and the man instantly fell silent. A quick glance told Ansel that Bertram's face had turned mottled red with indignation, though Ansel guessed it was directed more at him than at Lady Isolda.

"What do you wish with such a person?" she asked carefully. Her gaze again flicked to his sheathed sword, and he could see the wheels of her mind turning behind those pale green eyes.

"If I had come to do harm to Lancaster's son, I wouldnae have re-sheathed my blade," he said slowly, voicing what he suspected she was deducing. "Yer suspicion, along with the fear I see in yer eyes, tells me that the man I seek is in danger. Perhaps I am no' the first to come looking for him."

She held herself stock-still, but something flickered in her eyes that told him he'd hit a mark.

"That's the truth of it, is it no'?"

When she again refused to acknowledge what he'd said, the last thread of his patience finally shredded.

"I'm here to *protect* Lancaster's son, no' harm him," he snapped.

"What?" Shock briefly flashed across Lady Isolda's delicate features before she could train them into regal detachment once more.

"I have been sent to guard the man, to ensure no harm befalls him. Clearly he's in need of me, if this castle and one old soldier are the man's only protection." He swept a hand past Bertram to the half-built walls and gateless entryway.

"Who sent you?" Lady Isolda demanded, ignoring his censure.

Ansel took several deliberate steps toward her, effectively cutting Bertram out of their conversation, if it could be called that. He was a hair's breadth from losing what remained of his composure, but he willed himself to keep his voice level.

"The Earl of Lancaster himself."

Lady Isolda's lips parted on a sharp inhale. Her eyes rounded, and suddenly she looked more like a scared lass than a blustering noblewoman. With only a hand span between them now, he saw that she was younger than he'd initially thought. Her demeanor was severe and cold, yet she couldn't be more than five and twenty, and perhaps even younger.

"Why would—" He could hear her teeth click as she swiftly clamped her mouth shut. His gaze pinned her, searching for clues. What did this woman know of Lancaster? And what was she hiding from Ansel?

Lady Isolda struggled visibly to regain control of herself. At last, she seemed to find her tongue—and her cool bearing—once more.

"That is quite the claim. Do you have proof?"

He spun on his heels and strode to where he'd left Eachann untethered in the yard. With a sure hand, he removed a waxed parchment from his saddlebag. He unwrapped the parchment as he strode back toward her and handed her the Earl's missive without hesitating.

Although the missive bore neither Lancaster's seal nor his name, something about the look in Lady Isolda's pale green eyes told Ansel that she was acquainted with the man. He watched her closely as she accepted the piece of parchment.

She quickly skimmed the missive, then let her gaze settle on the signature.

"King Arthur," she murmured. Her slim throat bobbed as she swallowed hard. She refolded the missive and handed it back to Ansel, not meeting his gaze.

As he tucked the piece of parchment back into his saddlebag, the storm he'd just ridden through from the north descended on the castle. Fat drops of icy rain began pelting the yard. Though he was already soaking wet, he couldn't help but mutter a curse at his luck thus far on this mission.

Lady Isolda pulled the shawl around her shoulders tightly. Even as raindrops hit her expensive red brocaded surcoat, she hesitated for a long moment. At last, she muttered something under her breath, then turned to Bertram.

"See to Ansel Sutherland's horse," she said over the increasingly loud drum of rain.

"But my lady, I will not leave you with this—"

"It is all right, Bertram," she replied. Then she turned to Ansel. "This way, if you please."

Lady Isolda strode briskly across the yard toward one of the partially constructed square towers that butted up against the incomplete wall. Ansel hoisted his saddlebags over one shoulder and handed Eachann's reins to a narrow-eyed Bertram before following.

She shoved open the wooden door at the base of the tower and disappeared inside. *At least this one has a door*, he thought sourly. Though the tower lacked crenellation along its roof, it looked to be stoutly made of tightly fitted gray stone. The windows higher up were all shuttered firmly, which was more of a finishing touch than any of the other towers bore.

He stepped in behind her and booted the door closed with one foot. Once he'd dropped his saddlebags on the floor, he straightened and took in the interior of the tower.

The room was surprisingly cozy and well-appointed, though rather small for a noblewoman. A rectangular table with a few chairs next to it was pushed against the rear wall. The left side of the room was taken up by a small kitchen, with a hearth doubling as both the main source of heat and the site for cooking. Clean rushes softened the stone underfoot, and a few tapestries hung on the walls. To the right, a spiraling stone staircase led abovestairs.

"The rain has started up again, my lady. Shall I lay out a change of clothes—"

An older woman came bustling down the stairs, her voice echoing cheerfully against the stone. As the woman's eyes landed on Ansel, she froze. A strangled scream rose in her throat.

"All is well, Mary," Lady Isolda said quickly over the rising noise of the older woman's scream.

The woman, Mary, clapped a hand over her mouth, her eyes wide and still riveted on Ansel.

"Forgive my maid," Lady Isolda said to Ansel. "She is overly wary of…of strange men." She turned to the servant. "This is Ansel Sutherland. He was sent to protect the Earl of Lancaster's son."

Ansel didn't miss how deliberately she chose her words as she spoke to her maid.

"Ah," Mary said, slowly lowering her hand from her mouth. She nodded in understanding to her lady. "Indeed, forgive me, my lord." Mary's dark eyes darted between her mistress and Ansel with uncertainty.

What in bloody hell had happened at Dunstanburgh Castle to set everyone so on edge? Ansel ground his teeth against the desire to curse this mission once again.

"Mary, please have the guest chamber made up for Sir Sutherland and—"

"I'm no' a lord," he cut in. "Just Ansel."

Lady Isolda's lips tightened again almost imperceptibly. Something stirred in the pit of Ansel's stomach. It was strangely satisfying to wheedle a reaction—even a negative one—out of this stiff woman.

"Very well," she said, though he detected annoyance under the surface of her smooth tone. "Please have the chamber made up for Ansel. He will be staying this night—and no more."

Before Ansel could object, Mary's mouth fell open and she began chattering frantically.

"Oh, nay, my lady! This man cannot stay here in the tower with you! It is most improper! And is he Scottish? Oh, nay, my lady, *most* improper. Bertram and I will not allow—"

Ansel held up a hand for silence. The gesture sent Mary jumping, which gave him the opening he needed.

"I'll sleep in the gatehouse," he said. "But I'll no' be leaving until the threat to Lancaster's son has been eliminated. Dinnae think to stand between me and my mission."

"Nay," Lady Isolda said, her voice so quiet that Ansel had to take a step closer to her to hear. "You will leave tomorrow. I will provide you shelter from the storm, but then you will be on your way."

"Like hell I will," he snapped. "Where is Lancaster's son?"

Lady Isolda fixed her eyes on the rushes at his feet, giving her head the slightest of shakes.

"Enough games," Ansel bit out. "Where is Lancaster's son? Tell me."

Slowly, Lady Isolda dragged her eyes up to meet

his.

"He is not here."

Frustration burned hot in Ansel's veins. What a cursed mess this was. "Well, where the bloody hell is he?"

Lady Isolda's throat bobbed in a telltale sign of nervousness, but even still, she tilted her chin upward.

"Only I know where he is. And…and I will not tell you."

Chapter Four

Isolda clutched her hands in front of her to prevent twisting them in the brocade of her surcoat's skirts.

The enormous Scot took another step forward so that he towered over her. His eyes, which appeared nigh black in the hearth's flickering light, narrowed on her. Mary inhaled sharply from the stairs, but Isolda didn't dare take her eyes off Ansel Sutherland to glance at her maid.

"What do ye mean, only ye ken where he is, and ye'll no' tell me?"

He was so close that his scent reached out and enfolded her. He smelled of wood smoke and rain and horseflesh—purely masculine. She couldn't remember the last time she'd stood so close to a man. It was indecent. Improper. And yet she refused to step back.

"I mean exactly that," she replied, willing her voice to remain even.

Ansel shifted his weight irritably, and she had to drop her hands to her sides lest she brush against his—

Her eyes skittered over his large form once more. His shoulders were impossibly broad. The damp linen tunic he wore clung to his muscles, revealing clearly that he was not simply a big man. Nay, he was hard and honed everywhere she looked. Muscle corded in his shoulders and arms. His chest, which heaved with barely restrained anger directly in front of her eyes, appeared to be slab upon slab of pure strength. Even the blocks of muscle banding his stomach were plainly defined through his wet, clinging tunic.

When she ripped her gaze from his honed physique, his eyes had narrowed even more. The hard lines of his jaw were bristled with dark stubble. A slight cleft in his chin might have made him seem regal, but instead it combined with everything else about his rough, fierce appearance to make him look all the more like a wild Highland barbarian.

"I'll no' be gotten rid of so easily," he ground out, his own gaze boldly assessing her. "I'll have answers—if no' from ye, then I'll seek out Lancaster to settle this matter."

She felt her eyes widen slightly and silently cursed herself for giving him a reaction.

"Mary, please busy yourself abovestairs."

"But my lady—"

"Mary, please," Isolda said firmly.

At last, her maid reluctantly retreated up the stairs. Isolda waited until she heard the soft thump of a wooden door close behind Mary before taking a deep breath. She squared her shoulders and drew herself up to her full, if scanty, height.

"The Earl of Lancaster doesn't know where his son

is, for if he did, he wouldn't have sent you here to look for him."

Ansel crossed his arms over his chest. The bulge of his forearms nigh brushed against her breasts, but she refused to back down. He cocked a dark eyebrow at her, his mouth turning down sourly.

"Aye, I suppose I can grant ye that," he said, his low voice grudging. "But then ye must grant that Lancaster's bastard is indeed in danger. Why else would ye be hiding him from me?"

Though she tried to school her features, she must have flinched slightly at the word "bastard," for his eyes were once again keenly trained on her face.

"What is Lancaster's *bastard* to ye?" he said slowly, emphasizing the offending word. "And why have ye stowed him away?"

"I do not have to answer such rude questions from some Highland *barbarian*," she snapped, feeling a surge of ire heat her blood. "I am Lady Isolda of Embleton, and you…you are naught but a…"

"A Highland barbarian?" he parroted back to her. "Aye, I am that." A wolfish smile curved his lips, but his eyes remained hard and searching. "But I am here on the authority of the Earl himself. By his order, I am to protect his son. Whether ye choose to hamper me or aid me makes little difference, for I willnae be deterred."

"You will leave tomorrow morning," she asserted again, though she cursed herself for the subtle waver in her voice.

He must have sensed her cracking resolve, for he leaned in ever so slightly. Suddenly Isolda got the distinct impression of what a lamb must feel like as it was hunted by a wolf.

"Tomorrow morning will prove ye wrong," he said softly, flashing her another smile.

He leaned back on his heels, and she exhaled a breath she hadn't realized she'd been holding.

"For the time being, though, I am bone weary and sopping wet. I'd best retire to the gatehouse so that I can get a good night's sleep. I'll need to be refreshed for the work ahead of me tomorrow."

He stepped back and gave her a little mock bow, then turned and scooped up his saddlebags, tossing them over his shoulder. He yanked open the door that led to the yard and barreled out into the storm.

The rain was falling harder now. The yard had darkened considerably, both with the thick clouds overhead and the waning daylight of a fall evening.

As the wooden door swung nearly shut, Bertram caught it and ducked his head, now dripping wet, inside.

"Ah, thank God, my lady," Bertram said with a relieved nod of his head. "You've sent that Scottish...*man* away."

Bertram watched Ansel's back as he made his way across the yard, suspicion and distaste clearly written on his weathered features.

"Nay," Isolda said, suddenly weary. "He is staying in the gatehouse for the night."

Before Bertram could protest, she quickly went on. "Only for the night, though. I will send him away tomorrow."

Who was she fooling? If she had been able to keep the Scot away, he wouldn't be mounting the stairs to the castle's gatehouse at this moment.

"I'll see it done, my lady," Bertram said, straightening.

She nodded, but her mind whispered the truth to her. Bertram couldn't stop Ansel Sutherland. The Highlander more than proved that in the yard. How had he moved so swiftly, so fluidly when he'd drawn his sword on Bertram? She'd never seen a man move like that before.

Isolda pinched the bridge of her nose, feeling a headache forming.

"I think I shall retire for the evening," she said.

Bertram bowed. "Do you wish for me to stay and stand watch over the tower, my lady?"

The Highlander could likely barge into her little tower any time he wanted, with only old Bertram to slow him. She would have to make sure that Bertram didn't come to harm trying to enforce her wishes or protecting her from the Scot.

But for all of Ansel Sutherland's bluster and ire, she doubted he was a physical threat to her.

"Nay, that is noble of you, Bertram, but it will not

be unnecessary."

As Bertram slipped from the tower with another bow, she strode to the stairs and began making her slow ascent. The curving stairway was dim, but her feet knew this path all too well.

At the first landing, she reached for the door that led to her chamber. Blessedly, Mary was not within, though the maid had lit the fire in the hearth against the far wall.

She could call for Mary to help her undress, but Isolda longed to be alone with her thoughts.

The letter Ansel bore proved that he spoke the truth about his mission to protect Lancaster's son. The missive was in Lancaster's handwriting and was signed with Lancaster's pet name for himself to boot.

King Arthur. Isolda's mind flew back six years. Lancaster had spoken in hushed tones of his grand plans for himself. Isolda had been such a silly girl then. She'd hardly paid attention to his words, so entranced was she by Thomas's clever blue eyes and the power he carried as easily as a mantle over his shoulders.

Aye, she trusted that Ansel would not try to harm her this night. But that didn't mean the rough-edged man's presence didn't threaten her secret.

Isolda almost snorted. Ansel Sutherland wasn't rough-edged. He didn't have edges to speak of. He was rude, brash, impatient, and foul-tempered from what she'd seen so far.

But he was right about one thing—John, Lancaster's illegitimate son, was in danger.

She'd feared as much for nigh a year. The accidents weren't accidents at all, despite her desire to deny the truth. It was why she'd sent John away all those months ago. And it was why not even Mary or Bertram knew where she'd hidden him. It was too dangerous for them to know, for the knowledge alone could cost them their lives.

The fact that Thomas, the Earl of Lancaster, had sent someone to protect his son proved that the threat went far beyond her worst fears. Did such an action prove that Thomas cared about John after all?

Nay, she quickly pushed that line of thinking aside. She'd learned long ago that Lancaster didn't have the capacity for love, or even caring.

Just as Isolda had freed herself from the confines of her exquisitely made surcoat, a rap sounded against her chamber door.

"My lady?" Mary's weak voice drifted through the wood.

Isolda sighed. "All is well, Mary. I am tired. I can see to myself tonight."

"But what about your supper, my lady? And I can help with the tangles in your hair."

"Thank you, Mary," Isolda said, softening her voice. "But truly, I am fine. Tend to yourself this evening."

She heard Mary's footfalls trail away down the stairs.

With cold fingers, Isolda worked on the ties of the gown she'd selected to complement the surcoat. When only her chemise remained, she unbound her hair and took her bone comb to the windblown mess of locks.

At last, she slipped between the covers of her down-filled bed. All the riches surrounding her came from Lancaster, but none of them would protect her from whoever was after John. Perhaps Ansel could help...

Nay, she wouldn't divulge the secret of John's location to anyone—not Mary, not Bertram, and certainly not some irate Highland warrior who simply showed up at Dunstanburgh demanding to know where John was.

Unease tickled down her spine, so she burrowed deeper into the downy folds of her bed. Ansel Sutherland was determined. He'd vowed to protect John, with or without her help. And from what little she'd seen of him so far, he didn't seem like a man easily deterred.

She might just be stuck with the Scot for the time being.

Chapter Five

It didn't count as waking up if one hadn't truly slept, did it?

Ansel threw back the blankets of his bedroll when the first rays of morning sun slipped through the arrow slit over his makeshift bed and fell on the stone floor of the gatehouse.

He could blame his foul mood on the relentless hammering of rain all throughout the night, or on the fact that the floor he'd slept on, while dry, was harder and colder than any patch of forest dirt. He could find fault with the fact that he'd had to eat sennight-old biscuits and dried meat since his hostess hadn't offered him a warm meal or a mug of ale.

"Bloody English hospitality," he grumbled to himself as he donned a set of dry breeches and a tunic he'd removed from his saddlebags.

But if he were honest with himself, the real reason for his sour disposition this morning lay with a certain green-eyed, chestnut-haired Englishwoman who seemed hell-bent on thwarting his mission.

As if the idea of helping the Earl of Lancaster, an Englishman who'd fought against—and killed—Scots more than once in the last few years, wasn't bad enough. Now he had to get through the mysterious Lady Isolda, who clearly knew more than she was telling about both Lancaster and his bastard son.

"Doesnae matter," he muttered. He was a Highlander, damn it. He was a warrior. And he was sent by King Robert the Bruce himself. No wee English lass, noble or not, was going to best him so easily.

The hours of restless tossing and turning last night had given him plenty of time to plot his new approach to the lady in question—and form a plan of attack.

Ansel shoved his feet into his still-damp boots and buckled his sword to his hip.

He didn't bother fastening his shoulder-length hair at the nape of his neck, though. If she thought him a barbarian, he'd play the part, for it seemed to ruffle that cool, regal exterior she clung to. Perhaps if he could perturb her enough, he'd find an opening. And when he did, he'd strike.

He emerged from the gatehouse to find a surprisingly sunny, clear morning after last night's storm. The grass under his boots glistened with lingering raindrops as he crossed toward Lady Isolda's tower.

The yard was already abuzz with activity. Laborers were streaming through the gate and making their way toward various sections of the incomplete curtain wall. Ansel repressed a curse. He was going to have to talk with each and every one of them about what they knew of the lady of the keep—and Lancaster's son.

No matter, he reminded himself firmly. If this was the first task associated with completing his mission, so be it.

He rapped sharply on Lady Isolda's wooden door, but when it swung open, he found himself staring down at the wide-eyed maid, Mary.

"Where is yer mistress? I have some questions for her."

The woman slowly shook her gray-brown head, wringing her hands in the apron tied over her simple woolen gown.

"She isn't here at present my lor—er..."

"Just Ansel is fine, madam," he said, doing his best to place a smile on his face.

Mary blinked up at him, clearly disconcerted by his attempt at kindness. Well, he was out of practice. But he would have to find a way to put the jumpy maid at ease if he hoped to ever get a scrap of useful information out of her.

"And where is she? Hopefully no' tucked away with Lancaster's son, wherever that may be." He kept his voice light, though by Mary's continued hand-wringing, he had an uphill battle ahead.

"Nay, my lo—Ansel." Mary hesitated, her eyebrows drawing together as she considered something for a moment. "She is down on the Rumble Churn, below Gull Crag."

She pointed off toward where the cliff atop which Dunstanburgh Castle was perched fell away in a sheer drop to the North Sea below.

"Does she...go down there often?" The thought of the rigid, cold lady he'd spoken with yesterday scrambling down a cliff was rather incongruous.

Mary nodded. "Aye, every day. But she prefers not to be disturbed during such times."

"Thank you, Madam Mary," Ansel said with a bob of his head. "I will no' betray your confidence in me to your lady." He threw in a wink at the end, which earned him another blink and a blush from the maid.

Aye, he could do this, he thought as he strode from the tower toward the cliff's edge. Different people required different methods, but he'd have the information he needed eventually. Now all he had to do was figure out how to crack Lady Isolda's icy exterior.

He came to a sudden halt as his eyes landed on the lady in question. She was picking her way across a sea of rounded black rocks far below the cliff. She wore a blue surcoat with a creamy gown beneath, both of which were whipping frantically in the wind.

The wind revealed her figure to his riveted gaze. At a particularly strong blast of salty air, her garments plastered themselves to her legs, outlining every long line and delicate curve. She carefully lifted her skirts, uncovering a slim ankle wrapped in the thin leather of her boots. The thick braid of chestnut hair hanging down her back swung with each of her prudently placed steps.

So focused on her footing was she that she didn't

notice him at the top of the crag, watching her. But even without a witness to point out his staring, he knew the truth. The telltale heat coiled deep in his belly—and lower.

"Bloody hell," he murmured. The last thing he needed was to feel a bodily attraction to this haughty English noblewoman.

Suddenly her boot slipped on a damp rock. Her arms pin-wheeled as she attempted to regain her balance. Ansel's heart leapt into his throat and without thinking about it, he took a step closer to the edge of the cliff.

She managed to right herself before taking what promised to be a painful tumble on the rocks. With a little shake of her shoulders, she carried on. Ansel, too, had to give himself a jolt. What had he planned to do, leap from the nigh one hundred foot crag and swoop to the lady's rescue?

He watched the rigidness of her spine, the elegant way she held her head. Nay, she didn't need him. She could take care of herself.

His eyes traveled the edge of the crag until he found the trail he assumed she used to reach the rocks below. Though he took a step toward it, he stopped himself. She didn't like to be disturbed here, Mary had said. She'd halted and now stood gazing at the sun rising over the sea.

There would be plenty of time to question her—later. She could have this moment. He might as well get started with the others, though.

✧ ✧ ✧

"Lady Isolda! You'd best come, quick!"

Bernard stood at the top of the narrow path leading back up to the castle.

"What is wrong?"

"It is the Highlander, my lady."

Her stomach cinched into a knot. For some foolish reason, she'd held on to the sliver of hope that he would abide by her wishes and simply leave without a fuss this morning. Of course, that clearly hadn't happened.

"What about him?"

"He is questioning everyone in the castle about the Earl of Lancaster's son—and about you." Bertram's bushy eyebrows knitted together in consternation as he waited for her, his mouth turned down in clear ire as he spoke of Ansel Sutherland.

The knot in her belly tightened so hard that she gasped. She scrambled up the remaining few feet to the top of the path, no longer bothering to hold the fine blue silk of her skirts away from the ground.

"He asked me where Lancaster's son is, my lady. He also asked many questions about you—how long you've lived here and how far your knowledge of Lancaster and his heir goes. Of course I told him naught. When I wouldn't answer, he moved on to the laborers."

Isolda's nails bit into her palms as she squeezed her hands into fists. She barely resisted the urge to run across the yard. With all her willpower, she forced herself into a smooth but swift stride. Bertram fell in behind her.

She spotted Ansel's broad back and loose, dark hair, which rustled in the salty breeze, along the southwest section of the curtain wall. Lifting her head, she marched purposefully toward him.

"What is the meaning of this?" she demanded when she was close enough not to have to resort to an undignified shout to be heard over the wind and the noise of the laborers working on the wall.

Ansel turned slowly toward her, a dark eyebrow cocked arrogantly. As he pivoted to face her, she noticed that his tall, muscular body had blocked out the man to whom he was speaking. He had the Master Mason, Elias, nigh pinned against the wall.

Ansel acknowledged her with a little tilt of his head, but then turned back to Elias as if she hadn't just spoken to him.

"As ye were saying, ye never saw Lancaster's son. But ye've only been on the job for a few months, aye?"

Elias nodded, his gaze darting between Isolda and the giant Highlander questioning him.

"Aye, that's correct. I received a missive from one of Lancaster's men hiring me for this job. The previous mason's work was well done, from what I can tell, but apparently Lady Isolda sent him away and requested a new mason."

Isolda's heart hammered in her chest, nigh deafening her.

"How *dare* you question my workers about me as if I were some kind of criminal!" she hissed at Ansel.

"*Yer* workers?" Ansel turned back to her, that same wolfish look on his hard features. "If I am no' mistaken, this is Lancaster's castle. Ye are just the keeper—for the time being."

As she sputtered to find words for her rage at his blunt overconfidence, he spun toward where most of the laborers were working.

"Listen up, men!" he shouted over the noise of their labor. "I was sent here by order of the Earl of Lancaster. As he is the one paying ye, it's safe to say that he would demand yer cooperation with me. I'll have more questions for ye throughout the day—unless, of course, Lady Isolda prefers to answer them herself."

His dark gaze shifted to her, that cursed eyebrow raised expectantly.

Damn him. And damn Lancaster.

She was good and trapped now.

Chapter Six

A twinge of guilt pinched Ansel's chest even as he secured a small victory.

Judging from Lady Isolda's wide, outraged eyes and the way she clutched her hands at her sides so tightly that her knuckles were white, he'd cornered her. Aye, he'd finally get some answers. But it wasn't his way to manipulate a woman in such a way, lady or nay.

Lady Isolda's pale green gaze darted to the Master Mason behind him, then quickly scanned the two dozen or so workers who'd ceased their labor and were now looking on curiously. Bertram, the stubborn old soldier, gripped the sword at his hip, but there was nothing he could do for his lady now.

Suddenly he realized there was more than shock and outrage in her liquid green eyes—there was also fear. He'd exposed her, embarrassed her. She was clearly a woman with secrets.

He had his orders. But he'd proven his point. He didn't need to string her out further.

"Come, Lady Isolda," he said, lowering his voice. "Let us walk a pace. I think we have a few things to discuss."

Slowly, reluctantly, she nodded. He scanned the yard, looking for some place private they could talk, away from the curious stares of the laborers, the mason, and Bertram.

Other than the tower in which she resided, the only other completely walled structures were the stables where Bertram had stowed Eachann and the gatehouse.

He motioned toward the gatehouse with a little incline of his head. She raised her chin then, and Ansel felt as though she had just communed his death sentence, not the other way around.

That chafed. Her regal bearing made him feel like some rube—or the barbarian she'd called him. He gritted his teeth against the desire to tweak her pride publicly yet again. He wasn't here to play games with some arrogant noblewoman, though.

As she glided past him with the air of a queen, he snatched her wrist and threaded her arm through his.

"My lady," he said tightly as he guided her toward the gatehouse. Her eyes sparked green flames at him for his boldness, but she wouldn't do something as undignified as yank her arm out from under his—at least not in front of so many sets of eyes. It was a useful piece of information—though winks and charm worked on Mary, Lady Isolda responded better to the threat of public embarrassment.

"I have learned some most interesting details about ye, Lady Isolda," Ansel said softly as they made their way across the still-damp grass of the yard.

He felt her arm stiffen against his. "Is that so?"

"Oh aye," he drawled. "Bertram was…less than forthcoming, but the others provided some fascinating tidbits. I havenae had a chance to question Mary yet, but I believe she'll prove verra insightful."

She pressed her lips together for a moment. "What do you want to know?"

"As I've told ye, all I'm interested in is Lancaster's bastard son."

"And I told *you*," she snapped, "I'll not tell you where he is."

"Then we can do this the hard way." He kept his voice smooth, for several workers still looked on as they reached the gatehouse.

"Since ye are the keeper of the information I seek, it is ye who has become the focus of my inquiry."

"And what have you uncovered?"

"Oh, so far more questions than answers," he said with a nonchalant wave of his hand. He drew them to a halt just outside the gatehouse entryway. "But I am a verra persistent man. For instance, it strikes me as most odd that an English noblewoman has been placed in charge of the Earl of Lancaster's castle. Ye said ye were the Lady of Embleton, aye?"

Cautiously, she tilted her head in confirmation.

"Ye see, what's odd about that is that according to the laborers, Embleton is the nearest town off to the northwest. Many of them live there, in fact—but only for the last year or so. They tell me that the town didn't even exist before construction on Dunstanburgh began less than two years ago. Apparently, Lancaster planned to build the town along with the castle. For now, it is mostly just a place for the workers to lay their heads at night."

She stared at him defiantly, her eyes fixed on him. Yet tellingly, her slim white throat bobbed as she swallowed hard.

"Does that no' seem strange to you, Lady Isolda?" he prodded. "Why would Lancaster place his castle under the care of a woman who is a Lady of a region no' yet fully in existence?"

"Enough!" she snapped. "I do not see how impugning my name and title gets you any closer to finding Lancaster's son."

Color had risen into her cheeks, tinging her pale skin a rosy pink. He'd clearly hit a nerve. Like a hound on a scent, he longed for answers, but he'd tightened the screws on Lady Isolda enough for now. Time for a new angle.

"Verra well, my lady," Ansel said casually, "I shall stick to the matter at hand—Lancaster's bastard. I also learned that ye sent away the previous mason, along with all the laborers, less than a year ago. Neither Master Elias nor the workers I questioned have ever laid eyes on the man I've been sent here to protect, which indicates that ye sent Lancaster's son away at that time. None here can give me even the slightest description of the man I seek, though I imagine that Bertram and Mary could help in that regard—or ye, of course."

Lady Isolda spun on her heels and stormed through the gatehouse's open doorway. Aye, there was the crack in her perfectly cold façade he'd been looking for.

She swept through the empty stone chamber on the ground floor and made her way toward the spiraling staircase, the blue silk of her surcoat swishing around her legs. He kept pace with her easily, though he let her lead.

She didn't slow until she reached the very top, where the stairs ended abruptly on the unfinished roof. She approached the sharp edge, her back toward him. Her ribcage strained against her tight-fitting surcoat as her breath came short and fast. It wasn't from her swift ascent up the spiraling stairs, though, Ansel was sure. She was like a cornered animal, her options all evaporating.

"No more games," he said quietly, watching her carefully. "I am already close to the truth. Make this easier on yerself and simply tell me what I want to ken. Where is the man I seek? Where is Lancaster's bastard son?"

She spun to face him so suddenly that her skirts flared out in a swirl of blue and cream silk. The morning sun illuminated her, framing her dark hair and slim figure. Her eyes burned into him, shining with a depth of emotion he'd thus far never seen her display.

"Stop calling him Lancaster's *bastard*. His name is *John*. And he isn't a man. He's only a boy—a boy of just five summers." Her voice cracked on the last few words, though her eyes still held him, nigh glowing with liquid green fire.

Realization slammed into him like a punch to the stomach. Even as the pieces clicked together in his head, his heart twisted wildly.

"Ye are Lancaster's mistress. And the boy—John—he's…he's yer son."

Chapter Seven

Distantly, she registered the shocked look that crossed Ansel's features before they settled once more into their usual hard lines.

Panic seized her throat, nigh choking her. Yet the fire kindling in her chest demanded that she force out her voice anyway.

"I am *not* Lancaster's mistress," she bit out, willing herself to meet Ansel's searching eyes. "But I...I erred almost six years ago. I placed my trust in him, fool girl that I was. And I bore his son—*my son*."

Ansel took a slow step toward her. "So Lancaster placed ye here at Dunstanburgh—to hide ye from his enemies."

A broken, bitter laugh rose in her throat. "Aye, to hide us—from his wife and the rest of the nobles spreading vile rumors about him. The only danger John and I faced was public scorn at first. So Lancaster sent us here."

He took another cautious step toward her, as if approaching a wounded animal. "But construction on the castle began less than two years ago, and Embleton was naught but a handful of huts, according to the workers. Where did ye live?"

She lifted her chin. The last thing she wanted was this Highlander's pity. "We lived in a hut on the site where Lancaster planned to build the castle. For a few blessed years it was just Bertram, Mary, John, and me. But then construction began, and all the troubles started."

"What troubles? What caused ye to send John away?" His voice was its usual low rumble, but the sharp edge was gone from it.

Isolda swallowed hard. There was no point in lying, for Ansel would likely dig until he got the truth from her anyway.

"Accidents. Or so we hoped. One of the laborers dropped the pulley ropes while hoisting a stone for the wall. It almost landed on John, but at the last moment he scrambled out of the way. Not long after that, a drunken villager stumbled into the castle brandishing a knife. Blessedly, Bertram was there. He told me that the man appeared to be headed toward the tower where John and I slept, though. It all seemed too convenient."

She wrapped her arms around herself, trying to ward off the memories. Both cases were easy to explain away, yet some mother's instinct told her that they were connected.

"I sent John into hiding after the second incident. That was nigh a year ago, when I replaced the mason and the workers."

"And do ye ken why someone would be after John?"

Isolda exhaled wearily. "The Earl of Lancaster is the second richest man in all of England, behind only King Edward himself. Isn't it obvious? Someone likely hopes to take John for ransom and exact a steep fee for his return. Isn't that the way of things in these times of war?"

As soon as the words were out, she regretted the harsh implication. The Scots were reviled all over England for many reasons, but the nobles hated them especially for the toll they took on their coffers. The Scottish had a habit of taking noble captives, especially here in the Borderlands, and ransoming them back for exorbitant fees.

The insult was not lost on him. His dark eyes narrowed slightly, and his lips turned down behind the thick scruff bristling his face.

"I wouldnae expect a gently bred lady such as yerself to understand warfare," he said tightly.

The lie of her past knotted her stomach. But nay, he needn't know that particular truth. She would guard at least a few of her secrets.

"And if ye think that the only reason someone is coming after John is for a ransom payout, ye ken even less than ye think."

She tensed. "What do you mean? Why else would someone threaten him?"

To her surprise, the hardness once again fell away

from his features. His dark brown eyes flickered with something that could almost be called...sympathy.

"Come inside," he said softly, extending his hand toward her. "There is more ye ought to hear."

Suspicion had her narrowing her eyes on him. "Why? Why can't we remain out here?"

He exhaled through his teeth. "Bloody hell, woman, must ye fight me at every turn? Come into the gatehouse with me. Ye may want more privacy when ye hear what I have to say."

Her gaze fell to the yard below them. Though work had resumed on the wall after the scene Ansel had caused earlier, several sets of eyes still tugged up to the roof of the gatehouse where they stood, including Bertram's and Master Elias's.

When her eyes returned to Ansel, he had his arm extended toward her. Reluctantly, she reached out and placed her hand atop his forearm, allowing him to escort her from the roof. She hadn't noticed earlier when he'd taken her arm in his, but his skin was warm through the thin linen of his tunic. His muscles flexed and corded as her fingertips settled against them.

He guided her back to the stairs and down to one of the private chambers meant to house the Earl and his family one day. As she stepped into the chamber, she realized that this was where Ansel had slept last night. A bedroll lay slightly disheveled on the otherwise bare stone floor, his saddlebags at the foot of the blankets. An arrow slit let in the cheery morning sun, but the chamber was large enough that such a small gap in the stone left the rest of the room dim.

It felt strangely intimate to be alone with Ansel in the place where he'd slept last night. The chamber held a faint trace of his scent—a masculine combination of fresh air, wood smoke, and leather.

She pulled her spine straight and dropped her hand from his arm quickly. With a flick of her fingers, she smoothed her skirts now that they were out of the wind. Aye, she was well versed in hiding behind the role of a lady.

"What must you say that demands privacy? What other threat do you believe endangers John besides ransom?"

"Ye havenae asked me why Lancaster sent me, or how he reached me."

She blinked, caught off guard by Ansel's sudden change of subject.

"The letter you bear is proof enough that Lancaster wished for you to protect John. He must have sensed something was wrong when I demanded that he send a new mason and crew. I imagine you are some sort of...bodyguard for hire working to soothe English lords' fears of ransom attacks."

In truth, she'd been so focused on hiding the secrets of her past and John's whereabouts that she hadn't given Ansel Sutherland's connection to Lancaster much thought. But at Ansel's slow shake of the head, she felt a stone of dread sink into her stomach.

He eyed her for a long moment, then seemed to decide something. "I am part of King Robert the Bruce's inner circle of warriors and trusted advisors."

She inhaled sharply. She was in the presence of not just a Highlander, but a freedom fighter for the self-proclaimed King of Scotland—alone. Before she could comprehend the full implications of what he was saying, he went on. "Lancaster contacted the Bruce a fortnight ago requesting that the King send one of his best men to serve as a bodyguard."

"Lancaster is...working with Robert the Bruce?" She felt as if all the air had been knocked from her lungs. None of this made sense. Thomas was the cousin to King Edward II. Granted, she knew little of the politics and dealings of such powerful men, but if what Ansel claimed was true, Lancaster would be committing what was in effect treason.

"Aye, he is. And he has good reason to. Ye ken he opposes Edward?"

She nodded slowly, her eyes drifting to the stone floor between them. "He has been publicly critical of the King. He and the other nobles have tried to limit his power."

"Well, as ye can imagine, Edward has been none too pleased with Lancaster over that. Lancaster plans to make a move against Edward. And when he does, he fears that Edward will lash out at the one thread Lancaster has left dangling—John."

It was as if a pit opened up in the floor beneath her.

Isolda felt herself sinking even as the room seemed to tilt on its side. "You are saying...you are saying that Edward would *kill* John to thwart Lancaster?"

"Aye."

A sob ripped from her throat, echoing dizzyingly off the cold stone walls. Her head spun, her vision blurring with stinging tears as the ground fell away beneath her feet.

Suddenly hard arms encased her. Ansel's dark face swam before her, his brows pinched with worry.

"Isolda," he said, though his low voice sounded distant.

Her hands sank into the linen of his tunic. His arms tightened even more around her, binding her to the warm wall of his chest. That clean male scent surrounded her, cutting through the tempest of confusion that threatened to unmoor her. She clung desperately to him as if he were her anchor through the storm.

Another sob rose in her throat, but she forced it down. She couldn't fall apart. John needed her to keep her wits. She blinked back the tears filling her eyes and dragged in a deep breath.

Using every scrap of willpower, she unclenched her hands from Ansel's tunic and straightened. His arms loosened around her slightly, but instead of releasing her completely, his hands slid to her waist to steady her as she regained her feet.

"I am sorry to be the one to bring such news, lass," he said, his voice a husky whisper. "But John is in more danger than ye initially thought. Perhaps ye were right to send him away, but now his best chance for survival is under my protection."

"Nay," she mumbled, shaking her head to clear it of the intoxicating scent that seemed to curl around her. It made her feel…safe, for the first time in a long time. But that was an illusion. The only true safety to be had required that she keep John's location a secret.

Ansel's fingers tightened ever so slightly around her waist. "Ye still refuse to trust me. But *ye* may be in danger, too, if ye are the only one who holds the knowledge of John's whereabouts."

"Nay, I'm not in any danger—"

"Did the attacks stop once ye sent John away?"

"What?"

He pinned her with his dark gaze, his eyes searing her. "Once ye put John into hiding, did more unexplainable accidents befall ye?"

Ice shot through her veins even as she felt a flush rise in her cheeks at the hot brand of his hands on her waist. "A-aye. A month ago. I was in the marketplace in Embleton. A runaway cart almost struck me."

A muscle jumped in his jaw as she spoke. "Edward's men may be targeting ye as well, then. Either they seek information about John's whereabouts, or they hope to dispatch ye along with John."

Isolda's eyes widened and her lips slid apart. She must have looked terrified, for Ansel's eyes softened even as his brows drew together.

"I am no' yer enemy, Lady Isolda. I can protect both ye and John, but ye must *let* me."

So close to this strong, fierce man, she felt her resolve crumbling. Unbidden tears stung her eyes once more. How she longed to feel safe again—truly safe, not jumping at the sight of strange men or constantly looking over her shoulder.

But she had made a vow to herself to protect John with her life. If she had to carry the secret of his location to her grave, so be it. Although she longed to trust the man before her, she'd made that mistake once before. She'd trusted Lancaster, but never again would she err like that—not when her son's life hung in the balance.

"I...I cannot tell you where he is," she breathed, silently pleading with him to understand. She felt a hair's breadth from falling apart again under his searching brown eyes.

Slowly, he let his hands drop from her waist. He nodded, still holding her with his gaze. "I ken that ye want to keep yer son safe. But ye must understand that I have been given a mission by my King."

Her heart twisted in anticipation of another battle mounting between her and the unswayable Highland warrior before her. She drew in a shaky breath, trying to steel herself. But instead of hardening his features in preparation to spar with her once more, he quirked a dark eyebrow in thought.

"My mission is to protect John, and if ye are the only one who knows where he is, then it is also my mission to protect ye."

He nodded his head and crossed his arms over his chest as if the matter were settled.

She blinked in confusion. "But I have Bertram to look after me. I will be fine."

Now she got the full force of his scowl. "Nay, ye won't be, lass," he retorted. She inhaled sharply at the familiar address he'd given her—the second of this conversation.

"Forgive me, *my lady*," he said, still frowning. "But Bertram will no' be able to stop Edward's men if they are determined to reach John—which they are. Hell, this whole castle is working against ye and in favor of yer attackers. Ye've no gates, no walls, and no guards but one old man!"

Indignation over the insult to Bertram flared. "Bertram has served me faithfully and nobly for nigh six years," she shot back. "He is more than capable of protecting me—"

Ansel held up a hand to stop her.

"Ye havenae met many Scots, have ye, my lady?"

Her head spun once more at his abrupt change of topic. "Many Lowlanders have crossed the border to make their home here in Northumbria, and..."

At the slow shake of his head and the arrogant cock of his dark eyebrow, she trailed off.

"But ye have never met a Highlander. Suffice it to say that when we make a decision, it is final. I'll protect ye, and thereby John, as long as a threat exists."

She was at her wit's end. She'd never intended to tell him that John was her son, nor had she anticipated the news that both she and John might be in grave danger. She pinched the bridge of her nose, unable to muster any more steel for her spine.

"I cannot stop you from staying, or from appointing yourself my protector," she said. "But I ask that you stop questioning the people here about me or John. It is unseemly and—"

"Done," he said evenly.

"And I do not want you interfering with the work of the mason or the laborers. As you have already pointed out, they are in Lancaster's employ. They must be allowed to make progress on the castle."

"That I cannae promise," he said, his face set. "There will be some changes around here, if only for yer safety."

She was too weary to fight anymore. The tears she'd held inside throbbed in the back of her eyes and another headache was forming. All she could manage was a nod.

"Please excuse me," she said, scraping together the last semblance of propriety she could muster. She strode past him and to the stairs, then stepped carefully down to the yard. She had to will herself not to run straight to her tower and instead glided as a lady would across the grass.

But when she had climbed the stairs to her chamber and closed the door, she could hold back the tears no longer.

Both her and her son's lives were in danger, entangled by political schemers who spun them in a web as if they were no more than flies. And the only thing standing between her and death was a roguish Highlander with dark eyes and warm, strong hands.

Chapter Eight

Ansel splashed cool water over his face and bare chest. Though dreary clouds had dominated the sky for the last sennight, today had been a brilliant fall day. The sun had blazed in a crystal-clear blue sky, enticing the castle laborers to strip down to just their breeches.

He straightened, his eyes immediately traveling up the northwest tower to the window he now knew to be Lady Isolda's. Sure enough, she stood at the window, the wooden shutters drawn back to let the sunshine and warm air inside. Even from this distance, he could feel her gaze shift to land on him where he stood along the wall.

With a curse for himself, he ripped his gaze away. He couldn't deny his attraction—she was a beautiful woman, and he was a virile man, after all. But it was a distraction, one he could ill afford with so much to do still.

Over the last sennight, he'd taken charge of Dunstanburgh's construction, much to the vexation of the Master Mason, Elias.

His first order of business had been to shift the laborers' efforts from the patch of curtain wall along the southern edge of the keep to the gatehouse. Though having a completed wall was essential to properly fortify the castle, it was far more important to have a gate to block the primary entrance to the keep.

At least with the wall standing a minimum of a few feet all around, an assailant would have to scramble over it, wasting precious seconds of an attack, and potentially the element of surprise. In addition, no horses could be driven over the wall's thick base. But leaving the main entrance completely unbarred was simply unacceptable. Ansel himself had ridden in without so much as slowing his horse.

Of course, the problems had started immediately. Master Elias, the wiry little man with a sharp mind but a stubborn streak, had objected to Ansel ordering his crew of workers, especially when it meant pulling them off the task of completing the wall.

Master Elias's sole focus was to finish his task on time, lest the precious months before construction had to be halted for winter be wasted. But Ansel didn't care a whit for Elias's schedule if it meant leaving the castle—and Lady Isolda—vulnerable to attack.

After much debate, Ansel had at last convinced Elias that shifting to the wooden gates wouldn't set back his schedule, for the task needed to be done eventually anyway. But the portcullis wasn't going to be completed and delivered until next spring, according to the mason.

Though Ansel had wanted to throttle the man several times in only a sennight, he'd taken to spending his time with the mason and his workers. Partly it had been done out of convenience—he lent his strength to the task of fitting and erecting the wooden gates, and consequently took his meals with the men.

But he also had a strategic purpose in embedding himself amongst the laborers. The men flowed into the castle every morning at dawn, then walked back to the village of Embleton at dusk. It was hard to keep track of all of their faces. If Ansel wasn't able to seal Dunstanburgh's walls and lower its portcullis tight before winter was upon them, he could at least keep an eye on who came and went from the castle.

He cupped his hands once more in the bucket of cool well water at his feet and splashed away the day's labor. As he watched the workers file out through the new wooden gates, he felt that telltale itch between his shoulder blades.

Lady Isolda still watched him. He cursed himself silently. How was he expected to keep his mind sharp and his body focused with a beautiful—if haughty—English noblewoman watching him at all hours?

Ansel stomped toward the gatehouse, where he'd discarded his tunic and belt with his sword fastened to it.

"Bertram," he barked, startling the lingering laborers. They gave him a wide berth as they quickened their steps through the gates. Aye, he thought sourly, despite working alongside them for the last sennight, they were obviously still wary of the cantankerous Scot in their midst.

Ansel didn't bother donning his tunic, for though the sun was just slipping behind the mountains to the west, the earth still held the day's warmth. As he strapped his belt around his hips, Bertram came shuffling from Lady Isolda's unfinished tower.

Unbidden, Ansel's eyes shot from the door where Bertram emerged to the window where Lady Isolda had stood watching, but his gaze was a second too late. He caught a glimpse of swishing green fabric and then the shutters snapped closed.

Bertram fumbled for the sword on his hip as he crossed the grassy yard toward Ansel. The man's gate was stiff, likely from their little training sessions. Ansel had insisted that the old guard train with him from sunset, when the laborers headed toward the village, until the blue light of gloaming turned too dark for sword work.

Ansel pulled his sword free of its scabbard smoothly.

Without waiting for Bertram to take up a readied stance or raise his own sword, Ansel launched an attack. Bertram barely managed to get a handle on his weapon and deflect the blow. Their blades rang out across the quiet yard.

"Today's lesson is on preparedness," Ansel said, pivoting for a new angle of attack. He feinted right, then struck out at Bertram from the left.

"The lesson being that there is no such thing as being prepared enough."

Bertram blocked the attack but only had time to take a shuffling step back before Ansel lunged again.

Just as Ansel spun to level a mighty blow on Bertram's weaker side, the wooden door of Lady Isolda's tower thumped faintly.

Ansel halted abruptly in mid-turn, sword raised over his shoulder. Lady Isolda's pale skin stood out starkly in the falling twilight. Her emerald green surcoat was cut flat across the top, baring the curve of her shoulders to the evening air.

Bertram, already panting from Ansel's ruthless attacks, took the opening Ansel gave him. He thrust forward, aiming for Ansel's middle.

At the last possible moment, Ansel yanked his gaze away from Lady Isolda and parried the blow. He turned, letting Bertram's momentum carry him forward even as he grabbed the man's wrist. With a quick twist, he torqued the blade free of Bertram's grip.

Bertram stumbled forward with a grunt of surprise. When he turned to find Ansel with both blades cocked in his grip, he folded in a slump, his hands on his knees and his breath ragged.

"Is this really necessary?"

Ansel's head snapped back to Lady Isolda, who glided across the yard, emerald brocade swishing softly against the grass.

"Aye, it is." Ansel tossed Bertram's sword onto the ground at the older man's feet, then spun his own blade in his palm, readying for another attack. "Again, Bertram."

Lady Isolda stepped between Ansel and her guard. "Nay, Bertram, it is all right. You may rest for a moment."

"No, he may no'. Yer fierce guard here is rusty with a blade and sorely in need of the exertion."

Lady Isolda took several sudden strides toward Ansel. "There is no need to embarrass him. He is a good man," she bit out in little more than a whisper, thus shielding Bertram from her words.

Ansel exhaled slowly through his teeth. Aye, Bertram had never once complained over the grueling hour of training Ansel had put him through each evening. But Lady Isolda still didn't seem to understand how little her aging guard would be able to do against another attack by one of Edward's men.

"He needs this," he said, studiously keeping his voice low as well. "Hell, he needed this every day for the last decade. If he is to be ready when—no' if—another attack comes, he must train."

She raised her hand and waved it dismissively in the small space between them. The motion drew Ansel's gaze down. He immediately regretted it.

The low cut of her surcoat not only revealed the creamy skin of her shoulders, but also her delicate collar bones—and the soft curve of the tops of her breasts. They rose and fell gently with her breathing, but under his gaze, her breaths grew rapid and shallow.

His manhood surged to life despite the small voice in the back of his mind screaming that he shouldn't—couldn't—be attracted to this woman.

He forced his gaze from her breasts up the slim column of her neck, where he saw her throat bob in a swallow. When his eyes reached her mouth, her tongue darted out to moisten her lips.

Shite.

He was acting like the barbarian she'd called him by salivating over her like some starved animal. But when his gaze continued upward at last to her eyes, he was startled to find that she was actually staring at his bare chest.

Her pale green eyes almost seemed to glow in the fading light as they darted over his exposed form. Color rose in her cheeks even as she shifted her gaze to the ground between them. She visibly floundered to regain her regal air, but a long moment stretched, with neither of them saying anything.

Bertram shifted behind her, saving them both from having to find their tongues.

"It is all right, my lady," he panted, bending to retrieve his sword. "The training is doing me good. And Ansel is right—we must be prepared."

One thimbleful of tension drained from Ansel. At least he'd convinced Bertram of the reality of the threat against Lady Isolda. If only the lady herself wouldn't be so damnably stubborn.

She turned slightly toward Bertram, breaking the invisible spell that had held them so close. "We *are* prepared, Bertram. No harm has befallen me that you haven't been able to handle. I simply wish…"

She smoothed her hands down the front of her surcoat. "I wish for life to go on as normally as possible." She turned back to Ansel, her eyes firmly confined to his face. "You are unsettling Master Elias and the workers. Bertram is sore and tired. And I—"

"Aye?" Ansel said lowly. "Am I unsettling ye as well?" He leaned forward, all but obliterating the remaining space between them. He couldn't seem to help it—ruffling this noblewoman's feathers sent the blood hammering in his veins.

"Aye," she said, her voice suddenly breathy. "You are disturbing the peace here, Ansel Sutherland."

He snorted. For some reason, she couldn't seem to drop his clan name when speaking to him—at least in front of others. They hadn't addressed the fact that she'd fainted into his arms, or shed tears before him, since that day a sennight ago. She'd simply slipped back into her carefully cold demeanor once more. It must seem too intimate to discuss. Doing so would threaten her seemingly unflappable exterior—just like calling him solely by his given name or staring at his bare chest would.

"The peace here is an illusion," he said, the lust in his veins suddenly tinged with dark memories. "This is

Northumbria, is it no'? Peace and the Borderlands dinnae mix. And peace for someone who has been targeted by the King of England is impossible. Trust me—a Scot would ken."

Uncertainty flashed in her pale eyes, but she quickly replaced it with that stubborn defiance he'd seen often enough already. She tilted her chin in that regal way and parted her lips to argue with him, but just then an idea sparked in the back of his mind.

Before she could debate the need for his protection yet again, he interjected. "But if ye truly believe that all I'm doing here is unnecessary, perhaps ye'd be willing to put yer keep—and yer guard—to a test."

With her lips still parted, she tilted her head, but this time it was in confusion. Her dark brows came together over her eyes.

"What do you mean, a *test*?"

As the idea took shape, Ansel couldn't stop the slow smile that began spreading across his face.

"Ye think ye dinnae need my protection. Ye think that Bertram here is enough, and that all the changes I'm making to Master Elias's construction plan are unnecessary."

Guardedly, she nodded her agreement.

"And I wish to prove to ye that ye are a sitting duck here, with naught but an old man's sword and a few piles of stones to stand between ye and whoever seeks John's location."

She stiffened slightly at the mention of her son's

name.

"I mean no offense, Bertram," Ansel said with a shrug to the aging guard. "But ye dinnae understand what ye're up against—neither of ye."

Bertram came to stand by his lady's side, still slightly out of breath from his earlier exertion. Even still, Bertram's shoulders squared indignantly. "And what do you think you can do to make us...*understand*?"

Though Bertram had been willing to train without complaint, Ansel had found the edge of his willingness to go along with a Scottish outsider's plans. *Good*. Bertram would benefit from this demonstration just as much as Lady Isolda, then.

"I'm going to attack the keep—tonight. Put up yer best defense, and I'll prove to ye that it is past time ye get behind me in my efforts to shore this place up."

Lady Isolda blinked up at him. "You are going to *attack* the keep? What do you intend to do?"

"As I told Bertram earlier," Ansel said, re-sheathing his sword, "ye can never be prepared enough. Ye already have the benefit of the knowledge that I plan to attack tonight. If I was one of Edward's men, what would ye do to stop me?"

As Lady Isolda sputtered for the words to no doubt set him down a peg or two, he strode toward the gatehouse, where his tunic still lay in the entryway.

"I'll give ye an hour," he said, pulling his tunic over his head. "Then I'll come for ye."

He almost laughed as Lady Isolda indignantly

planted her fists on her hips.

"Come, my lady," Bertram said, guiding her back toward her tower. "Don't concern yourself with this game. He's just trying to prove a point, but we can prove one as well."

Ansel strode past the already-closed gate and toward a particularly low section of the curtain wall. He hoisted himself atop the thick stones, holding his sword in place on his hip.

"Good luck," he taunted before slipping down to the outside of the unfinished wall.

He caught a glimpse of Lady Isolda's face turning back toward him just before Bertram closed the tower's wooden door behind her and positioned himself in front of it.

This would be too easy.

Chapter Nine

This would be too easy.

Isolda paced the length of her chamber, then turned in front of the shuttered window and walked back toward her barred door. She pressed her lips together to prevent an unladylike curse of frustration from slipping out.

Had it been an hour yet?

Bertram had eaten a quick and simple meal with her and Mary, as was his habit, but then he'd returned to stand guard outside the tower. Mary had been in a flap about the prospect of Ansel attacking the castle, even if it was only to prove a point. Isolda had instructed her to take to her own chamber for the rest of the evening, knowing that the maid wasn't Ansel's target.

She was.

I'll come for ye.

For some reason, his words had sent a shiver down her spine. Even now they echoed in her mind, twisting her stomach into a hot knot that wasn't entirely accounted for by her trepidation for this little *test*, as he'd called it.

Of course, behind her bluster, she knew from the

moment he proposed his plan that they couldn't withstand his assault on the castle. She'd watched him work alongside the village laborers for the last sennight and spied on him as he trained with Bertram every evening. His body was stacked with hard-earned strength, his muscles coiled and taut under his sun-bronzed skin. The way he moved with his sword, it was as if the blade was an extension of his body. And his sharp gaze seemed to miss nothing—even her foolish staring.

But some part of her still didn't want to believe what he said was true—that John's life was in graver danger than she ever could have imagined, and now hers was, too. She longed to cling to her isolation here at Dunstanburgh, for even though John's absence was painful, at least she could pretend that sending him away had marked the end of the threat they faced.

But nay, this Highland rogue with a foul tongue and an even fouler mood insisted on proving just how vulnerable she was.

No matter, she told herself firmly, straightening her spine though her chamber was empty. She had a few tricks to show him yet.

She crossed to the window for the hundredth time that evening. A sliver of moonlight slid through the shutters. Night had fallen in earnest. Ansel was coming.

As she stood before the shuttered window, her curiosity bested her. Slowly, she unlatched the shutters. Just a peek into the yard, she promised herself. Careful to keep the motion as small and unnoticeable as possible, she cracked the shutters and peered down.

The half-moon hung brightly in the cloudless night sky. Its light bathed the yard in a silvery glow, though the gatehouse and parts of the curtain wall cast deep shadows. Her eyes scanned quickly for any hint of movement, but all was still.

If she angled her head just right, she could see Bertram where he stood at the tower's door. She almost smiled. Bertram normally slept in the wooden stables along the wall between her tower and the gatehouse. But at least for the sake of Ansel's game, he was a valiant guard this evening.

Isolda's mirth evaporated with that thought. Bertram had been with her since the moment she'd left Clitheroe, a crying newborn in her arms and not a friend in the world besides Mary.

It had seemed like an insult on Lancaster's part—or an afterthought—to send Bertram to watch over Isolda and little John. Whatever his intent, or lack of it, Lancaster had given her an angel in the form of the aging soldier. Bertram had protected John from the village drunkard wielding a knife. But compared to Ansel, Bertram seemed more suited to be a kindly companion rather than her sole protector.

Just then a shadow shifted ever so slightly near the stables. She inhaled sharply. From her angle looking down on the yard, she could see the faintly darker shadow moving along the wall, but the sight was blocked to Bertram where he stood at the tower's door.

She opened her mouth to give him warning, but then clamped it shut. How often did she stand guard from her chamber, scanning the yard for intruders? Nay, Bertram would have to meet the threat on his own.

The shadow disappeared behind the stables. A moment later, the stable doors burst open and a large form dashed out into the yard.

Isolda had to clamp a hand over her mouth to prevent from crying out in surprise. Her eyes darted after the huge blob darting across the yard. As the moonlight fell on it, she realized it was a horse, not a man.

She jerked her gaze to Bertram, who'd started at the sudden appearance of the horse as well. He had his sword drawn, and his gaze followed the animal.

Suddenly she saw the first shadow move again. It sprang from the cover of darkness along the curtain wall right next to the tower. Bertram, distracted by the horse, didn't see the attack until it was too late. A blade flashed in the moonlight, settling directly against his throat.

Bertram froze, his body tense under the blade.

"Ye're dead." Ansel's gruff, low whisper barely made it to Isolda's ears where she crouched in front of the cracked shutters.

The blade disappeared from Bertram's neck, and he visibly relaxed.

"Give me the key to the tower door."

"Nay!" Bertram shot back in a raised whisper.

She faintly heard Ansel's snort. "If I were a real attacker, I'd simply take the keys off yer dead body. Give them."

After a long pause, Isolda heard the key ring jangle as Bertram removed it from the pouch on his belt.

"Wait here," Ansel said. "And dinnae interfere—remember, ye're dead."

Now it was Bertram's turn to snort indignantly.

The key turned in the tower door's lock, and then she heard the soft squeak of the hinges as the door swung open.

Her heart hitched into her throat. Aye, it was only a game, but her stomach fluttered with anticipation. Ansel had made it into the tower, but that didn't mean the game was over.

She stood and stepped toward her chamber's door. With trembling fingers, she plucked the bejeweled dagger from her desk and took up her position. The dagger was ornamental, yet because it was never used, the blade was as sharp as ever.

Time stretched as she waited. Ansel must be slowly and systematically sweeping the tower, small as it was. How long would it take him to reach her chamber? It was on the first landing up the stairs from the ground floor, yet he seemed to be taking his time.

She nigh jumped out of her skin when her door rattled. He pulled and pushed for a moment, then cursed quietly in the stairwell on the other side of the thick door. Isolda pressed her lips together against the combination of anticipation and glee. He'd be realizing just now that her door didn't have a lock, which meant that his key ring wouldn't help him a whit.

The solid oak beam across her door vibrated as he tried to ram his way through, but both the door and the beam didn't budge.

Just as smug satisfaction began curling her lips, the tip of his sword slid through the thin gap between the door and the wall. Slowly, the blade worked farther inside as he carefully threaded it in the narrow space.

She almost cried out again as the blade abruptly jammed upward into the beam. The beam jostled but remained in place. Again, the sword whacked the slab of wood. After several more tries, the blade finally dislodged the oak beam, sending it tumbling to the stone floor.

The door swung open slowly, but she'd positioned herself so that the wood now hid her from the rest of the room, casting her in shadow. She gripped her dagger, willing her heart to slow and her feet to stay rooted until the moment to strike arrived.

At first, all she could see was Ansel's blade, illuminated weakly by the beam of moonlight slicing into the chamber from the cracked shutters. As he stepped cautiously into the room, his hand and then his arm came into her line of sight. At last, his broad back filled her vision.

"Ye can come out now, Lady Isolda," he said softly,

his gaze focused on her shadowy bed. She held her breath. He took another step closer to the bed, lowering his sword and re-sheathing it.

"I hope this little exercise has shown ye just how helpless ye are here."

Still he didn't turn toward her. Instead, he took another step toward the lumpy bed. She'd piled several pillows under the covers to make it appear as though she lay there. Her ruse had worked.

With two swift, silent steps on slippered feet, she closed the distance between them. Raising the dagger, she thrust it forward until it pinned the material of his tunic to his back.

Instantly, he tensed. She pressed the dagger ever so slightly harder.

"Not entirely helpless," she said, her voice swelling with triumph.

Like lightning, he spun around, catching her wrist in his large hand. In one smooth move, he torqued her arm so that her elbow bent and the dagger slipped behind her. She collided into the hard wall of his chest, her wrist restrained behind her back and her body flush with his. He squeezed the hand that was wrapped around her wrist ever so slightly, and despite her resistance, the dagger was suddenly pinned against *her* lower back.

All her triumph vaporized, to be replaced by a flood of hot panic. But it wasn't fear for her safety that made her squirm in Ansel's unyielding hold. Nay, it was the sudden and overwhelming contact with his body that turned her stomach into a scorching knot.

Her free hand rose to shove at his chest, but he caught her other wrist as well and bent it behind her. Impossibly, he bound both of her wrists with just one large, warm hand. His other hand plucked the dagger from her grasp. He tossed it casually on the bed behind him.

"Do ye intend to stand in hiding behind yer door while yer pillows take yer place in bed every night for the foreseeable future?" His voice was a low rumble that vibrated through her breasts where they were plastered against his chest.

She writhed in a redoubled effort to free herself, but it seemed to have no effect.

Nay, that wasn't entirely true. Ansel suddenly hissed a curse. Her head snapped up to find his face tight, a muscle ticking in his jaw. His eyes were a dark storm, but there was no trace of his usual ire there. Instead, raw, pure lust lay in their shadowy depths.

She inhaled sharply, but all it did was compress her breasts all the more fully to his chest. With each of his breaths, she could feel every corded muscle straining against his thin linen tunic.

He stared down at her, his heated gaze tearing through every last one of her defenses. She felt her regal façade crumbling. In his hard embrace, all that was left was the truth. She was just a woman. A woman who desperately wanted him.

The hand that bound both her wrists loosened ever so slightly. If she had wanted to, she realized distantly, she could have broken free with a swift yank. But she was mesmerized by the hunger in his gaze. What did he see reflected in her eyes? Did he see a longing that matched his own?

His free hand slowly rose toward her face. Callused fingertips brushed her neck, sending goose bumps racing down her arms and tightening her nipples beneath all the layers of fabric she wore like armor. His hand slipped to her nape, his fingers burying themselves in the base of her braid.

With slow determination, he tilted her head back. His hungry eyes dipped to her lips, which parted as she fought to control her breathing. Even though she knew what he intended, still she did not break free. Instead, her tongue slid across her lower lip involuntarily.

His fingers tightened in her hair at the unconscious act. He lowered his head to hers, his breath whispering across her lips for the faintest moment of hesitation. It was her last out, but she would not take it.

Instead, she lifted her chin ever so slightly, giving him all that he sought.

His mouth descended on hers then, no more hesitancy left. His lips were soft yet his kiss was demanding, claiming her with savage fierceness.

He tilted his head, fusing them together more fully. With a flick of his tongue, he tasted her lips.

And she opened to him.

At the first brush of his tongue against hers, a shudder tore through her all the way to her toes.

Their tongues entwined in silken heat, dancing and caressing. Somehow he pressed his body even closer until his warmth and scent completely engulfed her. Every angle and plane of him was hard and hot except for his velvety tongue.

She suddenly became aware of the rigid column of his manhood pressing against her belly. Passion-drunk, she arched her back, pressing into his hard shaft.

A groan ripped from his throat, sending tingles through her lips where they were fused together.

Suddenly he tore his mouth away, leaving them both taut and panting. Her lips and chin felt raw from his lust-filled kiss and the scrape of his stubble. Her nipples tingled from rubbing against his chest. Liquid heat pooled between her legs, unfulfilled need pulsing there.

She'd been kissed before, but never like that—never so demanding, so scalding with pent-up desire.

Suddenly shame mixed hotly with lust in her veins. Aye, she'd kissed before—and more. What had happened to her vow never again to let passion rule her? How could she have forgotten the consequences with a mere look from this rugged Highlander?

She took a wobbling step back and smoothed her surcoat with trembling hands. "We shouldn't have—"

"Did ye hear that?" he cut in abruptly, his dark brows descending.

"W-what?" She'd assumed he'd halted their kiss because it was wrong, not because some noise had distracted him.

She straightened, trying to salvage what little dignity she could. Just as she opened her mouth to reassert that the kiss had been out of line, a whinny drifted up from the yard below.

"Eachann," Ansel breathed. He strode to the shutters and pulled one back. Isolda followed, peering around his broad shoulder at the moonlit yard.

"Your horse?" she asked softly.

"Aye."

"There." She pointed to the far southeast corner of the keep, where the wall stood highest. A swish of the horse's tail flashed out of the shadows, followed by another soft whinny.

"Something is wrong."

Ansel's hard, flat voice sent unease rippling through her.

"What is—"

Before the question was out, the quiet night was shattered by the battle cries of a dozen men.

Chapter Ten

The shadows were suddenly alive.

Below Lady Isolda's window, the yard filled with swarming warriors, their drawn blades flashing in the moonlight.

Christ. Dread flashed for one blinding moment in Ansel's brain. They were under attack, but this was no game or test.

"Nay!"

Isolda stumbled back from the window, barely catching herself before she tumbled to the ground by gripping one of the thick posters on her bed.

Instinct suddenly fused with the long years of training, sending a strange clarity through Ansel's mind even as his body surged with energy.

"Stay here," he said, striding toward the door.

"What about Bertram?" Isolda's voice hitched close to hysteria.

"Dinnae fear. And bar this door behind me."

Even before he'd crossed through her chamber's doorway, his hand wrapped around his sword. The sound of metal hissing against leather as he unsheathed the blade was a familiar comfort.

As he bolted down the stairs, he heard the heavy thump of the beam being placed across Lady Isolda's door. She would be safe. He would make sure of it.

But as he reached the bottom of the spiraling stairs, he heard a bellow that sent a stab of foreboding into his belly.

Bertram.

Ansel dashed to the door, which he'd closed behind him when he'd entered earlier. He ripped open the door just in time to see Bertram slumping to the ground before it. A darkly clad man yanked his blade free of the old soldier, then turned toward Ansel in the open doorway.

Though his ears were filled with the roar of battle and the pounding of his own blood, Ansel's mind went quiet. Now was not the time for thinking. There was only the man directly in front of him.

He rooted himself where he stood, raising his blade in invitation to his opponent. The darkly clothed man charged with a wordless battle cry, driving his blade forward to impale Ansel.

But Ansel used the doorframe to his advantage. He twisted out of the way at the last moment, then pinned his attacker's blade between his own and the wooden doorframe. With a swift thrust along the length of the other man's sword, Ansel's blade found its home in the man's chest.

He barely had time to boot his dying opponent away before an identical attacker set upon him. His body turned liquid, each move so familiar that he might have been floating in a dream. But with every parry, with every lethal blow, with every strike that drove one opponent back, another would surge forward.

How many were there? Ansel was a fraction of a second too slow blocking the arcing blade of one of his attackers. His sword took the brunt of the force, but the blade sliced across his shoulder. The sting barely registered, but he knew distantly that when the battle lust cleared, the wound would need stitches.

Sweat and blood—his or his enemies', he couldn't say—mingled, stinging his eyes. His muscles burned dully, yet he sensed an ebb in the wave of attackers. He at last stepped from the protection of the doorway to meet the last man standing in the yard.

Moonlight glinted off the man's pale hair. He clutched his sword with two hands, but instead of his hands being positioned next to each other on the hilt, one was balled on top of the other. Something whispered in the back of Ansel's mind. This man was inexperienced with a weapon.

Ansel waited for the man to come to him. If his intuition was right, the man would attack first, as most beginners did, thus opening himself to a counterattack.

Just as he'd anticipated, the blond man let out a cry and charged forward, blade leveled at Ansel's chest. With an easy sidestep, Ansel spun and slashed his blade along the man's exposed back. The attacker fell to his knees, the sword tumbling from his hands before he slumped to the blood-darkened grass.

Ansel stood in a sea of bodies, their still forms gilded in moonlight.

The horrible memories stacked on top of each other, turning years of battles into one single nightmare. Ansel's ears rang with the echoes of battle cries, clanging metal, and dying screams of agony and fear.

This wasn't Bannockburn, he reminded himself with a little shake, nor was it any of the other battles for Scotland's independence he'd fought in. Nay, this skirmish was to protect Lady Isolda. Bannockburn was over.

A new scream tore through his thoughts, but this one didn't arise from his dark memories. It was a woman's cry of panic, real and present.

Isolda.

His gaze lurched from the attackers at his feet in the yard to her window above in the tower.

Fear, pure and white-hot, tore through him.

A grappling hook had been tossed through her window and was secured to the window ledge. A long rope dangled from the hook down the side of the stone tower and into the yard.

He bolted back into the tower, terror replacing the eerily calm battle haze from a moment before.

"Isolda!"

Chapter Eleven

Isolda had struggled to lift the thick oak beam and replace it across her chamber door. The fear coursing through her veins gave her a surge of extra strength. With a thud, the beam had fallen back into place.

A cacophony of battle cries rose from the yard and assaulted her ears as she paced back to the window. Just as she was going to peer out into the darkness past the open shutters, though, the clang of metal on metal rang out.

Ansel and Bertram were down there. Terror swelled until her throat closed and her head spun. She clapped her hands over her ears, but the sounds of fighting and death were only slightly muffled. Slowly, she sank to the floor, holding her head and praying for Ansel and Bertram's lives.

Time stretched nightmarishly. Screams of pain thrummed against her hands where they blocked her ears. Who was attacking them? Were those Bertram's screams? Ansel's? How much longer could this horror go on?

A much louder clang vibrated the stones beneath

her, cutting through her panic. Her head snapped up, her vision filling with a new terror. A large metal hook clung to her window ledge.

Renewed fear flooded her. The thick wooden beam across her door wouldn't save her now.

She scrambled to her feet, her hands flying to the hook. She clawed desperately at it, but it was wedged securely against the stone window opening. Her eyes traveled out the window to the rope fastened to the hook. Halfway up the tower, a shadowy man was scaling upward, his feet planted on the stones and his hands pulling him quickly up the rope.

Isolda frantically tore at the hook and the rope, drawing blood from her fingers, but it was no use. In a flash of clarity, she remembered the dagger Ansel had tossed onto her bed.

She dove toward the bed, her hands fumbling for the dagger's jeweled hilt. Just as her fingers closed around the cool metal, a shadow loomed in her window, blocking out the moonlight.

A scream rose in her throat as the shadow leapt in and landed in a crouch. He stood slowly, seemingly unperturbed by her terrified cry.

"We can do this the easy way," he said, his voice a soft whisper. "Or the other way."

He advanced on her, backlit by the weak moonlight coming in from the window. Her fingers tightened on the dagger within the folds of her bedding, but some distant voice of reason told her to wait, to bide her time.

"W-what do you want?" she breathed through trembling lips.

"The boy."

Icy fear stabbed her belly.

"He...he isn't here."

The man froze for a second as if considering her words. But then, as if from a nightmare, he advanced once more until he loomed over her where she sprawled on the bed.

"Where is he?"

Even through the terror twisting in her stomach, renewed courage surged within her. She would protect John with her life if she had to.

"I'll never tell."

The man's dark head tilted, and a beam of silver light caught the side of his face. To her horror, a soft smile curved his mouth.

"We'll see about that."

Like lighting, he fell on her, his weight pressing her into the bed. She screamed again, but his hands clamped around her neck, cutting off her air.

"Isolda!"

Ansel's voice ripped through the night from the yard outside.

She tried to call back to him, to beg for his help, but all that came out was a croak beneath the man's iron grip.

Suddenly the door vibrated with the force of a

powerful impact.

"Isolda!" Ansel's voice came again, right outside her door. The oak beam bounced across the door as he slammed into it once more.

The man's hands tightened until not even a wisp of air could slip into her lungs. Realization washed over her as she dragged futilely for breath. Ansel's trick to dislodge the oak beam with his sword would take too long. She'd lose consciousness before then—or she'd be dead.

Another blow assailed the door, but this time the wood creaked and groaned. Again, both the door and beam shivered under Ansel's attack, and now the sound of splintering rent the air.

The man looming over her darted his head toward the door nervously. Spots swam before her eyes as her lungs burned with the need for air.

Now, a distant voice whispered in the back of her mind.

Isolda yanked her hand free of the bedcovers, the dagger flashing through the air. She drove the blade into her attacker's side.

With a surprised grunt and a whoosh of air, his hands loosened around her neck. Even as she sucked in a greedy breath, she drove her knee up toward his groin. He blocked her intended target with his leg, yet he had to roll partially off her to do so.

She lashed out at him with every last thread of strength she possessed, clawing and kicking like a wildcat.

The chamber door suddenly exploded in a shower of splinters and chunks of wood. And then Ansel was launching forward, sword drawn and dark with blood.

Her attacker leapt to his feet and scrambled toward the window. Time seemed to slow as Isolda watched. Something bright flashed in the man's hands. Her brain, air-starved and overwrought with fear, was slow to understand what was happening.

But then the flashing object flew from the man's hand and sailed toward Ansel.

"Nay!" she screamed, but it was too late, for another flash darted from her attacker's grip and cut a line directly for Ansel.

Ansel somehow managed to twist away as the first dagger sped toward him. The small blade caught him in the arm rather than the chest, where her attacker had aimed it. But as the first dagger's impact jerked him back, he didn't have time to evade the second. The blade sank into his chest, the hilt quivering where it protruded.

And yet Ansel still staggered on toward the man at the window. Her assailant recoiled under Ansel's lurching advance. The man threw a leg out the window, then grabbed the rope with one hand, clutching his side with the other where Isolda's dagger still jutted. In a blink, he slid down the rope into the yard below.

Ansel stumbled to the windowsill and leaned his

head out.

"Shite," he muttered, his gaze shifting restlessly. "He's getting away."

He tried to leverage himself out the window, but when he lifted his sword arm, he winced and cursed in pain. His sword clattered to the stone floor next to the bed where Isolda sprawled.

She struggled to sit upright, but pain and fear left her weak. Her gaze locked on the two daggers bristling from his right arm and chest. Blood soaked his tunic and splattered his face. He looked like a monster—a monster who'd just saved her.

A sob tore from her raw throat. The sound must have broken through his embattled mind, for suddenly he moved toward her.

"Isolda," he ground out, his jaw clenched in obvious pain. "It is all right now. Ye are safe."

Chapter Twelve

Ansel's words didn't seem to penetrate through Isolda's fear, for her eyes remained wide on the daggers in his arm and upper chest.

"It is all right, lass," he said again, willing his voice to soften despite the fear that still hammered in his body. "Did he hurt ye?"

She blinked, her pale eyes clouding with confusion. "I am fine, but you…you are going to…"

He glanced down for the first time at the daggers. Aye, they hurt like the bloody Devil now that the adrenaline had ebbed in his veins. One was buried in the thick muscle of his upper arm—his sword arm, no less. The other jutted just below the outer edge of his collarbone, almost in his shoulder.

He reached up and took hold of the blade in his arm. The movement reminded him that his left shoulder would need tending to as well. He had ignored the slice he'd received earlier when he'd put his shoulder to Isolda's door and broke it down.

She gasped, and her hands flew to her mouth as he removed the first dagger with a swift tug. He grunted, but blessedly the blade was only as long as his little finger.

"I'm no' goin' tae die, lass," he bit out as he gripped the other dagger. "These are flesh wounds, naught more. Dinnae fash yerself."

"W-what?"

He jerked the second dagger free, warm blood trickling from the wound. "What do ye mean, what?"

"I...I can't understand you."

He would have laughed if he wasn't bleeding from at least three spots on his aching body. Without realizing it, he'd slipped into a thicker Highland brogue that she couldn't parse.

"Dinnae worry," he said, attempting to give her a smile. "I'll be fine."

She reached out a shaky, bloody hand toward him, her eyes filling with tears. But though she sought to comfort him, the sight of blood on her pale, perfect skin had him seeing red.

"Did he hurt ye?" he repeated, but this time he couldn't keep the hard edge from his voice.

She looked at her hand as if seeing it for the first time. She brought the other to join it in front of her eyes. Her fingertips were scraped raw, and one of her palms was smeared liberally with blood.

"I-I think most of it was...*his*."

As she lowered her trembling fingers, Ansel's gaze shifted to her neck. The delicate skin there was red, with the promise of deep bruises already showing.

Suddenly he had her by the shoulders, holding her

still. Slowly, he lifted a hand and tilted her chin so that he could see her neck.

"I should have followed him out that window," he bit out. "I shouldnae have let him get away."

Her eyes latched on to his. "He...he wanted to know where John is."

Tears rolled down her cheeks, silvered by the moonlight. Something cracked in Ansel's chest and he breathed another curse.

He dragged Isolda into his arms, pain and blood be damned. Her fingers twined in his tunic as sobs shook her slim frame. Her voice was ragged from that bastard's grip on her neck.

Suddenly she shoved herself upright, her eyes wide and shimmering.

"Bertram!"

Ansel jerked to his feet, snatching his sword from the floor along the way. He gritted his teeth against the bolt of fresh pain in his sword arm, but he forced his bloodied fingers to grip the hilt.

"Stay behind me," he said, helping Isolda up. Though his warrior's instinct told him the threat had passed, he didn't want Isolda to see the yard—or Bertram. He'd watched the man go down. He might still live, but it wouldn't be pretty.

He wrapped his hand around hers as he led her through the destroyed door and down the winding stairs. When they came to the ground floor chamber, he pulled her to the side of the open doorway.

"Wait here. And dinnae look, lass," he said gently, releasing her hand. He crossed through the door and moved carefully past the bodies to where he'd seen Bertram last. As he scanned the yard, the moon caught on the copper-gray of the old guard's hair.

Ansel fell to one knee, his hand flying to Bertram's chest. Though weak, a heartbeat still thumped there. Ansel exhaled slowly through his teeth, then resheathed his sword to free both of his hands.

His wounds screamed in protest, but he lifted Bertram with a grunt. Bertram groaned as well when Ansel hoisted him over his shoulder and picked his way back to the tower. When he entered the tower and lowered Bertram carefully to the floor, Isolda covered a cry of distress with her hands.

"He lives," Ansel said. "But he needs all the help we can give him."

Isolda's eyes darted up to his as realization flooded her features. "Oh God. Mary!"

Before he could stop her, she rushed past him and streaked up the stairs. He could hear Isolda calling to Mary abovestairs. Mary's panic-stricken voice replied in a barrage of terrified questions.

"I'll explain later, Mary," Isolda said, her voice growing more distinct as she once again descended the stairs. "But right now, Bertram needs us."

As Mary stepped into the main chamber, her eyes rounded with the scene before her. Ansel stood over Bertram, both men bloodied and Bertram lying prone and unconscious.

Before Mary could dissolve into hysteria, Isolda took her firmly by the shoulders.

"The castle was attacked. Bertram has been wounded. We must see to him."

Admiration for Isolda swelled in Ansel's chest. What sort of lady could put aside her own fear, confusion, and physical pain to take charge of the situation as she just had? Behind her normally cool, regal exterior lay a greater well of strength than he'd realized.

"Get water boiling. And see if you can find some linen to use as bandages. I'll check his wounds."

As Isolda spoke to Mary, a flicker of movement outside had Ansel's head snapping around.

Suddenly tense once more, Ansel eased back out into the yard. A wet cough drew his gaze to the middle of the grassy expanse, where a tuft of pale hair ruffled in the moonlight.

He approached the man who lay on his side in the yard, a weak cough making his shoulders shudder. It was the last man who'd stood against him, the blond-headed one whom Ansel had taken down so swiftly.

The man had somehow managed to roll from his stomach to his side. As Ansel crouched next to him, he flipped him onto his bloody, sliced back. The man groaned and panted in pain, his face contorted into a grimace.

Something clicked into place as Ansel looked down at the man's face.

"I've seen ye before," he breathed, dread sinking like a stone in his stomach. "Ye are one of the laborers from the village. Henry."

Blood tinged the young man's lips as he drew his mouth into a vicious smile.

"Aye."

Icy hatred replaced surprise as he stared at the dying man. "Why?" he ground out between clenched teeth. "Why would ye attack Lady Isolda?"

"Coin—more of it that a Scottish bastard like you will ever lay eyes on," Henry sneered.

"Who paid ye? Answer me!"

Henry coughed again, and this time, his mouth filled with blood. "Someone far more powerful that you. Someone…who will never…stop…"

Ansel shook the man's shoulder, but he had already slipped from this world. With a curse, Ansel straightened. Unease that had nothing to do with his aching, bloodied body spread through him.

Systematically, he went over each body strewn in the yard, checking to make sure they were dead, and then squinting in the moonlight to see if any of the others were from the village. Besides Henry, though, he didn't recognize any of the twelve men lying in the grass.

But there were thirteen attackers, counting the man who escaped. Ansel cursed himself once again for not killing the man for laying a finger on Isolda.

He retrieved Eachann, who stood faithfully next to

the wall where he'd first given the warning of intruders. Ansel secured the animal in the stables, then strode to the tower.

Isolda was already shaken from the night's events. Now he'd have to tell her about Henry and somehow convince her that they must flee.

They were no longer safe here.

Chapter Thirteen

Isolda jumped as Ansel closed the tower door behind him with a soft thud. She hadn't noticed him slip back inside at first, and for a horrifying moment, his movement and the sound of the door closing sent panic twisting like a knife in her belly.

Mary started as well where she crouched on the stone floor, cleaning a red gash across Bertram's chest.

Isolda's raw, shaking fingers fumbled with the needle she was trying to thread by the light of the kitchen fire. When at last she managed to thread the needle, she rose from the fire and turned toward Bertram, but when she stood, Ansel breathed a curse.

"Yer gown."

She looked down. The fine green brocade of her surcoat was blotched with dark blood, some her attacker's, some Bertram's, and some from Ansel when he'd embraced her.

She involuntarily smoothed one hand down the silk brocade, but it only left another smear of blood. Aye, the expensive garment was ruined, but she still had her life—thanks to the grim-faced Highlander before her.

"It is naught," she said softly, kneeling across from

Mary on Bertram's other side.

"How does he fare?" Ansel asked, coming to stand over her.

"The wound is deep but clean."

"Do ye have any yarrow?"

She blinked up at him, but then turned to Mary in askance.

"Aye, I think so," Mary said, rising and moving to the small kitchen.

"What does it do?" Isolda asked, shifting her gaze back to Bertram. His skin was white and his eyes were closed tight, but his chest still rose and fell gently beneath the vicious cut. She sent up another silent prayer for him.

"It will stop the bleeding and ward off infection," Ansel replied.

Again, she found herself blinking up at him in numbed surprise. "How do you know about healing herbs and medicines?"

A weary darkness settled over Ansel's hard features as he met Isolda's searching gaze.

"I've been in many a battle. I've seen men bleed out from wounds, or die of infection from small scratches. I've also seen men's lives saved by a few herbs or dried flowers."

Though his face was set rigidly, his dark brown eyes flickered with a deeper pain for a moment before he shuttered them. Something stirred in Isolda's chest, displacing her own fear and pain briefly. What had this man lived through? What had made him into the hardened warrior before her, and what old wounds still scarred him?

"Here is some," Mary interjected, holding up a dried bundle of the little white blossoms.

"Add those to the boiling water ye have in that caldron," Ansel directed. "Then soak the linen bandages in the yarrow water before applying them."

Mary set about the task silently, her shock likely still buffering her from what was now settling over Isolda. Bertram clung to life. The castle had been attacked. There was no more denying that some powerful force was still hunting John—and now her.

She dragged in a fortifying breath. She could not let the emotions barraging her sweep her away. Yet as she raised the threaded needle over Bertram's chest, her shaking fingers betrayed her.

Ansel crouched beside her, lowering his voice so that Mary might not overhear. "Have ye ever done that before, lass?" he asked, nodding toward the needle she held.

"Nay, not on a man," she blurted. "But I've spent all my life stitching." Just as she was about to say more, she caught herself. She sank her teeth into her lower lip. Noblewomen spent much of their time embroidering, an easy enough explanation for her words. It wasn't the same as the sewing of coarser fabrics she'd spent most of her life working on, but hopefully Ansel wouldn't notice the slip.

"I have stitched men on the battlefield. I can do it again if ye wish."

"I can do it," she said quickly. "I want to help."

He eyed her for a moment, but at last nodded.

With a steeling breath, she lowered the needle to Bertram's chest and began to set the stitches. To her relief, they were neat and small despite her nerves.

When at last she tied off the final stitch, Mary stood waiting with a damp, steaming strip of linen. Isolda rose, wiping her brow with the back of her hand. Mary set to work placing the yarrow-soaked bandages across Bertram's chest. Isolda didn't know if it was a blessing or a bad sign, but Bertram remained unconscious throughout.

"He has a good chance, thanks to ye both," Ansel said softly as Mary laid the last of the bandages on Bertram's long wound.

Mary let out a shaky exhale, bringing trembling fingers to her face. The maid looked suddenly older than Isolda had ever seen. She went to where Mary still crouched next to Bertram and placed a hand on her shoulder.

"Rest now, Mary."

Mary looked up at her with wide, tired eyes. "Nay, my lady. I cannot leave Bertram."

"Then rest here at his side, but we must make sure we are well enough to tend to him," Isolda said gently.

"But what about you, my lady? You must rest as well."

"Nay," she said, her gaze shifting to Ansel, who seemed so tall and large in the small chamber. "I'll tend to Ansel's wounds. You rest, and I'll rouse you when I need you."

It was a testament to just how exhausted and overwrought Mary was, for the steadfast maid didn't muster another protest. Instead, she nodded wearily and lowered herself directly onto the rushes next to Bertram. Within moments, her breathing slipped into the even rhythm of sleep.

Isolda moved toward Ansel, but he held up a hand.

"Dinnae concern yerself over me, lass—Lady Isolda."

She smiled weakly. "And you needn't concern yourself over my title. But as you said, men can die of small injuries left untended. Please." Her voice dropped to barely more than a whisper. "Allow me to see to your wounds."

Perhaps it was because they had to keep their voices low for Mary's sake, or perhaps it was her softly spoken plea, but suddenly a delicate intimacy hung in the air around them.

He nodded, then pulled a stool from the little dining table and positioned it in front of the kitchen hearth. He sat and slowly began peeling off his bloodied and torn tunic.

The fire cast dancing shadows over first the stacked muscles on his stomach, then the curving slabs of strength on his chest as he slowly lifted the tunic. His head disappeared into the garment for a moment as he lifted his arms with a grunt. Then he was entirely free of the tattered tunic, his skin glowing softly beneath the blood and grime of battle.

Isolda averted her gaze and moved to the caldron over the fire. She fumbled with a spoon to remove another strip of linen from the yarrow-soaked water. Her hands felt like wooden blocks once more, but it had less to do with the blood and cuts marring Ansel's flesh than the disconcerting intimacy of being so close to his hard, honed form.

She wrung out one of the rags and turned toward him, fortifying herself with a breath. As carefully as she could, she began dabbing the dagger wound on his right arm. At her first touch, he started slightly but didn't make a sound.

"I ken ye likely dinnae want to think on it, but I need to know more about the man who attacked ye," he said at last, his voice a low murmur.

Her hand stilled for a moment on his arm before she renewed her ministrations. "What do you wish to know?"

"What specifically did he say about John?"

She had to force her lungs to draw in air as the scene played out in her mind.

"He asked where 'the boy' was."

"So he kens yer son is a lad, but he may no' ken his name. That is good. What else?"

She shifted the yarrow-damp rag to the dagger

wound on Ansel's chest. This time, he flinched slightly, a muscle ticking in his jaw.

"I...I told him he wasn't here, and that I would never tell where he was. The man said 'We'll see about that,' and then...then he grabbed me and—"

"Shhh," Ansel soothed. His large hand came up and enfolded hers where she held the damp linen to his chest. His face softened as he looked up and held her gaze. Her vision wobbled as fresh tears sprang to her eyes.

"Forgive me, Isolda, but just a few more questions." His voice was like a dark, silken caress. Through her tears, she saw his eyes pinch with compassion.

She nodded, blinking the tears back and swallowing the lump of fear that had risen in her throat.

"Did ye get a good look at him?"

"Nay," she said, mining her memory with a slow shake of her head. "It was so dark and the moon was behind him. But his hair was likely brown or black."

"Good. What else? What about his voice? Was he Scottish? English? A Borderlander?"

"English," she replied. "He spoke...well. Not a Northerner's inflection."

"Aught else that ye can remember?"

Another tidbit floated to the surface of her mind. "His clothes...he wore no armor, but he did have on a fine leather doublet."

"How do ye ken it was fine if it was dark?"

Her fingertips tingled as she concentrated on the

memory of plunging the dagger into the man's side. "The leather—it was soft and supple, and with tight, small stitches running down the side seam."

Ansel's hand dropped from hers and his gaze narrowed on the floor in thought. "No armor, likely so that he could move quickly and quietly. But a finely made doublet means he is no commoner." He muttered a curse beneath his breath. "I cannae imagine it would be anyone other than one of Edward's men or the right hand of some other noble set against Lancaster."

It was all true, then—everything that Ansel had said was true, despite her desperate longing for it not to be so. A leaden knot of dread tightened her stomach.

Suddenly needing to busy herself, she moved around to his left shoulder, where blood dripped down his arm.

"There is something else I must tell ye," Ansel said, his low voice filled with reluctance.

Just then her eyes landed fully on the wound. She inhaled sharply. He must have driven that shoulder into her chamber door to split it open, for several large shards of wood protruded from the still-bleeding gash.

"I should have seen to this first," she breathed.

"Isolda, listen to me."

She shook her head. *Nay*, a voice whispered in the back of her mind, *no more bad news. I can't take any more.* She reached for one of the large splinters jutting from the wound, but he caught her wrist mid-air.

"Isolda."

"At least let me busy my hands while you tell me," she whispered, her voice cracking with a sudden rush of vulnerability. She was strong, she reminded herself as she clung to her composure. She'd survived worse than this—she had to, for John.

He nodded and released her wrist, his eyes flashing with understanding.

She reached out and gingerly took hold of the largest of the shards of wood protruding from Ansel's bloodied shoulder. With a swift tug, she pulled it free. Ansel grunted through clenched teeth.

As she took hold of another sliver of wood, he spoke.

"One of the attackers...he was..." He had to pause as she tore the wood from his flesh. "He was a laborer from the village. His name was Henry."

Her fingers froze on another splinter. Ice slammed through her veins. Although she only vaguely recognized the name, the thought of someone who'd been working so close to her for so long attacking the castle made bile rise in the back of her throat.

"He was the only one I recognized," Ansel went on quietly. "But it means that there may be more in the village who've been hired to work against ye."

She yanked the wood shard free, then nodded stiffly. A blessed numbness was descending over her mind like the fog that so often clung to the rocks of the Rumble Churn in the mornings.

"Ye are no' safe here anymore, Isolda. Even with all I've tried to do in the last sennight, there is no way to secure Dunstanburgh against another attack." Ansel's voice, though firm, was like a velvety balm, low and compassionate. Yet it barely reached her through the haze of detachment.

"But this is my home." The words sounded distant to her ears, like someone else's voice.

He turned suddenly so that his back was to the fire and he fully faced her. His thighs spread slightly so that she stood between them, his legs encasing her protectively.

Backlit by the fire, she couldn't read the emotion flitting across his features or the flicker of something dark in his eyes.

"I almost lost ye tonight," he said, his voice no more than a low breath. "I willnae take that risk again. We must leave here."

Just then, Mary shifted on the ground behind Isolda.

"And what of Bertram and Mary?" she said, glancing over her shoulder at her sleeping maid and the prone form of her loyal guard. "I cannot simply leave them here. It isn't safe. And Bertram isn't out of danger from that wound yet."

"We will ken by tomorrow morning if a fever has taken hold of Bertram. If it doesnae, I will send both him and Mary away. And we'll ride out as well."

"Tomorrow morning? But that isn't enough time! I

cannot—"

"Isolda." Ansel rose to his feet, taking her gently by the shoulders and holding her gaze steadily. "Listen to me. We will leave tomorrow morning, no arguments. Ye must keep John safe, and I must keep ye safe. To do that, we cannae stay here any longer than absolutely necessary."

Stark, cold reality settled deep in her bones at last. She couldn't fight Ansel any longer, not when deep down she knew he was right, knew she owed her life to him. But tonight had left her with no more words, no more tears. All she could manage was a broken nod.

She removed the last of the fragments of wood from Ansel's shoulder, then wearily stitched the two dagger wounds and the sword cut. As she tied off the last stitch, he gently took her hand in his.

"Rest now. Tomorrow will be a long day."

She let him lead her up the stairs and through her open, ruined doorway into her chamber. She recoiled slightly at the sight of her bed, for dark bloodstains marred the coverlet where she'd stabbed her assailant. He guided her to the far side of the large bed where the blankets were clean.

"I'll stay with ye until ye fall asleep," he said, pulling back the covers.

She didn't bother to remove her soiled surcoat. Instead, she slid wearily into bed, allowing him to pull the blankets around her.

He sat on the stone floor next to the bed, facing

her. The last thing she saw before her lids drooped closed and exhaustion stole her away were his dark, unreadable eyes watching over her.

Chapter Fourteen

Isolda woke with a start. She sat bolt upright, a gasp on her lips and her eyes flaring wide.

But the nightmare she'd torn herself from was the same as the reality she awoke to.

Her gaze fell on her window. Judging by the pale pink light of pre-dawn seeping through the open shutters, she'd only slept for a few hours. Her eyes traveled to the shattered door, and then the bloodstained coverlet on her bed. Aye, her nightmares had come alive last night.

Unbidden, her gaze landed on the floor below the window, but the two daggers Ansel had pulled from his body and dropped to the floor weren't there.

She let out a shaky breath, glad that at least one small piece of the horror from the night before was no longer there to greet her this morning. Ansel must have removed them when he'd left her side sometime in the middle of the night.

Her chamber was empty, though the memory of Ansel's dark gaze burning into her sent a strange pinch into her heart.

She'd almost completely fallen apart in front of

him. But now in the light of day, she needed to be brave.

She rose and quickly discarded her bloodied surcoat, gown, and chemise. After rinsing her hands and face in the basin of cold water on her desk, she went to her armoire.

Row upon row of expensive silks and brocades met her gaze. She selected a simple linen chemise, a gown of chestnut brown wool, and an unembellished surcoat of russet red. They were the only garments close to appropriate for riding while still being suitable for a lady. Ansel hadn't told her where they were going, but surely her title would help grease the wheels if they needed assistance.

She pulled a satchel from the back of the armoire and packed a few extra chemises, gowns, and one nicer surcoat along with her comb and the few other personal items that would fit. Then she slung her thickest wool cloak over her shoulders. Depending on where they were going, fall could be kind to them, or it could be cruel.

With one last look, she closed the armoire softly. Six years ago she could have never imagined possessing such wealth in the form of those expensive garments. Now she relied on them, for they were her armor, as sure as any knight's chainmail and plates of metal. Or perhaps the rich brocades and silks were her shield, for she hid behind them and behind the title of lady.

She pushed the dark thoughts aside. Aye, Lancaster

had bought her silence with the endless reams of decadent cloth. In that way, she was no better than a whore, just as her mother and father had called her the day they abandoned her at Clitheroe, her belly beginning to round with Lancaster's child. But she'd done what was necessary to survive—for herself, and for her son.

With the satchel slung over her shoulder, she stepped through her splintered door. When she reached the bottom of the spiraling stairs, she was surprised to find the ground floor chamber empty. Blood darkened the rushes on the ground where Bertram had lain, but he, Mary, and Ansel were nowhere in sight.

She pushed open the tower door and stepped into the yard. Although she braced herself for the sight of bodies, all she saw in the pink morning light was blood on the yard's grass.

Movement in front of the stables drew her gaze. A cart with a draft horse harnessed to it stood ready. Bertram lay in the back of the cart, with Mary standing by his side.

Isolda rushed to the cart, her heart suddenly in her throat.

"How does he fare?" she breathed.

"I could be worse." Bertram's voice was a grating whisper, but his pale lips quirked in a faint smile.

"Bertram!" Isolda took his hand as gently as she could and gave it a little squeeze. Relief stole her breath, and all she could do for a long moment was gaze down at the dear man's wan face.

"He woke not long ago," Mary said softly by her side. "He's been demanding to see you before we head out."

Isolda shifted her gaze to Mary, tears making the maid wobble before her vision.

"So he has convinced you that you must leave as well?"

"Aye," Mary replied, her voice pinched with emotion. "We both fought to stay by your side, my lady, but that Scot is as stubborn as a mule."

Just then, Ansel emerged from the stables drawing his enormous bay stallion behind him.

He wore a clean linen tunic and breeches, and his face and hands were free of the blood they bore last night. His hair was drawn back and tied at the nape of his neck, but dark stubble bristled thickly on his face, and his eyes carried shadows under them.

Isolda realized with a start that he had likely not slept at all last night. He must have removed the bodies of their attackers beyond the castle walls, gotten the cart ready, carried Bertram to it, and prepared his horse for their journey while she rested. Even still, he moved with the same fluid strength as he always did, with no indication of weariness other than the smudges under his eyes.

"Stubborn? Aye, I am that," Ansel said levelly as he approached.

"Where will they go?" Isolda asked, still clutching Bertram's hand.

"South, away from Embleton," Ansel replied, halting his horse next to the cart. "I dinnae ken if any of the other village laborers were hired to attack ye, but if they were, Mary and Bertram willnae be safe anywhere near the village."

"I have some family in York," Mary said. "It is a big enough town for us to disappear for a while—until we get word that you are safe, my lady."

Isolda threw an arm around her dear maid, drawing her into a fierce embrace. "I'll send word soon, I promise," she whispered, her throat nigh closing with a swell of emotion. "And you had better be up and back to your training." She turned back to Bertram, giving his hand another squeeze.

"Aye, my lady, you can count on it," he replied with a little nod of his copper-gray head.

Ansel helped Mary up into the front of the cart and handed her the draft horse's reins. As Mary clucked the horse into motion, Ansel strode to the newly erected wooden gates. He pulled one side open, giving Mary enough room to maneuver the cart through.

Mary waved one last time as the cart rolled slowly through the gates. Then Bertram's hand appeared from the bed of the cart, waving reassuringly. Isolda waved back, tears burning her eyes and choking her throat. Her only friends in the world pulled gradually out of sight.

Isolda's chest compressed painfully as a new surge of emotion stole her breath. Without realizing what she was doing, she turned from the gate and strode across the yard toward Gull Crag.

When she reached the edge of the cliff, she dragged in a lungful of the salty air. The sun was just cresting over the North Sea, its golden beams encasing her. Far below, waves crashed against the Rumble Churn, wrapping the black stones in white froth.

She sensed more than saw Ansel move silently to her side.

"We have limited time," he said quietly. "At best, we have a few days before the man who attacked ye reaches whoever sent him to deliver the news of his failure. At worst, we only have a few hours before some spy in the village realizes what has happened and alerts his compatriots, whoever they may be."

"Aye, I know." She drew in another breath, the brine burning her lungs and mingling with the tears welling in her eyes. "It is just...I may never see this place again."

She glanced at him and found his dark brown eyes riveted on her.

"Ye will live through this, Isolda. I swear it. I will protect ye."

A tear slipped from her eyes and burned a path down her cheek. The cold sea wind stung against the trail of moisture. "I know you will. I believe you. And I trust you. But..."

He tensed slightly, his muscles shifting under his tunic. "But?"

"But I still won't tell you where John is. Please understand. I fear that if the words cross my lips, my son will be in even graver danger than he is currently. I know it doesn't make sense, but—"

To her surprise, compassion flickered in the depths of his eyes. "Aye, I understand. A mother must protect her child. Ye dinnae need to tell me where John is—I'm no' asking. All I ask is that ye let me protect ye."

Another swell of emotion, this time tinged with gratitude, rose in her throat. "Aye, I will."

With one last, long look at the sea, she turned and made her way back toward his waiting horse. Ansel took her satchel and fastened it to his saddlebags, then helped her mount.

As he swung up into the saddle behind her, she finally had her emotions in check enough to speak.

"Where are we going?"

He snorted softly behind her. "We'll both keep our secrets for now, my lady," he said in her ear.

He took up the reins, and suddenly she realized just how intimate it was to share a horse with a man. His arms wrapped around her waist to grip the reins, and her bottom was nestled snugly between his thighs. The hard plane of his chest was flush with her back.

She could feel his thighs tighten slightly as he squeezed his knees into the horse's sides. The well-trained animal surged forward into a rapid walk.

Isolda barely had enough time to glance over her shoulder as they crossed through the open gate. The castle stood silently in the golden glow of sunrise. The unfinished towers and ragged curtain wall looked somber and desolate even in the cheery morning light.

Even still, this was the first place she'd called home, for her childhood had been one of constant travel to the next fair or grand market. This was the place she'd raised John until a year ago. This was the place she'd learned to stand with her spine straight and her chin raised.

And this was likely the last time she'd see it.

Ansel reined his horse to the north, though he angled far to the west to avoid Embleton, which sat quiet and still in the distance.

They were off.

Chapter Fifteen

Though he couldn't see her face, Ansel could tell by Isolda's slumped shoulders and lowered head that she was lost in her own world for most of the morning.

He never knew a woman's tears could have such an effect on a man. Aye, he'd drawn a few tears from his sister when they were just bairns, for which he'd been chastised by their stern father, but this was different.

He was taking her from her home, dragging her away from her only companions and upending her world. He was also going to keep her safe, by God, but that didn't mean that she wasn't struggling with the rest of it.

The image of her gilded in the golden light of sunrise, tears shimmering in her eyes and trailing down one cheek, was burned into his mind. She had never looked so hauntingly beautiful, wisps of dark hair dancing around her face and her chin held level even as pain flooded those pale green eyes. Something beyond lust had twisted his heart as he'd gazed upon her—something far more dangerous than mere physical desire.

He should have been grateful that once he'd mounted Eachann behind her, the deeper pinch in his chest had reverted back to simple lust once more. Yet he could not muster gratitude for his scrambled thoughts, thudding pulse, and throbbing manhood.

If only he could be lost in thought as she seemed to be. Instead, every nerve ending was on fire, molten need coursing through his veins. With each of the horse's brisk steps, their bodies rolled together. He prayed that she wouldn't notice the hard length of his manhood where it pressed against her bottom, but praying did little to relieve the heavy ache between his legs.

And her scent. *Bloody hell*. He'd noticed a faint whiff of it earlier, but now he could drag in his fill with each inhale, for the chestnut crown of her head was directly before his nose.

With his body humming with desire, his senses were sharp enough to dissect the subtle, complex scent drifting from her hair. There was a sweet, tart top note—lemon, he deduced. A luxury item like lemon soap would have had to be brought from Spain, or perhaps even the Far East. The tangy, expensive scent was a reminder of her elevated station.

But below the sharp sweetness of lemon, he detected the piney, earthy smell of lavender. The two scents twined together headily, one bright, one dark, until Ansel thought he'd grown drunk on the combination.

He gritted his teeth against the nigh unbearable desire to pull her plait free, drag her back flush against his chest, and bury his nose in her unbound hair while his hands found the soft curves of her breasts.

He jerked his head to the side, forcing his eyes to focus on their surroundings. If he wasn't careful, he'd guide them dangerously close to a village or town. Or worse, he'd lose hold on the last thread of self-control he possessed and do just what his body demanded.

The one benefit of her being lost in her own thoughts was that she hadn't probed him with questions about where they were going, nor had she been paying attention to their surroundings.

But even as he counted that small blessing, her chin tilted up and she glanced around. She shifted as she craned her neck to take in the position of the sun. It was past midday now, and though the sun was warm and pleasant again today, the autumn evening would be descending soon.

"We are riding north."

It wasn't a question, yet she didn't mask the confusion in her voice.

"Aye."

She shifted again, twisting so that she could look back at him. Her movement sent her bottom rubbing against his groin. He clamped his mouth shut on a colorful curse.

"Why?"

"Because it is safer."

A crease appeared between her dark eyebrows. "I don't see how heading farther into the Borderlands could be—"

Her eyes widened on him in understanding. "You are taking me into Scotland, aren't you?"

"Aye."

Suddenly, a look of fear flickered behind her pale green eyes.

"Why?" she repeated, but this time the word was guarded.

What could riding into Scotland possibly mean to an English noblewoman? And why did he sense there was something she was hiding? Ansel tucked the thought away. She was tired and raw from the events of the night before. No need to push her on the matter just yet.

"For starters, because the English willnae follow us. Edward's men will think twice about pursuing ye into Scotland," he said evenly. "With Bannockburn hanging around their necks, they'll no' likely charge past the Borderlands again."

"Bannockburn," she said softly. "You were there, weren't you?"

Surprise flashed through him as she continued to hold his gaze, her head swiveled on her slim neck. Before he could ask her how she'd guessed, though, she went on.

"You spoke of seeing many battlefields when we

were tending to Bertram last eve. And...and I noticed when I was stitching you that you bear a few fresh scars."

Heat coiled low in his belly. So, she'd been staring at his body, more than just to see to his most recent wounds. But the lust was also tinged with a different heat—the darker burn of all the memories of battles that still haunted him.

"What do ye ken of Bannockburn, lass?" His voice bore a low edge he hadn't intended, but he wouldn't apologize, even though she recoiled slightly.

"Only that King Edward sought to relieve Stirling Castle from Scottish attacks last June," she breathed. "Robert the Bruce beat the English back, and Edward was forced to flee. You have already told me that you work closely with the Bruce. What was your role at Bannockburn?"

"I dinnae like to talk of battle."

She bit her lower lip, drawing his eyes there.

"Forgive me," she said softly. "It is only... I know so little of you, and now we are riding into Scotland. Alone."

He released a slow breath. She was right, of course. He wasn't naturally a trusting or forthcoming man, but she only had him now. She needed to trust him, which meant that he had to overcome his own reticence and guardedness.

"I have fought by King Robert's side for seven years," he said quietly.

Her lips parted in surprise, but he went on. "Bannockburn was one of many engagements I've participated in for Scotland's independence. It wasnae the bloodiest, but we were outnumbered two to one. Even in the thick of things we all sensed something—that it would be a decisive battle, one way or another." Ansel snorted softly to himself. "Luckily for us, we were on the winning side."

It was the most he'd ever said about the battle to someone who hadn't been at Bannockburn. It was a small offering, but relief seeped into him at Isolda's nod of understanding.

"You said that the English wouldn't likely follow us into Scotland, but that it was only one of the reasons we are riding north," she said. "What are the other reasons?"

Ansel let his gaze scan their surroundings again. Soft, rolling green hills were broken up by patches of plowed farmland and clumps of trees turning the vibrant reds and yellows of fall.

"I'm no' verra familiar with the English countryside," he said, cocking a brow at the tame-looking landscape. "I'm from the Highlands, ye ken."

She nodded again, so he went on. "If the men after ye and John *do* decide that it's worth risking their English hides on Scottish soil, I need to be familiar with the land. I need to be able to use our surroundings to my benefit." He shrugged "And I ken the Highlands like the back of my hand."

Her eyes rounded slightly. "So we are going all the way to the Highlands, then?"

He felt a satisfied smile twist the corners of his mouth. Suddenly he was reminded that Isolda was a proper English lady—her tone revealed her horror at the idea of traveling into the heart of the wild, uncivilized Highlands.

"Aye, I've a place in mind—somewhere safe, somewhere the English arenae aware of."

Her brows furrowed, and again he was rewarded with a surge of roguish gratification.

"And you won't tell me where it is?"

"Nay, for as ye ken well, sometimes just speaking a secret, even into a trusted ear, will cause trouble."

Color rose into her cheeks, but she reluctantly nodded her understanding again. "But how long will we be traveling? Surely the Highlands of Scotland aren't too far away."

"If we ride hard every day for a sennight, we'll reach our destination—if the weather cooperates, that is."

At her shocked expression, he went on quickly. "That reminds me—did ye bring any other clothes more…suitable for travel?"

His gaze slide down to where her wool cloak split open over her snug, finely made russet surcoat. Her breasts strained against the layers of material as she inhaled.

She looked down as well, her brows rising in desperation.

"Nay, these are the closest things I have to riding clothes."

"It's just that they'll likely be uncomfortable for the long days in the saddle ahead of us. And they are a wee bit...conspicuous for the Highlands," he said carefully.

Truth be told, she'd stick out like a rose in a field of wildflowers in Scotland wearing the getup of an English noblewoman. None but the wealthiest in the likes of Perth and Edinburgh even wore surcoats and gowns of the quality and fabric that Isolda owned.

"You didn't tell me where we were going, and I didn't have time to—"

"Aye, ye're right," he said evenly, trying to soothe her rising panic. "We'll just have to trade for some new garments for ye when we reach an inn."

Her delicate features still bore the creases of discomfort at that. Aye, he enjoyed pricking her pride, but he didn't truly believe she was some spoiled chit. Perhaps there was something else behind her unease at losing all her finely made garments. Another question to stow away for later, he thought with a flicker of apprehension.

"Are we...sleeping in an inn tonight?"

Her voice was so hopeful that he actually felt like the savage she'd once called him for disappointing her. "Nay, no' tonight. We have to get through the Borderlands first, and I willnae risk drawing suspicion from the English and Scots alike in a village or town. We dinnae exactly make a likely pair."

For the briefest moment, surprise and then amusement scuttled across her face. The faintest curve of her full, pink lips insinuated a smile.

"Aye, you are right about that."

But then her face sobered to its usual serious cast.

"Where will we sleep then?"

He gestured broadly across the landscape surrounding them. "Outdoors."

Isolda pressed her lips together but didn't say anything. She only nodded tightly and turned back around, settling herself facing forward in the saddle.

Disappointment warred with respect in his mind. Aye, he enjoyed getting a rise out of his English lady, but he couldn't deny his admiration for her grit. His blood pumped hotly in his veins and his manhood jolted to life once more as her bottom nestled between his legs.

This was not exactly the mission he'd had in mind when he'd left Dunrobin. It would be a long journey back to the Highlands.

Chapter Sixteen

Clemont jammed his fist into the still-bleeding wound in his side as he swung down from his horse. Since he hadn't fallen dead during the long, hard ride back to Clitheroe Castle, he deduced that it was only a flesh wound. Still, he grunted and cursed when his feet hit the cobblestones inside Clitheroe's gates.

"Go tell your lord that I have returned," Clemont bit out to one of the two pages rushing forward to take his horse. The lad bowed swiftly and darted into the castle.

Slowly, Clemont forced his legs to move. The long night, followed by a full day of hard riding, would have left him stiff and sore even without the bleeding gouge in his side.

He strode across the yard and toward the squat little keep. Luckily, the whole castle was so small that he only had to struggle through a few paces before reaching the keep. Although laborers were hard at work outside the curtain wall building several more structures, the keep itself was necessarily cramped and short. Ironic, Clemont thought not for the first time, given the man who owned it.

He crossed through the doors and into the narrow, low-ceilinged ground floor chamber. The room was empty, for one of the new structures outside the wall was to be an enormous, elegant great hall more fitting for its owner's station. Clemont moved immediately to the stairs, knowing where he could find the lord of Clitheroe Castle.

As he made his way up the stairs, the page he'd sent ahead of him darted down. The lad averted his gaze—so, the lord was in a foul mood, was he? Clemont's news wouldn't help matters, but the throbbing ache in his side dulled any lingering impulse to care.

When he reached the door he knew to be the man's study, he didn't even bother knocking. Instead, he strode in, sweeping the door closed behind him.

The Earl of Lancaster sat at an enormous wooden desk, which was strewn with papers. Weak light streamed in through a series of narrow slits in the thick stone. The stark little room bore no other furnishings, leaving Clemont to come to a halt before the desk.

Once again, he was struck by how incongruous Lancaster's primary seat for official business was. The Earl was the second richest man in all of England, behind only the King himself, yet the squat, square keep with the dark, cramped chambers didn't exactly send the Earl's enemies quaking. Perhaps that was why Lancaster seemed to be in a perpetually foul mood.

Lancaster rose slowly from behind the desk. Of

course, the man tried to make up for his inadequate keep in other ways. He wore silks and brocades from head to toe, as usual. The arrogant tilt of his dark head spoke of unquestioned power, and the smooth, pale hands he placed on the desk between them nigh reeked of wealth.

"I hope you have good news for me, Clemont," Lancaster said softly, though his pale blue eyes were sharp. They took in the sight of the blood dripping from Clemont's fist where he held his side.

"Nay, my lord," Clemont said.

Lancaster's delicate hands fisted on top of the piles of parchment and missives. "What happened?"

"I gathered a force of men, as you instructed—quietly. One of the laborers in Embleton gave me the details I needed—the castle's layout, where the woman slept, and so forth. But I began to hear rumors in the village that a stranger had arrived at Dunstanburgh. Indeed, my man among the laborers confirmed it—a Scot."

Something flickered in Lancaster's icy eyes. Even though his mind was dulled from pain and fatigue, Clemont didn't miss Lancaster's little tell.

"You wouldn't have aught to do with a Scot arriving at Dunstanburgh, would you, my lord?" he said, narrowing his eyes on the Earl.

Lancaster held Clemont's sharp gaze but didn't speak.

Rage, sharp and hot, surged in Clemont's veins.

"Because if you did, your contract with my employer would be void. We would collect full payment, though, of course."

Clemont shifted slightly, the subtlest of threats.

Lancaster lifted his hands slowly from the desk. "Remember to whom you speak. I am the Earl of Lancaster, cousin to King Edward II—and the future King of England. You are no more than a man for hire, a bounty hunter, and your employer—"

Seeming to seek composure once more, Lancaster slid a hand over his already-smooth hair.

"You hired someone else," Clemont said flatly. "Despite the fact that my employer guarantees a satisfactory completion of your...requested terminations."

Lancaster's mouth lifted in a little smile. "Aye, I hired the Scot, but not to do your job. I have every faith in your abilities, Clemont. Or I *did*. I ask again—what happened?"

"We attacked the castle, just as planned. But the Scot..." Clemont pressed his hand harder into his side, sending a fresh wave of pain through his body. He had been bested. And he was never bested. "The Scot took out my men."

"And yet you stand before me, bleeding," Lancaster snapped, annoyance tightening his mouth.

"I made a move for the woman. She gave me this." Clemont peeled his hand away from his wound and pulled the jeweled dagger from his belt. He'd had to wrench the dagger from his side while riding at a full gallop.

Lancaster snatched the bloody, jewel-encrusted dagger from Clemont's hand.

"That bitch," he breathed. "I gave her this."

"She said the boy wasn't with her, and from what my laborer on the inside said, she spoke the truth."

Lancaster muttered an oath. "It is as I thought, then. She has hidden the boy somewhere."

"I could have gotten the information from her if the Scot hadn't been there. He drove me away." Clemont shifted again, but this time it was to reapply his fist to his aching side. "I gave him a few of my own daggers, though. He couldn't give chase."

Lancaster's cold eyes jerked from the dagger in his hands to Clemont. "Did you kill him?" he asked sharply.

Clemont felt another stab of bitter distaste for Lancaster. "I don't know, for I was forced to flee. It seemed as though the Scot was there to protect the very woman you sent me to kill once I found and killed the boy. Why?"

Again, Lancaster's mouth quirked, but his eyes remained icy. "Ah, Clemont. There is so much more at play than the murders of my bastard son and his mother, but a simple bounty hunter like you wouldn't understand."

Clemont gritted his teeth even as he repressed an inward smile. Aye, Lancaster was a rich, powerful man and Clemont was no more than a hired killer. In fact,

Clemont's employer practically owned him.

But the tables could so easily be turned. If some other rich English nobleman had wished for Lancaster's head delivered on a gilded platter, Clemont would have gladly seen to the task.

Killing had long ago lost the flush of emotion for Clemont—fear, pleasure, anger, all of it had worn away into the flat necessity of the tasks his employer gave him. Yet if his employer would let him, he'd relish extracting a slow death from this arrogant whoreson. He'd use his short throwing daggers to draw out the fear and the pain.

"Try me."

Lancaster waved at the paper-strewn desk with the dagger that still bore Clemont's blood. "If I am to be King of England, alliances must be made—including with the barbarian Scots. Hiring a bodyguard binds me closer with their fool King, Robert the Bruce. Besides, I had my suspicions that Isolda has stowed our son somewhere in Scotland—who better to sniff the boy out than one of the Bruce's lapdogs?"

Realization washed over Clemont. He kept his features emotionless though. "So you contracted with my employer and hired me to hunt down and kill the boy and the woman. But you also hired a bodyguard for her. You reasoned that if I failed, you'd still have the Scot in play."

"And your arrival today confirmed that I was right to have a backup plan," Lancaster said, his gaze sliding over Clemont. "You look like hell."

Aye, the woman had done a number on his face with her claws, and his clothes were soaked with his own blood and the grime of a night and a day of hard travel.

"So what is your next move, my lord?" Clemont said levelly. "Is the Scot a bounty hunter as well? Do you have no more need of my services?"

"Don't be so defensive, Clemont," Lancaster purred with a lifted eyebrow. "Of course I still need you. In fact, you've played your part perfectly thus far. Your attack has likely spooked Isolda and the Scot. I thought the other...*incidents* I put in her path would have done the trick, but she is a stubborn little bitch. But nay, this time she cannot be mistaken. If the Scot is worth a sliver of what the Bruce claims, he'll insist that he and Isolda flee."

"And how does that help me complete my task, my lord?" Clemont said, barely maintaining his threadbare patience.

He was used to dealing with rich, pompous asses who thought themselves superior to him, but Clemont did the work they were too weak or cowardly to do. He spilled his marks' blood and he watched the life drain from their eyes while his employer took coin from the likes of the soft-handed Lancaster.

"Clemont, use a little imagination," Lancaster said reprovingly. "If Isolda fears for our son's life, the first thing she will do is seek him out to reassure herself that she has hidden him well. Isolda has proven…difficult to control, but at the end of the day, she is like all other mothers—blinded by some foolish protective instinct and completely unreasonable when it comes to her child."

Lancaster walked around the desk, his ornate, wood-heeled shoes clicking softly on the stone floor.

"All you have to do is pick up their trail, and I guarantee they'll lead you right to my son. If you are up to it, that is." He waved casually at Clemont's bloodied side.

Clemont raised an eyebrow. "Aye, I am up to it. I am not one to leave a task unfinished."

"Your employer assured me the same about you," Lancaster said, his eyes sparkling. "The village healer can stitch you up, then I would suggest you head out. Surely they can't have too great a lead on you."

"Tracking them won't be a problem."

"I am truly impressed with your employer's services," Lancaster said. He spun the dagger around in his hand and extended it, hilt first, toward Clemont. "I think you've earned this."

"Nay," Clemont said, eying the jewel- and blood-encrusted dagger. "My employer only allows me to take payment from him."

Lancaster shrugged and set the dagger down on his desk. "Suit yourself. Your employer certainly is a demanding man."

Uninterested in talking with Lancaster any longer

than necessary, Clemont gave a stiff nod of his head, then spun on his heels to seek Clitheroe's healer.

"Oh, and Clemont." Lancaster's casual voice halted him at the door. "Your failure to extract the necessary information to find my son was part of my plan—this time. But if you fail again…"

He didn't need to voice the rest of the threat. Clemont knew very well that if he didn't deliver the heads of Lancaster's bastard son and the boy's mother, he would face the consequences. And anything Lancaster could dream up would be far more pleasant than what his employer would do to him if he failed.

And that was why he wouldn't fail.

Chapter Seventeen

Isolda gritted her teeth to keep them from chattering. She would *not* complain, she told herself over and over as she held her spine rigid and her head level beneath her cloak's hood. She would *not*.

Last night had sorely tested her. After a long and grueling day in the saddle, Ansel had guided Eachann into a copse of evergreen trees away from the road. They'd made a simple camp and eaten hard biscuits and dried meat that Ansel had apparently procured from Mary.

When it was time to hunker down for the night, Ansel had given her a length of blue and green plaid he'd removed from his saddlebag. Taking another thick wool plaid for himself, he stretched out on the opposite side of their little fire and had gone to sleep.

Though saddle-sore and exhausted from the horrors of the night before, Isolda had struggled to fall asleep. And she couldn't blame her status as a lady for her discomfort. Nay, she'd spent many a night sleeping on the ground wrapped in stout wool up until six years ago. The true reason was that the plaid she'd wrapped around her cloak enveloped her in Ansel's heady, masculine scent.

It was almost a relief when the clouds that had threatened earlier that evening unleashed a heavy rain on them. The dark trees overhead dripped noisily, and fat raindrops pelted her huddled form, distracting her from the dangerous direction of her thoughts.

But when the fire hissed out and the ground grew soft beneath her, she silently cursed her situation thoroughly.

She was on the run from the forces of evil who would kill her and her son. She didn't have a friend in the world who could help her other than Ansel. And all she could think about was being alone with this Highland warrior who smelled of wood smoke and fresh air, whose hard body had rubbed against her all day in the saddle, and whose eyes bore dark secrets she longed to know.

She only had one defense against her own traitorous lust—playing the part of a lady. She had learned over the last six years to bear the title like a shield, to hide behind the armor of expensive clothing and a rigid, haughty air.

The problem was, how could she hide her desire for Ansel behind her regal bearing when she was soaking wet, cold, saddle-sore, and muddy?

It had been a long night, indeed.

The gray light of morning brought no relief, however. There had been neither time nor a place to change her soaking, too-tight surcoat and gown, so she was forced to mount Eachann in garments she now realized were a terrible choice for this grueling journey.

The rain continued throughout the day, though blessedly it weakened to a misty drizzle. Yet despite her wool cloak and Ansel's plaid, which she still had wrapped around her, the cold, damp air seeped into her aching bones.

By the time the sky turned from light gray to the muted blue of a cloud-obscured sunset, Isolda's teeth were firmly clamped together and her lips pressed tight against the nigh overpowering need to plead for mercy from their punishing trek.

As if reading her thoughts, Ansel spoke low and gentle behind her in the saddle.

"We'll be stopping soon, my lady." His voice was like a silken balm on her bedraggled spirits.

Ansel had been quiet all day as they'd ridden through the drizzle. She had never been this far north, but she could guess from his rigid watchfulness of their surroundings that they'd crossed through the Borderlands and were in the Lowlands of Scotland by now.

Isolda pried her lips apart and willed her jaw not to chatter noisily. "Where will we stay tonight?"

"At an inn this time. I fear ye'll need to be wrung out if we sleep in this rain another night."

Despite her weariness and discomfort, she felt a weak smile tug one corner of her mouth.

"And where are we? I gather we are no longer in England?"

"Aye, we are south of Stirling."

Sharp fear cut through the cold and numbness in her mind and body. "Stirling? But isn't that where…"

"The Battle of Bannockburn was decided back in June, Isolda," Ansel murmured, though she didn't miss his hands clenching slightly on the reins in front of her. "Besides, it's no' like we will be riding directly to the castle and asking Sir Phillip Mowbray for a bed. We are going to an inn well outside the town and away from the castle."

She nodded woodenly, but she couldn't ward away her unease. "And what will those who fought for Stirling Castle and Scotland's freedom think of an Englishwoman in their midst?"

"I've been meaning to speak with ye about that. Now that we are in Scotland, I'll no' be calling ye 'Lady'—just Isolda. And ye'd best no' speak overmuch, if at all—yer accent will only draw unwanted attention to us. Understood?"

Suddenly Isolda felt like a soldier taking orders from the gruff Highland warrior sitting behind her. She swallowed hard.

"But I thought you said that the battle was over and decided in June," she said, unable to stop the waver that broke through her voice.

He exhaled and shifted in the saddle, his chest brushing her back. She'd been trying all day to keep a respectable distance between their bodies, but even with the slight touch, tingling heat jolted through her frozen bones.

"Some willnae take kindly to an English noblewoman, it's true. Many are still raw over Bannockburn—they lost their families, their homes, and their farms to the English. It will be best no' to test anyone's allegiances, ye ken?"

She nodded again, her jaw too achy from trying to keep from shivering to say more.

Just as the drizzling rain finally let up, Ansel reined Eachann off the road. In the falling darkness, Isolda could make out a little clump of buildings ahead. Ansel drew them to a halt when they reached the largest of the structures, which rose from the center of several squat wooden shops.

Ansel slid off the horse and landed with a splat in the mud. He turned to retrieve Isolda from Eachann's back, but when his hands wrapped around her waist and his gaze met hers, he cursed.

"Why in the bloody hell did ye no' tell me ye were so cold, lass?" he bit out. "Yer lips are nigh blue and ye are trembling like a leaf!"

Aye, she must look a sight. Her plait was a wild mess beneath her hood, she was rigid as an oak knot from trying to keep her shivers at bay, and her once-fine clothes were sodden and streaked with mud.

"I did not wish to be a nuisance," she said tightly. "I know we must move with haste, and I don't want to hinder you further than I already have."

That wasn't the entire truth, of course. Aye, she

knew now just how badly she needed Ansel's protection, and she didn't want to stand against him as she had back at Dunstanburgh. But if she were honest with herself, she would admit that playing the part of a proper English lady—sitting straight-spined in the saddle, not touching him, and maintaining her threadbare hold on propriety—was the only thing keeping her from falling into his arms and begging for his warmth, his touch, his kiss.

"Aye, well, ye'd be more than a nuisance if ye keeled over from exhaustion—or worse, died of a chill—just because ye were too proud to tell me how ye suffered."

His hands tightened around her waist and he pulled her gently from his horse. But when her feet came into contact with the soft ground, she gasped and moaned.

Her feet had gone blessedly numb by midday. Now they throbbed under her weight, somehow burning cold and hot at the same time.

Isolda tottered precariously and tumbled directly into Ansel's chest. Like strong, warm bands of iron, his arms wrapped around her, steadying her and preventing her from falling to the mud.

He cursed again, the sound rumbling through his chest. Despite her now-uncontrollable shivers, a warm flush crept to her cheeks. Once again, they were plastered together, his arms around her and his head tilting down toward hers.

Her breath caught in her throat. She'd tried all day

to maintain a proper distance between them, and her blasted body betrayed her yet again. The truth was, no matter how much she tried to hide it, she wanted him—wanted their hot lips melded together, his hard body forcing her soft one to yield to it, those rough hands of his holding her close.

Just then, the door to the building behind Isolda opened and light flooded out.

"Who is that out there?"

At the sound of a woman's voice, Ansel's head snapped up, his gaze darting over Eachann's back toward the wooden building before which he'd stopped.

"We are in need of a room for the night," Ansel responded, his hands still firm on Isolda's waist. "And we will happily pay extra for the late hour and the inconvenience."

The unseen speaker grumbled about the mud, but from the sound of squelching, she was making her way toward them.

"Just the two of ye, then?"

Isolda still couldn't see the woman who spoke, for she was short enough to be blocked by Eachann's brown flanks.

"Aye," Ansel said. "Though I'll also throw in another extra coin for the care of my horse."

At last the woman emerged from behind Eachann. In the yellow light spilling from the open door, Isolda took stock of her.

She was short and wide of hip. Though her garb was modest, she had a crisp, clean apron tied snugly around her waist. Her hair was pulled back in a simple bun, the light revealing it to be dark blonde. Her cheeks were rosy, yet she wore a slight frown on her face as she took in the sight of them.

"I suppose ye'll only want one room?" The woman's eyes slid down to where Ansel's hands still gripped Isolda's waist. In a burst of embarrassment, Isolda tried to pull away, but Ansel's hold only tightened, keeping her in his grasp.

"Aye, my *wife* and I only require a warm, dry place to sleep."

Ansel's pointed word seemed to set the woman slightly more at ease, but a torrent of hot mortification flooded Isolda.

"Ah, verra well," the woman said, her gaze turning less critical. "I'll have my husband see to yer horse when he returns from the castle shortly, but I can take him to the barn now and then show ye to a room. I am Margery, and my husband and I run the Rose and Thistle—ye can guess which one I am."

Ansel removed his saddlebags from Eachann and Margery led the animal behind the inn, disappearing from the band of light streaming from the still-open inn door.

"Can ye walk?" Ansel said softly.

Isolda's legs felt like pudding, but it wasn't because of the ebbing numbness from their long, cold day of riding. "Your *wife?*" she hissed, rounding on him.

He grunted, but it sounded dangerously close to a snort of mirth. "Aye. It will attract less suspicion. How else would ye have me explain my arrival at an inn after dark with a beautiful woman in my arms?"

The air whooshed from her lungs at his words. *He thinks me beautiful?* Even as she struggled to form a response, her heart skittered against her ribcage.

Just as she opened her mouth, Margery came squelching back around the corner holding up the hem of her skirt distastefully against the mud.

"Come on then," she said brusquely, beckoning them toward the open inn door.

Ansel took her arm in his then started toward the door, though he went slowly enough for her to find her legs and totter alongside him.

Tears almost sprang to Isolda's eyes as she stepped into the inn. Warm light from a roaring fire filled the room. There were a few tables and chairs, where several small clumps of either villagers or the inn's patrons sat drinking mugs of ale and talking quietly. The smell of seasoned stew sent a rumble through Isolda's stomach.

Margery snatched an unlit candle from one of the unoccupied tables and lit the wick in the hearth's fire.

"This way," she said, leading them toward a flight of wooden stairs at the back of the room. At the top of the stairs, they followed her down a narrow corridor lined with doors to the last room.

"It's small, but it's watertight and clean," she said, swinging open the door. The light from the candle in her hand illuminated a simple but tidy chamber. Shutters were closed tight against the day's rain, and the wooden floor was swept clean, with nary a cobweb in sight.

But when Isolda's eyes landed on the bed, she had to swallow the knot that rose in her throat. As Margery had said, it was a clean, dry place to sleep—but the bed was so small that it would hardly accommodate even one person.

"Thank ye, Madam Margery," Ansel said smoothly, stepping into the room and drawing Isolda after him. "This will do perfectly."

"Will ye be joining us belowstairs for a meal, or perhaps some ale?" she asked, eyeing them again. "Ye both look like ye could use some hot food and a drink to warm ye."

"Aye, we'd greatly appreciate a meal, though we'll take it up here, if ye please."

Margery raised an eyebrow. She looked like she wanted to probe them further on their late arrival and bedraggled appearance, but instead of pressing, she simply nodded. She deposited the candle on the tiny wooden table opposite the bed then silently departed, closing the door behind her.

Isolda quickly scanned the little chamber once more. Unbidden heat rose to her face at the sudden intimacy of being alone with Ansel in such a small space—a space with little more than a narrow bed in it.

She jumped when Ansel dropped the saddlebags he'd hung over his shoulder onto the floor.

"I'll go see about Margery's stew. Ye should get out of those wet clothes," he said gruffly.

Before she could form a response, he'd slipped out the door and closed it behind him.

Isolda dragged in a fortifying breath. She'd been alone with Ansel last night, hadn't she? Yet he'd been sleeping well away on the other side of the fire, and there hadn't been a bed—a bed that reminded her of his lie to Margery.

My wife. His Scottish burr had enfolded the word, making it sound strange and new.

She gave herself a little shake. Now was not the time to dwell on such silliness. She fumbled with wooden fingers at her cloak's tie at her throat, eager to be rid of her wet garments. Once she was free of the sodden wool, she draped the cloak, along with Ansel's borrowed plaid, over the chair pushed up against the little table by the door.

But when her cold-stiffened fingers reached the ties lacing down the back of her surcoat, she realized the threads had knotted. She blew into her hands, trying to work some feeling and dexterity back into them.

As she reached again for her surcoat's ties, her fingers slightly more nimble this time, she realized to her horror that the threads were swollen with moisture. The knot wouldn't budge, tug and fumble as she might.

Heavy boot-falls drew closer in the corridor outside the little chamber. She yanked desperately at her surcoat, but to no avail.

Ansel's fist rapped on the door. "Isolda? Are ye finished?"

Defeated, she exhaled shakily. "Aye, you can come in."

He opened the door, two bowls of steaming stew held against his chest with one arm and two mugs of ale held together by the handles in his free hand.

His eyes raked over her as he stepped inside and booted the door closed.

"Why are ye still wearing those wet clothes?"

She swallowed hard, her cheeks burning.

"I'm stuck. I need your help to undress."

Chapter Eighteen

Ansel set the mugs of ale and bowls of stew down carefully on the tiny table to buy himself time.

His mouth was suddenly dry, and he feared that if he looked at Isolda directly, he wouldn't be able to stop himself from doing what his body longed for.

"What do ye mean, ye're stuck?" He kept his voice level as he arranged the mugs and bowls slowly.

"The laces on my surcoat—they are knotted and swollen with rainwater."

Bloody hell, did her voice have to be especially breathy all of a sudden? He dared a glance at her. Despite the comely flush to her cheeks, she still looked far too pale. Her damp clothes clung to her, and as she shifted under his gaze, he noticed that she still trembled.

All at once, hot, irrational anger surged through him. Aye, anger was good—better than the lust threatening to overpower him. He embraced the ire thrumming in his veins, for it gave him a safer outlet for his pent desire.

"Ye shouldnae have let me abuse ye so greatly on our journey," he snapped, lowering his brows at her.

"Ye should have spoken up, told me ye were so cold and wet."

A flicker of indignation kindled in her eyes. Good—he'd get her blood pumping, even if it wasn't in the way that his body craved.

"What would you have me do? Demand that you stop for several days until the rains passed and I grew more accustomed to spending every moment of daylight in the saddle?"

"Aye! Are ye no' an English noblewoman? I thought making demands was exactly what ladies did best."

She sucked in a breath through chattering teeth. Dark fear flitted across her pale features for the briefest moment.

"Of course I am a lady," she snapped, quickly regaining her composure.

What had he just witnessed? He hadn't meant to question her title, so why had her thoughts gone in that direction? What was she hiding?

Then again, her outrage could have just as easily arisen from his harsh tone and the ire he was directing at her.

The air bristled with a taut silence for a long moment. She boldly met his gaze, her delicate brows lowered and her mouth set defiantly.

He was being a bloody arse, he knew. Ansel clawed his damp hair back from his forehead and muttered a curse.

"It is no' yer fault," he said, the sharpness edging his tone a moment ago filed down now. "It is mine. I ken verra well that ye are a lady and no' used to hard travel in the saddle or being out of doors in all weather. I should have watched ye more carefully."

He was not used to making mistakes—or apologizing. It grated that he had done both, and that Isolda had borne the consequences.

Surprise flitted across those pale green eyes, which looked iridescent in the light of the single candle on the table. Isolda opened her mouth, but he held up a hand, willing himself to go on despite his stubborn pride.

"Nay, dinnae. It is my job to protect ye, whether it be from Edward's men or from the elements." He snorted wearily as his eyes raked over her. "As it is, ye look more likely to die of a chill on my watch than by some hired assassin."

She puffed out a breath that held a hint of mirth in it. "Will you help me, then?" she asked softly, turning slightly so that he could see the laces trailing down her back.

But instead of looking at the ties, his gaze involuntarily slid from her slim shoulders to her narrowly cinched waist, then lower to the flare of her hips and the perfect roundness of her rear.

It was as if a boulder suddenly crushed his chest, for his lungs compressed and he struggled to draw in a breath. The only reason he didn't curse himself to high heaven was because his tongue abruptly refused to move.

He was going to undress Isolda. And somehow he was going to have to find the strength not to touch her.

The room was so small that he was nigh flush against her back in one easy stride. He forced his gaze on the rain-swollen knot at the small of her back, just before that mouth-watering flare of her hips and bottom. Aye, she was good and stuck.

Ansel squinted in the low light. When he'd moved toward her, his frame had blocked the candle's rays from falling on Isolda's back. Unconsciously, he reached out and took her by the hips, angling her slightly to catch the light.

But with his fingers sinking into the wet material encasing her hips, a new surge of lust crashed through him. He could take her like this. He could spin her around, never loosening his hold on those perfect hips, then toss her skirts up and wrap her legs around his waist. Or he could simply bend her over and claim her, one hand tangled in that wild chestnut hair while the other held her steady as he sank into her.

He snatched his hands away from her hips as if he'd been burned. He was on a mission, damn it. The last thing he should be fantasizing about was claiming Lady Isolda's tantalizing body.

It was bad enough that she was English nobility. There was no denying that it rankled his Scottish pride to find an English lady appealing.

Far worse, though, her presence was a distraction

from his assignment. What if he was too busy smelling her hair to notice a stealth attack? Or too engrossed in wrapping her legs around his hips to detect a threat?

"Any luck?" she said over her shoulder.

Damn it all. "No' yet."

He fumbled with the waterlogged knot, his fingers feeling clumsy and large. "I fear I'll have to cut it."

She glanced over her shoulder again, her brows creasing. "Cut it? But…"

"I ken it's a fine garment, but ye willnae be wearing it again, for a time anyway. The surcoat marks ye as far too wealthy to be traveling alone on a single horse with the likes of me."

Reluctantly, she nodded. "Very well. Cut the ties."

He drew the dagger strapped to his boot and with a clean swipe, he sliced the knot from the laces.

Isolda exhaled, but instead of sounding disappointed at the damage done to her surcoat, she actually sounded relieved. The laces along her back swelled to accommodate the expansion of her ribs as she drew in a deep breath.

Ansel realized suddenly that part of Isolda's ever-rigid posture wasn't simply a haughty air she put on—her garments held her bound, limiting her mobility to the point that she had to remain stiff and unbending nearly all the time.

"Why do ye wear such ridiculously tight clothes?" he said, sliding his fingers in the lacing to further loosen them. He hadn't meant for his words to come out so sharply, but he was having a hard time concentrating on anything but the feel of her back beneath the layers of damp fabric.

She stiffened beneath his fingers where they worked the surcoat's laces. "It is the style. A well-cut garment reveals the skill of the tailor and makes the most of a woman's form."

"But ye cannae move—ye can barely breathe."

"Aye, well…it is what the noblewomen of England wear."

"Thank God we are in Scotland now," he muttered.

At last the laces were loosened enough. Isolda's hands came to her shoulders and she began to peel the tight, wet garment down. Yet the russet surcoat clung to the chestnut brown gown underneath. Her fingers were pale and unsteady as she fumbled with the fabric.

Ansel gritted his teeth. "Let me help ye with that as well."

As he reached out, his hands brushed hers where they tugged at the material on her shoulders. Her fingers were icy and trembling.

He cursed himself silently once more. She was a lady, after all. She wasn't used to such grueling conditions, and like an arse, he hadn't been attentive to her. Perhaps she'd been right when she'd called him a barbarian.

Even still, he couldn't deny the swell of respect that rose in his chest—she hadn't complained in the slightest. Now, however, she was paying for it.

He stilled her fingers, holding them in his for a long moment to try to warm them. With a little noise, she drew her hands away and blew into them.

Gripping the wet fabric, Ansel began working it down her shoulders. The surcoat slowly peeled away like a second skin. First her shoulders and arms came free, then he tugged the surcoat down her back to her waist. With each inch gained, his hands slid against her body.

His manhood pulsed despite the fact that he, too, was cold and wet. Each contour was so delicate beneath his hands. What would her skin feel like beneath all these cursed layers of wet fabric?

With a yank that was perhaps more forceful than necessary, he pulled the surcoat over her hips.

"Thank you. I can see to it from here," Isolda said, her voice a breathy whisper.

Had the feel of his hands on her body affected her as much as it had him? Ansel bit back an oath for the traitorous line of his thoughts. Now even his mind was in collusion with his body to thwart his mission. He needed to protect Isolda—and perhaps that meant protecting her from his own lust.

She pushed the surcoat to the ground and stepped out of it. But now Ansel noticed that the chestnut gown underneath it had laces as well—laces that were swollen with rainwater, just like the surcoat.

"Do ye…" He had to clear his throat, for it was

suddenly thick. "Do ye have a spare chemise and gown, lass?"

"Aye."

"Good." He snatched up his dagger once more and sliced through the gown's ties as well.

"What are you—"

"Ye can get new laces when ye are safe," he said, his hands grasping the gown. "But ye cannae continue to linger in these wet clothes. Ye are soaked to the bone."

He peeled the thin wool gown away, only to reveal the clinging layer of her linen chemise.

This time he couldn't stop a low curse from slipping past his lips. The white linen stuck to her skin, revealing the expanse of her flawless, creamy back.

"Ye'd better see to the rest of it," he said, spinning on his heels.

She must have hesitated for a moment, because the room fell so quiet that he could hear her shallow, uneven breaths. Finally, a wet thump on the wooden floorboards told him that she'd removed her gown. Only the faintest rustle alerted him to the fact that she was discarding her damp chemise.

He clenched his fists even as his cock pulsed urgently. She was standing only a foot or two behind him—naked. All that silken flesh was exposed to the air. If he reached out backward, his fingertips would brush against her creamy skin.

"Can you…can you hand me a dry chemise?"

Her tight voice snapped him out of his reverie. Glancing at his feet, he realized that he stood directly over his saddlebags and the satchel of hers he'd attached to them. He bent and dug in her satchel until his fingers brushed soft, finely spun linen.

Christ, is this what touches her skin at every moment? His cock once again surged. He pulled the chemise free, letting the material slide through his fingers.

With a yank on his self-control, he stood swiftly and spun away from the bag. But too late, he realized what he'd done.

She gasped and turned partially away, clutching her wet chemise to her front. In the split second before Ansel thought to jerk his head to the side, his eyes feasted on the slim, milky length of her.

The soft glow of the candle encased her in golden light. It caressed her long, supple legs and clung to the inward sweep of her waist. Half of her shapely bottom was warmed by the light while the other was cast in shadow. Her unruly plait was almost completely undone. Wet tendrils of chestnut hair clung to her slim back and shoulders.

Ansel ripped his eyes away. "Bloody hell," he hissed, extending the chemise in his hand toward her while keeping his head averted.

She snatched the chemise from his grasp. The whisper of dry material over skin told him she was once again hidden from his hungry gaze.

Desperate for something to do with his hands other

than drag her against him and lay claim to her, Ansel turned to the little table.

"Here," he said, bluntly shoving a bowl of stew into her hands.

She kept her chin ducked, but there was no mistaking the hot flush in her cheeks. She took the stew and sat in the small chair. As she moved, the linen chemise danced across her skin, taunting him.

He stormed back to his saddlebags and yanked free a dry tunic and breeches. Giving her his back, he quickly kicked off his boots and pulled his wet tunic over his head.

"What are you—" Isolda squeaked.

Ansel glanced over his shoulder just in time to see her snap her head away, her gaze studiously focused on the stew she ate.

"Ye dinnae expect me to stay in wet clothes either, do ye, lass?" His voice bore an edge, but it was better to sound cross than lust-addled.

"Nay, of course not."

He stripped away his waterlogged breeches, his cock springing free readily. Damn it all, but no amount of cold, wet fabric could tame his eager manhood. He yanked on the dry breeches, followed by the tunic, then turned toward the table.

Just as he took up his own bowl of stew and mug of ale, Isolda rose.

"I am weary. I think I'll turn in."

"Ye can take the bed," he said. "I'll sleep on the

floor."

She nodded, her features flashing with relief. As he took up her chair, she moved to the narrow bed and drew back the covers. She settled herself with her back to him and pulled the blankets up to her chin.

Ansel downed his ale in one long gulp. By all the saints, this was going to be a long night. He finished the stew, letting its warmth seep into his weary body, then drank Isolda's untouched ale as well. By the time he rose and blew out the candle, his body hummed with heat.

But as he stretched himself out below the bed in the dark, he could hear Isolda's teeth chattering still.

"Bloody hell," he muttered to himself. He sat up and slowly raked a hand through his hair. Was this God testing him, or the Devil?

"Ye cannae seem to grow warm, aye, lass?" he said softly.

"A-aye," she replied.

"Then no amount of blankets will help. The only thing to do is…to let me warm ye."

"What?" Panic edged her voice, but he'd seen the way she looked at him and felt the way she'd responded to his kiss back at Dunstanburgh. She wanted him, too. And like him, she was afraid of the strength of that desire.

"I promise no' to compromise ye in any way." His voice was a low rasp in the dark.

He heard her breath catch in her throat. After a

long pause, she finally spoke. "You know very well that I am no innocent maiden. There is naught to compromise."

All the air left his lungs in a long, slow hiss. Why did she have to say things like that when he was barely keeping his cock in his breeches?

"Ye are still a lady, Isolda," he managed after a moment of struggle. "I'll no' insult ye by behaving…inappropriately. I am yer protector—naught more."

"Aye," she breathed.

Slowly, so as not to spook her, Ansel rose and placed a hand on the edge of the bed. She scooted away toward the wall, though it only created a sliver of space for him.

He eased back the blankets and slid in behind her, his chest to her back. By God, they fit perfectly together. Her head tucked under his chin, her bottom nestled perfectly against his groin, and their legs folded together as if they were made for each other.

Once he had the blankets pulled back up around them, he slid his arm around her front. His hand brushed past one of her breasts, and they both inhaled sharply. She trembled against him, but he couldn't be sure it was entirely from the chill that had set upon her.

"Goodnight, Ansel," she said, a wobble betraying her otherwise firm voice.

"Goodnight, Isolda," he managed.

Slowly, her shivers eased and her body went limp in his embrace. But long after her breathing grew steady within the little cocoon of warmth their bodies made, his manhood throbbed against her. At long last, exhaustion claimed him, but his sleep was filled with heated visions of Isolda.

Chapter Nineteen

Isolda was drifting on a sun-warmed cloud. She inhaled, her nose filling with the clean scent of wood smoke, fresh air, and something familiar—something that both soothed and thrilled her at the same time.

She burrowed her nose into the pillow she was lying upon, drawing in another breath of the heady scent. The firm yet warm pillow shifted. She threw her arm and one leg around it to hold it in place, nuzzling it with her face once more.

"Christ, lass," her pillow hissed in a rasping Scottish brogue.

She jolted fully awake with such a start that her eyes snapped open and her head jerked up from what she now realized was Ansel's chest. With her swift movement, her nose bumped into his.

Ansel's arms, which were wrapped around her like bands of iron, tightened to prevent them both from tumbling out of the narrow bed due to her sudden start. She was held immobile, her arm thrown over his chest and one of her legs entwined with his. Their noses still touched, with only a hair's breadth separating their mouths.

"Christ," he muttered again, his breath tickling her lips. She blinked up at him and suddenly felt like she was drowning in the dark pools of his eyes. Hunger lay there—a hunger so fierce and raw that her breath stuck in her throat.

Caught in his gaze, bound in his arms, there was no room to think, to put up her usual walls.

She sank her fingers into the front of his tunic. Even that small motion was all it took to close the distance between their mouths.

Ansel's lips were impossibly soft considering every other inch of him was as hard as forged metal.

At the first brushing contact of their mouths, he inhaled sharply through his nose, his fingers clutching her to him all the more tightly. He held her so close that she could hardly breathe. Her breasts crushed against his chest, with only the thin linen of his tunic and her chemise separating them.

He tilted his head, deepening their kiss. As if they had a mind of their own, her hands massaged his chest. Her fingers brushed hot skin when they found the opening in the front of his tunic. Crisp hairs tickled her fingertips as she greedily delved inside his tunic, longing for more contact.

One of his hands slid up to her hair, which had come completely free of its plait. His fingers sank into her locks, sending tendrils of sensation through her scalp. Her nipples tightened against his chest, and damp heat began pooling between her legs.

His tongue flicked against her lips in askance, and she readily opened to him. Their tongues mated in a needy, velvety embrace.

Unbidden, her knee rose against his thigh, bringing her womanhood fully against his hip. She moaned into his mouth, her body desperate for more of him.

Suddenly he rolled them both so that she was flat on her back. His broad frame loomed over her, though he bore some of his weight on his elbows. She dragged in a ragged breath, but their mouths were still fused together in their passionate kiss.

Slowly, he slipped a knee between her thighs, pressing up until he met with that aching spot. She moaned again at the delicious pressure against her throbbing sex. Her fingers turned to claws against his chest. A growl rose in his throat and vibrated against her lips, but her nails only seemed to fuel his lust.

He shifted slightly to free one of his arms from underneath her. The movement suddenly brought the hard thrust of his manhood against her hip. She writhed against his knee where he pressed between her legs, which made her hip rub more fully against his cock.

Flexing his pelvis against her, she felt the full extent of his arousal. His cock strained against his breeches, pulsing into her hip.

With another unintelligible curse against her lips, his now-freed hand cupped one of her breasts. Just the contact of his palm covering her already-taut nipple through her chemise sent her arching greedily into his hand.

"Ansel," she panted.

He groaned in response, sliding his callused hand over her breast. She gasped, pleasure shooting through her whole body. The sensation was building on itself, surging like a rising tide. She undulated against him, silently begging for more.

A sharp knock at the door had her jumping nigh out of her skin. She shrieked in surprise, but the sound was muffled by Ansel's lips.

"If ye wish to break yer fast, porridge is being served belowstairs."

It was Margery's curt voice on the other side of the door.

"Thank ye, Margery. We'll be down momentarily," Ansel bit out between gasps for breath.

As the innkeeper's footfalls drew away, Ansel rolled from the bed. Isolda clutched the covers to her chest as if she were naked. The truth was, she felt more than naked. She'd let her guard down, dropped her imperious air for a mere moment, and look what she'd almost done.

Hot shame crept up her neck and into her face. She was a wanton woman, just as her parents had said—just as Thomas, the Earl of Lancaster, had said.

Ansel gazed down at her, his eyes still smoldering with passion. He dragged a hand through his hair.

"We shouldnae have—"

"Aye. It was a moment of weakness. It will not happen again."

He nodded slowly, though his dark eyes still carved into her with unspent desire. "Aye."

He gave her his back as he set about stuffing his feet into his boots and clamping his belt and sword on his hip.

Isolda slid her feet onto the floor, careful to smooth her chemise where it had ridden up her legs. She pushed the blankets aside and rose, but as she stood, every muscle screamed in protest.

She groaned and wobbled on legs that somehow simultaneously felt like pudding and burned like the Devil.

Suddenly Ansel had her by the arms, his brows lowered and his mouth turned down behind the bristle of stubble darkening his face. "What is wrong?"

Isolda shifted gingerly, only to be rewarded with another flood of discomfort from her overwrought muscles.

"It is naught. Just the result of two days in the saddle and a night spent on the ground in the rain," she said through clenched teeth.

Ansel muttered an oath. "I shouldnae have pushed ye so hard."

His gaze swept over her, and a fresh wave of mortification washed through her. Despite the lack of comforts in her childhood and adolescence, she had let herself grow weak and soft living the life of a lady these past six years. And now she was so saddle-sore and achy that she'd be hard-pressed to walk, let along spend another sennight traveling north with Ansel.

"I'll be fine. I'm just a little stiff, that's all."

His eyes narrowed on her in assessment. "Nay," he said at last. "We'd best stay here for at least a day or two, lest ye grow far worse with the travel that lays ahead."

"But what about—" She lowered her voice, though she doubted anyone was listening. "What about Edward's men?"

A muscle ticked in Ansel's jaw as he considered for a moment. "As I said, it is my job to ensure that no harm befalls ye. We must be watchful for another attack, but my hope is that either Edward wouldnae send men into Scotland, or that they havenae picked up on our trail. In either case, I'd be doing ye no service if I rode ye into the ground. Ye need to rest."

His gaze searched her again, this time dropping to her mouth. For a breathless moment, she thought he was going to kiss her, but then his hands dropped from her arms and he stepped back consciously.

"I'll fetch us something to eat," he said, his voice level with reserve.

"Nay," she said quickly, her gaze flitting involuntarily to the bed. If she stayed in this cramped room with nothing but her memories and Ansel's lingering scent, she just might go mad. "I'll join you belowstairs in a few moments. I just need to gather myself."

"Verra well," he said. "But remember—try to wear something simple, and avoid speaking. Ye are no' an English lady here."

He slipped silently from the door, leaving her alone with her burning cheeks and a body that ached with a need for far more than just rest.

Aye, she was no lady.

Chapter Twenty

Ansel dragged his hair back and fastened it with a bit of leather as he descended the inn's wooden stairs. He could only hope that the small act of smoothing his hair would hide any traces of the turmoil that raged inside.

Christ, what had he almost done? He had never failed to put his duty and honor before all else, yet his desire for Isolda threatened to undo that. He was supposed to be serving his King, not tumbling with some Englishwoman whose son he was meant to protect. For some reason, Isolda made him feel like the wild barbarian she'd called him all those days past.

Ansel slid into a chair in the corner farthest from the door, hoping to go unnoticed. A few of the inn's patrons had already taken up tables and chairs as they waited for their breakfast. They were all quiet and kept their eyes down, some likely as uninterested as he in being questioned, and others slumping wearily from too much ale the night before.

Just then, the inn's door opened and a tall, thick-set man entered.

"Margery!" he bellowed.

The woman came bustling out of the kitchen that was attached to the inn's main room.

"Well it's about blooming time!" she snapped.

Ansel glanced casually at the large man who'd just entered. A scraggly blond beard obscured the lower half of his face. He stood easily as tall as Ansel, who towered over most Lowlanders and Englishmen, but was several stones heavier. His eyes were red-rimmed and as he stomped toward Margery, Ansel caught a whiff of stale ale.

"I dinnae need yer sharp tongue this morning, woman."

"*Woman?*" Margery squawked, planting her fists on her wide, aproned hips. "That's *wife* to ye, Fagan!"

Fagan, apparently the other keeper of the Rose and Thistle, slumped into a stool next to the kitchen. Margery resumed stirring a caldron of porridge over the hearth, not bothering to close the door between the inn's main room and the kitchen.

"And what kept ye all night?" she demanded over her shoulder, though she lowered her voice so as not to disturb the other patrons. Ansel strained to listen without being noticed.

"Mowbray refused to hear the petition," Fagan grumbled, crossing his meaty arms over his chest. "All fifteen of us waited until the guards turned us away, but we never even saw the English bugger's hide."

Margery straightened and darted her head around the room. Ansel studiously pretended to be engrossed in picking at his nails, but he didn't miss Margery's furtive looks.

"Dinnae speak of Sir Philip that way," she hissed, dropping her voice even lower. "He may have sided with King Edward, but he is a Scot, and he is with King Robert now."

Ansel clamped his teeth together to prevent from snapping an oath. Aye, Philip Mowbray was a Scot—and a traitor. The man had sided with Edward and held Stirling Castle for the English. When the Battle of Bannockburn had forced him to turn over the castle to Robert the Bruce, for some reason Mowbray had been allowed to stay on as the castle's keeper, this time for the Scots. The Bruce was a more forgiving man that Ansel would have been.

"Aye, well," Fagan muttered. "Nevertheless, he wouldnae even hear the petition to lower the innkeepers' tax. Mowbray grows fat on our backs behind Stirling's walls."

"And let me guess—after ye all were sent away, ye decided to grouse into each other's ears all night?"

Fagan straightened on the stool. "We talked, aye. At the Dragon's Head. The innkeepers' guild will hear of this, ye ken. We'll no' stand for Mowbray leeching us dry, just like the bloody English did." He waved a large hand dismissively at his wife. "But ye wouldnae understand. Ye've never had a head for business."

"Ye spent all night—and likely all our coin—drinking at the Dragon's Head instead of earning yer keep in yer own establishment, and *I'm* the one who doesnae understand business?"

Margery waved her porridge-encrusted wooden spoon at Fagan. When her husband didn't respond, she grumbled something and began doling the steaming porridge into wooden bowls.

With her hands and arms full of bowls, Margery began moving around the tables and chairs, distributing the simple fare to the inn's other patrons. When she reached Ansel, he quirked an eyebrow at her and lifted his mouth into a grin.

"And I thought *ye* were supposed to be the thistle of the Rose and Thistle," he said softly.

She snorted as she set down his bowl. For the first time that he'd seen, her frown flipped into a smile. "Aye, well," she said, shooting a glance at Fagan. "Even roses have thorns. Och, and dinnae fash yerself about yer horse. When it became obvious that my husband wasnae going to return last night, I saw to him myself. He's a fine animal."

Something tickled in the back of Ansel's mind. Was Margery again trying to get an explanation out of him for why he and Isolda had shown up in the rain at such a late hour last night? Like as not, she was just simply curious—as an innkeeper, she no doubt saw all manner of people passing through. Still, Ansel would have to tread carefully to avoid drawing too much attention.

"Thank ye, Madam Margery," he said, bowing his head a little in an overdone show of manners. "Ye are most kind."

She simpered under his praise. "Of course, milord. Will ye and yer wife be staying long?"

"A few days, perhaps. Hopefully the rains will stay away until—"

The room, which had already been quiet, suddenly fell dead silent. A flicker of movement on the stairs caught Ansel's eye, and all at once he realized that he'd made a terrible mistake.

Isolda stepped carefully down the stairs, one hand on the railing and the other lifting her skirts past her toes.

She wore a simple gown with no surcoat, as he'd instructed, but the wool was clearly spun finely and dyed a rich emerald green. Even from across the room, he could tell that it was tailored expertly, for it fit every one of her delicate curves like a caress. And the creamy linen chemise that peeked out at her wrists and along the modestly scooped neckline spoke of more precious coin for the fabric and tailoring.

But it wasn't just her garments that spoke of wealth. It was the way she carried herself with that damned regal air. With her shoulders back and her head held at a carefully tilted angle, she looked like a queen deigning to descend toward her subjects as she reached the last step.

Ansel's gaze quickly darted to the other patrons. Dread sank into his stomach. The men had completely forgotten the porridge in front of them and were staring open-mouthed at Isolda. But to Ansel's horror, they weren't simply looking at her with awe or reverence. Nay, lust lit their eyes and had their mouths hanging slack.

The green gown drew attention to those ethereal eyes, which now sought the room for Ansel. Her lips were rosy and slightly swollen from his demanding kiss. A flush pinkened her otherwise pale skin. Though she'd tamed her chestnut locks into a tight plait, it still shone lustrously in the light of the inn's fire.

She inhaled as her eyes finally landed on him, which caused the faintest hint of the upper curve of her creamy breasts to swell along her neckline.

Ansel gritted his teeth until his jaw ached to keep from cursing. Aye, he'd made a terrible mistake. He'd been a fool to think that he could travel inconspicuously with such a great beauty as Isolda. And by staying at an inn, he very well may have drawn unwanted—or even dangerous—attention to them.

Isolda made her way across the room, seemingly unaware of the eyes that followed her as she moved.

"There ye are, *wife*," Ansel said louder than necessary.

Isolda's step faltered for the briefest moment, but she managed to keep her features smooth. She sat across from him at the little table in the corner.

Margery placed a bowl of porridge in front of Isolda, eyeing her surreptitiously.

"As I was saying, we'll be staying a few days—and

of course we'll pay ye for the fine accommodations and yer extra attentions to my horse," Ansel said levelly to Margery.

The innkeeper nodded, her eyes flickering at Ansel's less-than-subtle implication that he'd also pay extra for her discretion—and for giving them privacy.

Margery moved back to the kitchen, but Ansel could feel Fagan's probing gaze on them.

"Would ye care for a bath to ease your aches, sweeting?" Ansel said, taking Isolda's hand in his.

Her eyes rounded for a moment at the endearment and his touch. She opened her mouth to respond, but then she seemed to remember his instructions about not speaking. She clamped her lips shut and pressed them into a forced smile, bobbing her head in a nod.

"I'll ask Madam Margery to see to it," he said, keeping his voice light.

As Isolda ate her porridge, most of the other patrons of the inn slowly rose from their empty bowls and reluctantly made their way outside or abovestairs. Many cast hungry glances toward Isolda, despite the fact that Ansel still had her hand folded in his.

When at last Isolda was done and the room was almost empty, Ansel called Margery over.

"A bath for my wife, if ye please," he said, willing the tight tension from his voice. "Perhaps this evening, after supper."

Margery bobbed into a quick curtsy and reached for Isolda's empty bowl.

"Thank you," Isolda said absently as Margery cleared the table.

Margery's hand froze on the bowl, her eyes shooting to Isolda. "What did ye say?"

Too late, Isolda compressed her lips, her gaze darting to Ansel.

Shite. Dread twisted like a knife in his belly.

Fagan rose slowly from his stool and stalked toward their table. "Well, well. It seems as though we have an Englishwoman in our midst."

Chapter Twenty-One

Fagan's blue eyes narrowed on Isolda as he loomed over their table.

"And what is an Englishwoman doing in an inn not far outside Stirling?"

Ansel's heart pounded, sending blood coursing through his veins. If he had to, he would be ready to fight.

The few patrons who had lingered in the inn's main room were suddenly alert, their gazes fixed on the little corner table. They pushed back from their tables, their chairs squealing against the stone floor. Ansel's gaze shot to them, but he couldn't tell as they stood and looked on sharply if they meant to cause trouble or prevent it.

Studiously, Ansel leaned back in his chair, letting his thumb swish lazily over Isolda's trembling hand.

"Och, ye ken how it is, I'm sure," he said evenly, forcing one side of his mouth up into a roguish grin. He glanced between Margery and Fagan, but both still stood rigidly over their table, their brows lowered.

Ansel shrugged, letting his grin widen disarmingly. "We are no' far from the Borderlands, after all.

I…came upon Isolda here in a carriage a fortnight ago. And well…now we are headed north."

Isolda looked at him, her eyes wide with confusion, but Margery relaxed a hair's breadth.

"Ye're saying ye stole her, then?"

Ansel forced a chuckle to rise in his throat. "Such things are common enough, are they no'? I had us wed no' long ago in Edinburgh as we passed through, and…well… I havenae heard any complaints from the lass since."

That drew a few chuckles from the patrons who looked on, but Isolda's hand clenched into a fist underneath his palm. Her lips tightened slightly, an angry flush staining her cheeks.

Margery lifted an eyebrow at him in guarded amusement. Fagan, on the other hand, was still glowering at Isolda behind his bushy blond beard.

"Ye said ye were headed north?" Fagan asked, not taking his sharp gaze from Isolda.

"Aye, I hail from the Highlands," Ansel replied.

Margery nodded. "I thought I detected a Highland brogue to yer voice. Where are ye from?"

Ansel's mind raced. If he told the truth, he'd in effect be creating a trail by which anyone—Scottish or English—could follow him and Isolda. But Margery had seen them arrive last night with his Sutherland plaids wrapped around their shoulders. If he lied, she might catch him in it.

"Sutherland territory," he said obliquely. Margery

nodded again, seeming satisfied. The tension knotting Ansel's entire body eased ever so slightly.

Fagan grunted, shifting his eyes to Ansel before returning them to Isolda. He sniffed as if she smelled foul. "I dinnae abide sheltering the English under my roof."

"Och, it's no' just yer roof," Margery said tartly, rounding on her husband. "It's mine, too. These are *my* patrons, since ye saw fit to stay out all night drinking instead of seeing them settled."

Even still, Margery cast a distasteful glance at Isolda. "English," she muttered, turning back to the kitchen to clean up after the simple breakfast.

"We dinnae want any trouble," Ansel said, keeping his voice low enough that only Fagan would hear. "We'll be on our way in a few days' time, and ye'll never see us again."

Fagan glowered down at them. "Aye," he said at last. "No' a bit of trouble."

The man turned away, muttering under his breath.

Unease trickled down Ansel's spine, but he was careful to keep his body relaxed. He stood and drew Isolda to her feet by the hand he still clasped. He made a show of strolling toward the stairs, bobbing little nods to the other patrons who still stood watching them as they passed.

At last, the remaining patrons seemed to relax and began filtering out of the inn. Some cast glances at them as they made their way upstairs.

When they reached their door, Ansel's grip tightened on Isolda's hand.

"Get inside," he whispered. "And stay there for the rest of the day. Dinnae answer the door to anyone but me, ye understand?"

She stared up at him, fear rounding her eyes. "Don't leave me here alone!" she choked out.

Ansel exhaled. He opened the door to their chamber and brought her inside, closing the door after them against any prying ears.

"It will be all right," he said softly.

"But the way that man—"

"Isolda, listen to me." He took her gently by the shoulders, holding her frightened eyes with his gaze. "No one will harm ye, I promise. Fagan is full of piss and vinegar, but he wouldnae dare aught, nor would any of those others."

She nodded weakly. "I am sorry I spoke."

"Dinnae fash yerself," he whispered. "In truth, we have drawn suspicion since the moment we arrived. I still plan to stay another day or two to let ye rest, but we need to be more careful. As it is, I need to see to Eachann."

"Why?" she said, fear once again pinching her voice.

He ran a soothing hand down one of her arms. "It isn't aught to worry about. But I'd like to see to him myself to ensure that he is in good form. I may even need to get him re-shod."

She swallowed but held his gaze. "Because we may need to flee, is that it?"

He exhaled slowly once more. "Aye." He let his hands drop and turned toward the door. "Remember what I said. Dinnae open the door unless it's me."

"Ansel," she breathed, halting him.

"Aye?"

"How could you say that you had stolen me from England and wed me?"

He pinned her with his gaze. Normally the haughty tilt of her chin and the lowering of her delicately curved brows would have sparked his ire—or at least encouraged him to ruffle those uppity feathers of hers. But at the moment, he took her indignation as a good sign. It meant that her fear had ebbed enough to make room for exasperation.

"As I said belowstairs, it is common enough for Scotsmen to kidnap their brides. If nothing else, that explanation is more believable than the truth—that ye are being targeted by King Edward II and that yer former lover, the Earl of Lancaster, hired a Scot to protect ye and yer illegitimate son."

Isolda sputtered in an attempt to respond, but before she could form words, he slipped out the door. As he closed her inside their chamber, he flashed her a reassuring smile.

"Welcome to Scotland."

Chapter Twenty-Two

Isolda brought the precious bar of soap she'd tucked into her satchel up to her nose. She inhaled the luxurious scent of lemon and lavender, letting it fill her lungs.

Gingerly, she threw a leg over the high-sided wooden tub Margery had brought to her chamber not long ago. The water inside steamed blissfully.

She eased herself into the water an inch at a time, for Margery had made it exceptionally hot. Once she was halfway in, she unplaited her hair with her fingers.

Isolda had spent the day alone in the dim, cramped chamber, too afraid to even open the shutters. She'd paced restlessly for a while, but she was still sore from all those hours in the saddle, so she'd stretched out on the little bed she'd shared with Ansel the night before.

That hadn't been particularly restful, though, since the bedding still held his earthy, masculine scent.

When Margery had knocked sometime in the early evening, she'd nigh leapt from her skin with fright, so tightly was she wound.

Though Ansel had told her not to open the door to anyone, Margery had already lugged the deep tub up the stairs by herself. Isolda feared that if she refused to admit her, it would only cause more trouble and suspicion, so she'd let Margery inside.

After several trips up the stairs for Margery, a bucket of water weighing her down, Isolda was left alone with her bath.

She had truly grown soft in the last six years.

Nay, that wasn't entirely true, for the first few years after John had been born were challenging, even with her new title of Lady. She, Mary, Bertram, and John had lived in little more than a hovel before construction started on Dunstanburgh Castle nigh two years ago. It was no worse than she'd grown up with, but she was used to being surrounded by her cheery, hardworking family. The isolation at Dunstanburgh had almost been enough to break her.

But as the physical comforts of life at Dunstanburgh had increased and Lancaster had plied her with money for her silence and invisibility, she'd grown into the role of Lady that had at first been such an act.

She had become unused to hard conditions and had begun to take simple pleasures like soaking in a hot bath with her beloved, fragrant soap for granted.

Never again, she promised herself as she sank all the way into the steaming water. She doubted if a bath had ever felt as good as it did in that moment.

She worked the soap between her hands, then began lathering her hair. There had been so little time to gather her thoughts of late, so little time to slow down and relax. Though the dark looks Fagan had given her this morning still haunted her, at least for the moment she was alone and could undo some of the knots of fear and exhaustion that had taken root since—

Since Ansel had arrived in her life. Even the thought of him sent a tight warmth low into her belly. Though danger had swirled at every turn, she felt impossibly safe in his presence. Safe—and desirous of his gaze, his touch, his kiss.

But she was no silly girl nurturing her first infatuation. She should know better than to let passion rule her—she'd already learned the hard way what could happen when she let her lust have free rein. It was an indulgence she could not afford again.

Her heart twisted painfully, stilling her hands in her hair. *Never again*, she whispered to herself once more. Never again would she succumb to her cursed desire, no matter how much she longed to.

So lost in thought was she that too late, she registered the sound of boot-falls outside the door.

"Isolda, I asked Margery to bring us supper up here again, for—"

A cry of warning turned into a shriek of surprise as the door flew open. Ansel stood stunned in the doorway, a lit candle in his hand and his eyes locking on her.

She clapped her hands over her chest, barring her breasts from view. Ansel's gaze dropped at her motion, and his lips parted on a hissing exhale.

Seeming to regain a shred of his wits, he stepped into their chamber and swiftly closed the door behind him.

"What are ye doing?" he rasped, his eyes still fixed on her.

"What does it look like?" she squeaked.

His eyes darkened even as they remained pinned on her. "I told ye no' to open the door to anyone."

Just then, hurried footsteps sounded in the corridor beyond their chamber.

"What is all the fuss?" Margery's voice drifted through the door a moment before she rapped sharply. Not waiting for a reply, she opened the door, huffing from the stairs.

"It is naught," Ansel said smoothly. "My wife…simply thought she saw a mouse, but she was mistaken."

"Ah," Margery said, her gaze sliding between them. "Verra well. When supper is ready I will bring it to ye, as ye asked."

She closed the door behind her, but Ansel waited until the sound of her footsteps disappeared. He rounded on her once more.

"I thought I made myself clear," he bit out.

"Aye, well," she shot back, her heart still in her throat from his sudden appearance. "Margery brought the bath early, and I didn't want to simply turn her away."

He considered that, dropping his gaze to the floor.

"I'd best leave ye, then," he said slowly.

"Nay!" She swallowed to try to temper her voice. "If you go belowstairs now, Margery will be all the more suspicious."

Ansel set his candle on the table next to the unlit one from the night before.

"Aye, ye're right." He gave her his broad back then. "Ye'd best finish before Margery returns."

Hurriedly, she set aside her precious soap and cupped her hands to rinse the suds from her hair. As she lifted her arms to dump water over her head, she inhaled sharply at a fresh twinge of pain. Two days on horseback had introduced her to muscles she didn't even know she had, let alone ones that could become so knotted.

"Ye're still sore, are ye no'?" Ansel's voice was a dark caress behind her.

Something twisted deep inside her. Silently, she cursed her traitorous body for the sudden flush of heat his voice sent through her.

"Aye, but I'll be all right," she breathed. As if to defy her, another twinge of pain shot through her back as she tried once more to rinse her hair.

"Let me help ye."

Before she could respond, his warm hand brushed past her shoulder. She stiffened, but when she glanced down, she realized that the light from the candle shimmered on the surface of her bathwater, affording her a sliver of modesty.

He lifted his cupped hand and let the hot bathwater trickle down through her sudsy locks. He repeated the motion again and again until her hair streamed down around her shoulders, clean and free of soap.

"Thank you," she said, her voice strangely thin.

Ansel grunted, but instead of standing and giving her his back once more, his fingers brushed over her shoulders and to her back.

She inhaled sharply as his hands began to knead her sore flesh.

"Ye dinnae need to be so rigid in the saddle," he said lowly.

She started, for his mouth was close to her ear, and his warm breath sent goose bumps over her skin despite the steaming bathwater.

"I..."

"I ken that yer surcoat was responsible for some of it, but all the same, ye should have leaned back against me."

She sucked in a breath as his fingers found a particularly tight knot in the middle of her back.

"Ye needn't be so proper all the time. I could have eased yer discomfort earlier."

Her head spun hazily as waves of pleasure washed over her where his hands worked. Was he talking about riding, or something else? Her fuzzy brain couldn't parse the implication of his whisper-soft admonition.

"Aye..."

Was she agreeing with him or urging him on? She didn't know, nor did she care at the moment, for his hands moved lower, below the waterline.

He massaged her lower back, and she arched shamelessly at his touch like an attention-starved cat.

"Bloody hell," he muttered, though the words seemed more directed at himself than at her.

His hands slid around her waist, pulling her against the side of the tub.

"What are ye doing to me, Isolda?" he breathed, his lips brushing her earlobe. His callused palms rasped against her stomach below the water, one moving upward, the other downward.

A tiny alarm bell rang in the back of her mind, but she was too far gone to heed it. All her fortitude and resolution to hold herself at bay be damned—Ansel's arms bound her, his hands burned a path along her skin, and his mouth brushed against her ear. She was lost to the moment—lost to him.

One of his rough-padded thumbs slid along the underside of her breast. A moan escaped her lips, wordlessly urging him on. The fingers on his other hand brushed the top of the curls between her legs.

Unbidden, her knees parted slightly, beckoning him farther. He ground out a curse. Simultaneously, his thumb rasped across her nipple and one fingertip slid across the seam of her sex.

Isolda gasped, her head falling back onto the edge of the tub. The motion exposed her neck to him, which he quickly took advantage of. As he began slowly circling the thumb on her nipple, he sank his teeth into the soft flesh of her neck.

Sensation jolted through her like lightning. It was as if every nerve ending in her body sizzled with sparks of passion.

His finger slipped between her folds and found that spot of pure pleasure. Her knees fell completely open, sloshing water against the sides of the tub.

"Damn it all. I want ye," he growled against her neck, his tongue flicking her sensitive skin there. "Now."

Chapter Twenty-Three

Isolda's head spun at the force of the passion burning through her. Ansel's stubble scraped the sensitive skin of her neck, his soft lips giving stark contrast as he rasped the words.

"Aye," she panted, arching into his hands all the more fully. "Aye, Ansel. I want you, too. Now."

Suddenly she was lifted into the air, water cascading from her body into the tub beneath her. His arms bound her to his chest, and where her skin touched him, his tunic grew wet.

In two strides, he reached the narrow little bed they'd shared almost chastely last night. As he lowered her, still dripping wet, toward the mattress, she clung to him.

"The blankets," she breathed. "They'll get soaked and—"

"I dinnae care," he growled, dipping her the rest of the way down. He straightened and looked down at her. With the candle behind him, he loomed like an enormous shadow over her, but his eyes burned with fierce desire as he gazed at her.

For a moment she felt too exposed, too bared before him where she lay naked on the bed under his scorching gaze, but then he began tearing at his own clothes with such urgency that she forgot to be ashamed of her nakedness.

His gaze held her captive as he yanked on the ties at the neck of his tunic. He unbuckled his belt while he kicked off his boots, and all the while his eyes feasted on her with a hunger she'd never seen before. The only time he broke his stare was to pull his tunic over his head.

Now it was her turn to stare, captivated by the sight before her. Her eyes raked over every hard plane and ridge. She was mesmerized by the hypnotic rippling and coiling of his corded muscles. She'd seen his bare chest before, but now she needed to touch it, to feel its heat and hardness pressed against her.

His hands tore at the ties on his breeches. With a sharp exhale, he yanked the material down, freeing his engorged cock. The hard, thick length of him jutted toward her, and her breath quickened and caught in her throat. She knew exactly what they were going to do next—and she wanted it as badly as he did.

Stepping free of his breeches, he lowered himself over her, his large, honed frame engulfing her. Instinctively, she spread her thighs to give him room to settle between them.

Though he supported most of his weight on his elbows, the air whooshed from her lungs. Surely this was madness, but any last shred of rational thought fled her mind as the full length of him rubbed against her, skin to skin.

His mouth fell to her neck, and he began alternating kisses and bites. Each petal-soft brush of his lips was followed by a shiver-inducing nip until her whole body quaked from the inside out.

His hands found her breasts, which were already arched for his touch. Then he trailed his lips downward until they captured one of her nipples.

She gasped and groaned, liquid fire shooting through her. Involuntarily, her hips bucked, bringing his cock into contact with her damp folds.

Now it was his turn to groan. He undulated against her, his cock gliding against the folds of her womanhood in a delicious tease.

"I cannot take any more," she breathed. "Please, Ansel. Now."

One of his hands slid between them, guiding his cock to her entrance. He held himself there, his thumb finding that perfect spot just above.

She cried out, half in ecstasy and half in desperation for more.

His thumb strummed against that spot in an achingly slow rhythm until she feared her whole being would fly apart into a million pieces. Slowly, deliberately, he drove into her.

With each pulse of his thumb and each inch he pushed deeper, her breath broke on a cry of pleasure. At last he was sheathed fully inside her, and she could feel his cock pulsing with his own need.

She threw her arms around his neck, her nails sinking into his shoulders to urge him on.

He growled, and she knew the last thread of his control had snapped. He withdrew and thrust into her, wringing a desperate moan from both of their throats. Again, he drove deep, and again.

Isolda's body could climb no higher. She began to quake as cascade upon cascade of pleasure broke over her, within her, through her. She cried out, her body arching against his as she greedily reaped every last drop of ecstasy from their joining.

His own climax ripped a shout from him. He thrust hard, holding himself deep as he spent himself inside her.

He collapsed on top of her, careful to roll to his side to avoid crushing her. She could barely hear his exhausted panting over the thundering pulse in her ears. Gradually, her heart slowed as the last tendrils of pleasure melted away in her body.

Her fingers grazed up his arm, where she brushed against the stitches she'd placed there only a few days ago. She inhaled sharply.

"I didn't hurt you, did I?"

In the flickering light of the candle, she could see the neat row of stitches she'd made. The skin underneath was neither swollen nor red, both good signs. Her gaze darted to his chest, then his other shoulder. All the wounds appeared to be healing quickly.

A low chuckle rumbled through his chest. "Nay, ye didnae hurt me, lass. Quite the opposite."

His dark brown eyes were filled with a liquid heat as they held her. He brushed a wet strand of hair from her forehead, taking his time to tuck it behind her ear and trail his fingers down her throat.

She swallowed against his fingertips as cold reality leeched back into her mind.

"Ansel," she whispered, a terrible dread sinking into her stomach. "We shouldn't have—"

His hand lifted from her neck and hovered in the air between them to halt her words.

"Nay, you must listen," she said, her throat tight with shame. "We cannot do this. I—"

"Shh." His brows dropped in concentration. He cocked his head, his gaze slipping from her to the floorboards beyond the bed.

Confusion flickered through her. She strained to hear what had caught his attention, but the only sound was the muted rumble of voices seeping through the floorboards from the inn's main room.

"Something isnae right," he muttered. He swung his legs from the bed and stood, quickly snatching up his breeches. He dressed swiftly as she watched in bewilderment.

Was he leaving her? Pain sliced through her heart, reopening the old wound Lancaster had inflicted almost six years ago. Lancaster had turned cold and callous after he'd gotten what he wanted from her.

She'd thought Ansel was different, but she'd been wrong before.

She didn't fight the shame that washed over her. How could she make the same mistake twice?

"Ansel…" Pain cracked her voice and tears burned in her eyes as she watched him.

"Just hold on, lass," Ansel said, darting to the door. He eased it open and brought his ear to the gap.

Now the noise from the main room drifted more distinctly up the stairs and down the corridor to their door. But what Isolda heard turned her blood to ice.

What she'd mistaken for simple voices belowstairs were actually shouts—angry shouts. The Scottish brogues overlaid each other, each more adamant than the last about the source of their anger—the English.

Isolda clutched a blanket over her nakedness as she sat bolt upright. She sucked in a ragged breath as Ansel's gaze collided with hers.

"It will be all right," he said softly, but he couldn't mask the sudden tautness in his body. "They are likely just drunk and releasing a wee bit of pent energy."

Fagan's voice rose above the others then, cutting sharply through the noise and reaching them clearly.

"And why else would that bastard Mowbray deny us?" he snapped. "Because he's a bloody English sympathizer!"

The floorboards rumbled as those belowstairs shouted their agreement, with some calling for Mowbray's traitorous head.

Isolda pressed her lips together to stop the frightened whimper that rose in her throat.

"Get dressed," Ansel commanded. "And gather all of our things. We may need to leave in a hurry tonight."

He looked at her fully for a moment, his eyes clouding with some emotion she couldn't read in the flickering candlelight. And then he was gone, slipping silently from the room and closing the door softly behind him.

Chapter Twenty-Four

Ansel crept on silent feet down the corridor toward the inn's stairs. The warm glow of firelight filled the stairway ahead of him, but the scene was far from cheery, for angry shouts rent the air.

Though every instinct told him to grasp his sword hilt and slide the blade's familiar weight into his hands, he resisted. There was still a chance that the night wouldn't end in violence, and he would not be the one to start it. And if it came to that, he would have to call upon every last shred of skill and strength to ensure that Isolda was safe.

He eased down the stairs, moving slowly to keep from drawing attention to himself. The inn's main room was crowded with restless men, their bodies warming the ale-scented air.

As he slipped into the back of the crowd, Ansel quickly scanned the room. Fagan stood in one corner, his foot propped on a chair. Though the other men stood as well, Fagan's height made his dirty blond head tower over the others.

"...hands are stuffed with English coin, yet he wants more Scottish gold, too."

The crowd rumbled indignantly in agreement with Fagan's words.

Just then Ansel caught sight of a short figure squeezing through the tightly packed group of men.

"Margery," he hissed when the woman pressed by him.

The woman's head snapped up and she froze next to him. Her hands bristled with empty ale mugs.

"Ye'd best stay abovestairs with yer wife," Margery said, her gaze darting around the room. All eyes were still focused on Fagan, though.

Ansel bowed his head so that she wouldn't have to speak up to be heard over the crowd. "What goes on here?"

Margery glanced around again, but at last she spoke.

"My husband serves as the head of the Stirling chapter of the innkeepers' guild, though he fancies himself the entire guild's leader. He and the others have been attempting to petition Mowbray to lower their taxes."

"And Mowbray wouldnae see them yesterday," Ansel said. "What happened today?"

"Mowbray finally heard their petition this eve," Margery said. "But he denied them. They came back here an hour ago already drunk and with their dander up." She shook her head disapprovingly. "I told Fagan not to serve any more ale, but he wouldnae listen."

"...might as well be English, for he has Scottish

blood on his hands and Scottish coin in his pocket."

The crowd roared in response to Fagan's latest shouted declaration.

"As I said, ye'd best stay abovestairs," Margery said quickly before slipping back into the mob and weaving her way toward the kitchen.

"We all ken verra well that there are still English among us, even after Bannockburn," Fagan said, dropping his voice. The men responded by spitting on the ground and muttering about filthy English in their midst.

"They take our money, just like Mowbray, and some even report back to England. They say even women can be spies for Longshanks's snot-nosed son, Edward."

Ansel's head snapped up, only to find that Fagan's hard blue eyes cut across the throng to pin him.

The mass of drunken, angry men muttered again, some in surprise at the suggestion of female spies, some with a few choice words for all Englishwomen.

"Aye, it's true," Fagan went on. "The English are everywhere, watching us, stealing from us, sneaking onto our lands."

Fagan dropped his boot from the chair he'd propped it on and slowly pushed his way through the crowd. Fire and ice collided in the pit of Ansel's stomach. He tensed as Fagan approached, but he willed his hands to remain clenched at his sides.

"And how do these filthy English set their claws into Scotland? Why, with the aid of Scottish sympathizers like Mowbray."

Fagan came to a halt directly in front of Ansel. The blond giant crossed his thick arms over his chest, but Ansel refused to move. He narrowed his gaze on the innkeeper, his lips curling back in a warning snarl.

"Who among ye is a sympathizer with the English?" Fagan said, spittle flying from the corners of his mouth.

The men roared denials and curses for any Scotsman who would aid the English.

Ansel held his ground, his teeth clamped together so tightly that his jaw throbbed.

"And what about ye, *friend*?" Fagan said, leaning even closer to Ansel. "Where do yer loyalties lie?"

"I fought by the Bruce's side at Bannockburn," Ansel said, his voice carrying across the suddenly hushed room. "And at Loch Doon and Dunbraes Castle. And countless other battles. So dinnae question my loyalty, *friend*."

Many of those gathered shifted uneasily, but judging from the glint in Fagan's eyes, he wasn't done yet.

"Ah, but that is the funny thing about men's loyalties, is it no', lads?" he said, commanding the attention of the room once more. "Sometimes loyalties lay with a man's country, and sometimes they lay between his woman's thighs."

Confusion flitted through the room as tension once again thickened the air.

"Ye see, friends, the man before ye ruts with an Englishwoman, who is abovestairs at this verra moment."

Shite.

A cacophony of outrage filled the small space. Someone bumped into Ansel from behind. There were too many bodies pressing against him to allow him room to draw his sword.

"Leave him be, Fagan!" Margery's high voice cut from the kitchen, but no one heeded it.

"Perhaps the English still havenae learned their lesson!" Fagan shouted over the uproar, drowning out Margery's distant protests. "Perhaps we should teach it to them again!"

Another bump, this time harder, threatened to knock Ansel off balance. A hard shove came from his other side. It was time to act.

Like a bolt of lightning, Ansel drew back his fist and unleashed it with a wicked snap. His knuckles collided with Fagan's nose, producing a loud crack. Fagan stumbled backward, blood spurting from his broken nose.

The room erupted in chaos. Blessedly, the angry mob's overindulgence of ale would work in Ansel's favor. As they staggered backward in surprise around Fagan, he leapt toward the stairs, yanking his sword free.

The crowd's shock faded, to be replaced by renewed anger.

His moment of surprise was up.

Two dozen drunk, livid Scotsmen who thought he was an English sympathizer turned on him as one.

Chapter Twenty-Five

Isolda dressed hurriedly by the light of the single candle. She did her best to squeeze out the remaining moisture from her hair and quickly plait it, but her braid hung wetly against the hood of her cloak.

As Ansel had instructed, she grabbed their few possessions and stuffed them into their bags. With a start, she remembered the precious scented soap she'd set aside as she'd bathed. How long ago that deliciously hot bath—and Ansel's scorching touches—seemed now.

She shoved the thought aside and retrieved the bar of soap, carefully wrapping it in linen before stuffing it into her satchel. She could dwell on their shared passion, and the flood of shame that followed, some other time, but not now.

She gasped and started as another rumble sent the floorboards vibrating. Although she could no longer make out what the voices were saying, their rage was obvious.

Clutching herself in her arms, she paced across the narrow room. Was Ansel safe? Was she? If only she hadn't spoken and revealed the fact that she was English. Though Margery had been kind, if a bit thorny, Fagan had clearly been suspicious of her that morning.

Just as she turned to nervously cross the room once more, noise erupted in the direction of the stairs. This time she didn't manage to suppress the cry of fear that ripped from her throat. The din was suddenly different. It was sharper and more intense—and closer.

There was a loud thump on the stairs, followed by another at the far end of the corridor. A scream of pain sliced through the door.

Isolda's heart leapt into her throat, her pulse hammering in her veins. Hands trembling with fright, she snatched up her satchel and Ansel's saddlebags, which were still attached.

A scuffle sounded right outside the door. Someone grunted in pain, then there were more thuds of contact.

Her eyes darted around the room. It was so small that there was nowhere to go, nowhere to hide. She backed toward the shuttered window, holding the bags before her like a shield, her eyes wide and riveted on the door.

"Isolda!"

Ansel's harsh cry was unmistakable even muffled by the door's thick wood.

"Ansel!" she shrieked, her voice hitching with terror.

The door suddenly exploded inward. Ansel launched himself inside, then slammed the door closed.

A heavy thud reverberated through the wood a second later as some large body flung itself against the door.

Ansel drove his shoulder into the wood, keeping the door shut even as it bounced with another assault.

"Go out the window!" he shouted at her. "Get Eachann from the stables and bring him to the alley below us."

"What? But we are at least a dozen feet off the ground!"

"Go!" Ansel barked, struggling to keep the door shut against the mob outside. "Now!"

Renewed panic surged through her. She spun and yanked the shutters away from the window. Night shrouded the ground below in shadow.

Isolda swallowed hard. Voices bellowed on the other side of the door. Ansel grunted with the effort of holding it closed, his shoulder shoved into the wood even as his boots slipped against the floorboards.

She threw their bags to the ground. They landed with a muted thump a moment later.

That will be me in a moment.

Heart in her throat, she swung first one leg and then the other over the window ledge. She gripped the wooden sill, her nails clawing for purchase.

Drawing on every drop of willpower she possessed, she lowered herself until she dangled from the sill, her feet twisting in nothing but air. Dragging in a breath, she said a prayer and let go.

Night air whooshed passed her for a terrible,

stretching moment. Then her feet slammed into the ground, sending bolts of pain through her legs. She rolled to the side and bumped into their bags.

Fear numbed the pain as she stumbled to her feet, clutching the bags. She staggered toward the stables attached to the back of the inn.

Inside, Eachann was easy to spot even in the dimness. He was the biggest horse by far, fit to carry Ansel's large frame. She ran a soothing hand across the bay's nose, then slipped his bridle on. She struggled with the heavy leather saddle, her fingers trembling as she worked the buckles underneath the large animal's belly.

Whispering a word of reassurance into Eachann's velvet brown ear, she boosted herself on his back and guided him out of his stall.

The horse's ears twitched at the shouts coming from the inn. Just as Isolda spurred Eachann into the alley above which their window stood, light and noise erupted from the front of the inn. The men inside were now spilling out in search of them.

She reined Eachann into the shadows along the inn's wall, praying her trembling body wouldn't spook the animal and give their assailants warning. Her gaze shot up to the window she'd fallen from.

"Please," she breathed, no more than a whisper of air crossing her lips.

As if in answer to her plea, Ansel appeared in the windowsill. He jammed his sword in its scabbard before launching himself into thin air.

Isolda clapped a hand over her mouth to muffle her scream as she watched him fall. He landed and rolled far more gracefully than she had, though he cursed when he rose to his feet, wavering.

Large bodies blocked the light from the window overhead.

"There he is!" someone shouted.

More shouts answered behind them as the men who'd come out the inn's front door rounded the corner and saw them.

Isolda spurred Eachann toward Ansel. He staggered forward, flinging himself onto Eachann's back as they passed him without slowing.

The mob closed in behind them just as Isolda dug her heels into Eachann's sides. The horse, well-trained and bred for battle, surged forward mightily, nearly unseating both Isolda and Ansel.

Ansel wrapped his arms around her and grabbed the reins, jerking Eachann to the right. The animal exploded onto a wider road, breaking into a full gallop. The road flew by under Eachann's pounding hooves.

At last, the angry shouts faded behind them. The town shrank away and soon they were riding by the weak light of the partially obscured moon, dark woods surrounding them on either side of the road.

Isolda slumped backward against Ansel, terror suddenly replaced with quaking exhaustion. He grunted sharply when her back connected with his chest.

"Are you hurt?"

He grunted again and suddenly yanked the reins to the left, pulled Eachann off the road. Blackness surrounded them as they slid under the cover of the thick pine trees lining the road.

"I'll be fine," he replied at last, though his voice was tight behind her. "Just a few scrapes and bruises."

"What...what happened?"

"Fagan worked those men into a froth of ale and anger," he said disdainfully. "They decided to turn their resentment against us."

"Did you...kill them?" She hated the sound of her own voice, but even more, she hated the swirl of fear she felt at the thought.

"Nay," he said, his voice suddenly softening. "They were riled up, but they werenae evil men. Still, they needed stopping—or at least slowing."

She dragged in a shaky breath. Once again, he'd saved her. "Thank you."

His hand tightened possessively around her, but then suddenly he released his hold on her.

"It was my fault that ye were in danger to begin with." His voice was hard and flat, and she could feel tension radiating off him where he sat in the saddle behind her.

"Nay, Ansel," she breathed. "It was my fault. I spoke when I shouldn't have and revealed that I am English."

"Nay, lass," he ground out through his teeth. "I

mean I shouldnae have…seduced ye."

Heat flooded her face even as the night air ruffled the cloak around her shoulders. "I let you…I wanted you, too…"

"Aye," Ansel said, his voice a low rasp. "But I am yer protector. I was supposed to keep watch, to be ready at all times. Instead, I lost myself. I let myself be distracted."

His words burned, yet there was a note of truth to them. That was what it had been between them—a distraction from all the pain and fear of late. Nothing more. She swallowed the ache that rose in her throat. He was right. She knew their attraction was wrong, too, but he was strong enough to say so.

"Because I let my guard down, I didnae hear the trouble brewing belowstairs," he went on stiffly. "I must beg yer forgiveness. And I promise that it will never happen again."

"Aye," she breathed, blinking back the tears of hurt and shame. "Never again."

Chapter Twenty-Six

Ansel pulled Eachann to a halt next to a gurgling forest creek.

"We'll rest here for a wee bit," he said flatly.

Isolda nodded stiffly and threw her leg over Eachann's neck. Without Ansel's assistance, she slid down Eachann's side and landed on the soft forest floor.

It was one of a hundred little ways she had found in the last sennight to avoid having to come into physical contact with him.

Ansel should have been grateful to her for that, for even the most innocent jostling contact atop Eachann's back or brush of their hands when he passed her his waterskin was enough to send hot longing shooting through him.

He silently cursed himself as he swung down from the saddle.

Over the last sennight of hard riding, neither of them had spoken of their lovemaking at the inn or Ansel's harsh words along the roadside when they'd fled the village.

Aye, he'd been harsh when he'd told her that they

shouldn't have succumbed to their lust, that he was choosing to put his mission to protect her above his desire to claim her as his. And yet, she seemed to have her own reasons for keeping a cool distance between them, though she hadn't shared those reasons with Ansel. All he knew was that the last sennight had been long and painful.

Of course, the conditions only worsened their grueling journey into the Highlands. God seemed to be enjoying putting them through their paces as they traveled.

The last of the summer heat and sunshine had evaporated, leaving the cold, damp air of true fall in its place. It had rained for much of the last sennight. Even now, heavy clouds hung threateningly low over the trees where they had stopped to rest.

Ansel had explained to Isolda that after the disaster at the inn outside Stirling, they wouldn't be staying in any more inns, nor would they pass through even the sleepiest of villages. They wouldn't even be using the roads. Instead, they would make what would have already been a difficult five-day journey into a sennight-long slog through forests and moors, plains and mountains in order to avoid unwanted attention.

She hadn't complained, only nodded, lifting her chin in that noble way. Her regal bearing was back again, despite the fact that none of the comforts suited to a lady were possible on this journey.

It seemed like ages ago that he'd taken pleasure in

ruffling those haughty feathers of hers to get a rise out of her. Now Ansel recognized that stiff air for what it truly was—an act. He'd seen the pulsing passion Isolda bore just below her mask of formality. The only thing he didn't understand was why she hid behind that rigid, cold façade even now that he knew the truth. Something about it spoke of desperation.

Ansel guided Eachann toward the babbling stream, then dropped the reins so that the weary animal could drink the cool, clear water.

The patches of forest had grown smaller and were separated by greater expanses of rugged land as they'd ridden north. The shelter of the trees and the cheery stream were a relief from the difficult, rocky terrain they'd been crossing all day.

This was the Highlands—his home. The hardness of the land was a comfort of sorts, a reminder of who he was. This land had forged him. It had made him as strong as the rocky ground, as sharp as the biting fall wind, and as steely as the cloudy sky overhead.

Isolda bent next to the creek and cupped her hands in the water. She lifted them to her mouth and drank long and slow. When she dropped her hands, beads of sparkling water clung to her rosy, full lips.

Bloody hell. Highlander or nay, Ansel didn't feel particularly strong at the moment. Desire surged through him. She didn't even have to touch him to nigh bring him to his knees.

She rose from the creek slowly, placing her hands

on the small of her back and arching against the undoubted stiffness that knotted her body.

He'd been careful to watch her for signs that she was pushing herself too hard again. He wouldn't make the same mistake twice and put her health in danger. He'd given her two plaids, which she kept wrapped around her over her cloak at all times. The sight of her wearing Sutherland colors twisted something deep in his chest, but he wouldn't let himself consider what it meant.

Though Isolda fared better than he would have expected in the last sennight, she couldn't completely hide her discomfort behind that mask of nobility. Her delicate hands kneaded her lower back just above where her gown's laces ended and her bottom curved sensuously.

She had on the brown woolen gown she'd first worn under the red surcoat. Ansel had insisted she pack away the expensive surcoat, though even the simple brown gown with laces borrowed from another garment was too fine for the journey he'd put her through.

His mind shot back to that night when he'd sliced through her garment's ties and caught a glimpse of her creamy flesh for the first time. Unbidden, his manhood throbbed to life in his breeches.

Damn it all, he had to get his thoughts—and his body—under control.

He tore back the flap on one saddlebag and began

rummaging in its depths just to give his hands something to do. His fingertips brushed cool metal, and he withdrew one of the two daggers he'd tucked away there when they'd departed Dunstanburgh.

They were Isolda's attacker's daggers—the daggers Ansel had been forced to pry from his own flesh. He'd examined them already, though neither gave him clues as to who their assailant had been.

He held up the small throwing dagger again anyway, grateful for the pretense of busying himself with something other than staring at Isolda. The blade was short but fat, almost oval-shaped, likely so that it would do more damage when it made impact with its target. Neither the hilt nor the blade itself bore any markings or etchings, however.

Isolda turned from the creek and strode to where Eachann stood. When her gaze fell on him, she started in surprise.

"I noticed you removed those…things…from my chamber that night," she said, her eyes locking uneasily on the dagger. "But I didn't realize you brought them with us."

Ansel shrugged in his best attempt at nonchalant detachment. "I thought to study them for clues, though they offer none."

"But…you don't think that whoever attacked us has followed us into Scotland, do you?"

He didn't miss the sudden tremor in her voice.

"Nay," he replied brusquely. "Even if Edward's

men had crossed the border after us, our trail should be cold. No one has seen us since the village, and the rains will have obliterated our tracks, even so far off the road."

She absently ran a hand down Eachann's neck, apparently unaware of Ansel's eyes following her every move.

Though her tight-fitting, expertly tailored surcoat had made the outline of her body quite clear, Ansel savored seeing her in a simple gown, her chemise peeking out at the sleeves and along her collar bones. For some reason it felt more intimate to be able to see her body moving against the slightly less snug garments. He imagined what her skin must feel like brushing along her soft linen chemise, her hips swaying gently within the folds of her woolen gown.

Ansel silently cursed himself again and snapped his eyes from her. He was acting like a bloody starved animal when he should be concentrating on his mission. He'd made a terrible error in thinking he could indulge in his lust for Isolda instead of focusing on protecting her.

"Are we close to our destination?"

His gaze darted back to Isolda. She still stood stroking Eachann's neck, her back partially turned toward Ansel. Surprise flitted through him. It was the first time in a sennight of hard travel that she'd asked if their harrowing journey was almost over—another indication of just how exhausted she must truly be.

"Aye, we are." He squinted past the copse of trees in which they stood. "Though we cannae see it from here, the North Sea is just off to the east." He pointed with the little dagger toward the flatter land to their right that marked the coastline.

Isolda's gaze followed the blade, but then snaked back up his arm and over his chest. Her pale green eyes flicked to his face ever so briefly, but then she shifted her gaze away.

Ansel cleared his throat. "Dunrobin Castle, the clan seat of the Sutherlands, lies over there." He shifted the dagger slightly to the north.

"Is that where we are going? To Dunrobin Castle?"

Though Isolda kept her voice level, he detected a note of yearning in it.

"Nay," he said reluctantly.

She pressed her lips together. "Is the castle not safe?"

Ansel clenched his teeth against the sharp pang of shame that stabbed him at her words. It was his job to protect her, to make her feel safe at all times. Yet her voice held an edge of fear that clearly revealed his failing.

"Aye, the castle is verra safe."

"How do you know?"

"Because I have lived there for many years."

Her eyes darted back to his, her dark brows arching with surprise before she regained control over her features. "Oh?"

"Aye. The castle is surrounded by a thick stone wall, and there are several towers where guards and watchmen stand at all hours of the day and night. It is one of the finest strongholds in all the Highlands, for it must protect the Sutherland Laird."

Despite her casual nod, he saw curiosity lurking in the depths of her eyes.

"And that is your home?"

He shrugged. "As I said, I've lived there for many years of my life. But my true home is just there." He drew the blade slightly inland from where Dunrobin lay. "Brora Tower. That is where we are headed."

Though several rolling hills and clumps of forest stood between them and Brora, blocking the view, Isolda's eyes nevertheless searched where he pointed. Her curiosity sent a pinch into his chest. How he wanted to pull her to him, tell her all his secrets and draw out all of hers. How he wanted her to *know* him.

"Brora Tower," she repeated. "Is it safe there, as it is at Dunrobin?"

Again, the edge of concern in her voice cut him. The swell of longing in his chest was swiftly replaced with hot guilt.

He turned fully toward her, holding her eyes with his. "I was wrong to think us safe outside Stirling. Though the Lowlands have been quiet since Bannockburn, Scots' memories are long. Edward has ravaged Scotland for so many years—as did his father, Edward Longshanks, before him—that Scotland will be many years in the healing. I shouldnae have taken the chance in assuming that the tensions of war had eased."

Isolda's gaze softened and her lips parted. "Do not be so hard on yourself. You could not have predicted the actions of an angry mob. Besides," she said with a little shake of her shoulders, "those men were fools, not truly evil, as you said. They were not working for Edward to hunt John and me down."

"Aye," Ansel said, some of the tension easing from his shoulders. "It seems that we have shaken Edward's men."

She nodded, a relieved exhale slipping through her lips.

"And the Highlands are different than the Lowlands," he added. "Though war has reached us even this far north, we have no' been ravaged by the English like the Lowlands and Borderlands have been. An Englishwoman in the Highlands will certainly draw curiosity, but no' hatred as it did farther south."

A crease appeared between her eyebrows as worry once again tightened her features. "Will I be the subject of much…attention where we are going—Brora Tower, you said?"

Ansel couldn't help the flutter of fondness that pulled up one corner of his mouth. "Nay, for there aren't many there to bother over ye. Ye'll see soon enough. We should reach the tower in a few more hours."

He felt her hesitant gaze follow him as he turned

and dropped the throwing dagger into his saddlebag.

"We'd best be on our way." Unconsciously, he stepped to her side and gripped her waist to help her into the saddle. She stiffened beneath his touch but didn't pull away as he lifted her onto Eachann's back. It wasn't much, but even getting to touch her again sent a swell of heat through him.

As he swung into the saddle behind her, she studiously leaned forward slightly, creating the same small gap between their bodies that had existed for the last sennight.

It was right of her to do so, he reminded himself firmly, but that didn't ease the ache in his chest.

He spurred Eachann forward, cursing himself silently for longing so desperately for what he could never have.

Chapter Twenty-Seven

If it were possible, Isolda felt her shoulders and back tighten even more as they rode.

Ansel's home.

She couldn't deny the lure of knowing more, but she'd bitten her tongue to keep from prying. It was better that she not contemplate what kind of man rode behind her.

An honorable man. A protective man. A man whose hard exterior shielded a noble heart.

Foolish thoughts, she chided herself. She'd believed those same things about the Earl of Lancaster. *Ansel is not the same as Thomas*, a voice whispered in her head, but she shoved it aside. She was ruled by passion, just as her parents had said. And passion would be her undoing unless she could guard herself against the warmth that blossomed in her heart at the mere thought of Ansel.

So lost in her own dark contemplations was she that it wasn't until Ansel spurred Eachann into a gallop that she snapped her head up and took in her surroundings.

They had entered hilly country, with stark mountains to the west and flatlands to the east. A lake ruffled with the cool afternoon breeze to their left.

And then she saw it.

A stone tower several storeys tall rose from the top of the highest hill in the area. She squinted against the gray sky behind the tower. A few outbuildings surrounded it, but otherwise it was completely isolated, with no thick curtain wall or village nestled around it.

Brora Tower.

Her heart hitched into her throat with uncertainty. What awaited her there?

A flicker of movement at the tower's base had her squinting again. A figure darted down the grassy hill and across the open space between them and the tower.

At first Isolda thought the figure was a man, but as he drew nearer, she realized with a start that it was actually a child.

Something in her chest twisted painfully. The lad couldn't be much older than John. In the many months since she'd last seen her son, he'd turned five. She'd missed his birthday. A knot rose to her throat as she watched the lad run toward them.

"Uncle Ansel!" the boy shouted when he had almost closed the distance between them.

Shock replaced pain as Isolda registered the words.

"Uncle?" she murmured over her shoulder.

Ignoring her, Ansel pulled Eachann back into a walk. His chuckle made her jump, so foreign was the sound. She turned partially in the saddle to find a wide grin splitting Ansel's face.

A jolt of heat tore through her. He was so handsome, his face transformed by the warm smile for his nephew.

"Go on back to the tower, Niall," he said, still smiling down at the lad. "Tell yer mother and father that I am here."

Niall tore off in the direction he'd come, leaving them behind as Eachann plodded toward the tower.

"Mama, Papa, Uncle Ansel is here!" the boy shouted gleefully.

The wooden door at the base of the tower opened, and out emerged a large man with a brightly colored plaid belted around his hips and an extra length of material thrown over his shirt-clad shoulder. The plaid was of a different pattern and coloring than the one Ansel had given Isolda to drape over her cloak—the man's was red and green, while the one she wore was blue and green.

The man strode a few paces away from the door and waited for them to approach. Behind him, a woman burst from the doorway, her gaze latching onto them.

"Ansel!" the woman cried, rushing forward.

At the base of the hill atop which the tower perched, Ansel reined Eachann to a halt and swung down from the animal's back hurriedly. Before he could offer Isolda assistance down, the woman launched herself into Ansel's arms.

"Brother," the woman breathed. "I have missed ye."

Isolda felt her eyes widen as she looked on from the saddle. The woman broke her fierce hug with Ansel and held him back to examine him.

Now that she was so close, Isolda could see the resemblance between the two. Like Ansel, the woman had thick, dark brown hair, which was secured in a simple braid. Her eyes shone with emotion. They were the same rich chestnut as Ansel's.

"I have missed ye and the wee ones, too," Ansel said, his voice soft.

Just then, the woman shifted her gaze to where Isolda sat perched atop Eachann's back.

"And who is this?"

Isolda stiffened, though the woman's eyes held nothing more than kind curiosity.

Ansel slowly opened his mouth to answer, but before he could speak, the man who'd emerged first from the tower strode to them. He clapped Ansel soundly on the shoulder, then extended his forearm to him. Ansel took hold in a firm shake.

"Ansel! It is good to see ye," the man said. "But by God, man, ye look like a bloody Englishman in those breeches and tunic."

"Burke," the woman said gently. "No' in front of the children."

Isolda's gaze tugged toward the open tower door,

where a dark head had just appeared. A little girl no more than three years of age stood almost entirely hidden by the doorframe, her gaze wide and shy on them.

"Forgive me," the man, Burke, said. "But it is no' every day yer brother arrives dressed like an Englishman and with a woman sharing his horse with him."

Burke's light brown head tilted up toward her, his night-blue eyes fixing on her with the same curiosity the woman's gaze held.

"This is Lady Isolda of Embleton," Ansel said.

At the surprise flitting across the faces staring up at her, Isolda cringed internally. Ansel had used her title, even though he knew Embleton was a farce. Not so long ago, he'd openly questioned the validity of a ladyship associated with an unfinished village like Embleton, yet now he was allowing her to keep her secrets.

Ansel reached up and wrapped his hands around Isolda's waist, sliding her with ease from Eachann's back. When Isolda's feet hit the ground, Ansel's sister bobbed into an apprehensive curtsy and Burke dipped his head.

"Nay," she said quickly. "Please don't. And just Isolda is fine."

As they both raised themselves from their genuflections, their eyes again locked on her. The woman's lips fell apart, and Burke raised a sandy eyebrow in surprise.

Once more, Isolda had forgotten that her English accent would draw curiosity at best and ire—or even violence—at worst. The breath froze in her lungs as she waited for their reaction.

At last, Burke whistled softly through his teeth. "I take it there is quite the story behind this, Ansel."

"Aye," Ansel replied gruffly.

"One that can wait until we have seen to the comforts of our guests," Ansel's sister said, deliberately shooting a glance at Burke. She turned back to Isolda and Ansel. "Ye look as if ye both have been through quite a journey. Let us prepare a bath and a meal for ye."

"Thank ye, Sister, but I'll swim in the loch," Ansel said, his gaze darting to Isolda. She felt color rise to her cheeks as the memory of her last bath—and what had come after—flooded her.

Once again, she felt the woman's perceptive eyes searching her. Isolda stiffened her spine against the urge to duck her head and hide her blush.

"Ah, well," the woman said slowly, her gaze shifting between her brother and Isolda. "Just a bath for Isolda, then."

Ansel nodded curtly and unfastened Isolda's satchel from his saddlebags. Then he removed the bags, slinging them over his shoulders.

"If ye wouldnae mind seeing to Eachann, Sister," he said. "I'll be back before supper."

Burke's sandy brows lowered as he looked between

them all. "I'll join ye at the loch, if ye dinnae mind, Ansel," he said carefully. "Niall and I were going to go fishing there this afternoon anyway."

It was the barest of movements, but Isolda didn't miss the look that passed between Burke and Ansel's sister or the slight nod of thanks the woman gave him.

As the two men and the lad strode past the tower to the lake that sat behind it, the woman turned kind but curious eyes on Isolda.

"Och, that oaf brother of mine didnae even introduce us. I am Meredith Sinclair, née Sutherland. That was my husband, Burke Sinclair. I believe ye met my son Niall."

At Isolda's nod, Meredith pointed surreptitiously toward the doorway, where the dark-headed little girl still peered at them. "And that is my daughter, Fiona. She's a shy one, but a true angel."

"Th-thank you for your hospitality," Isolda managed. She was still reeling from learning that they were staying with Ansel's sister and her family. But perhaps even more shocking was the kindness they were showing her.

"It is naught," Meredith said, taking Eachann's reins. "Now, I should see to this wearied horse." She rubbed Eachann's nose, and the animal immediately nuzzled her back.

"I hope it is not too much of an inconvenience, Madam Sinclair," Isolda said. She silently cursed herself for her awkward formality, but Meredith only smiled kindly.

"Please, call me Meredith. And nay, it is no inconvenience at all. I have a way with animals, ye see. Ansel kenned that I would enjoy tending to Eachann." To Isolda's surprise, Meredith snorted ruefully. "*Eachann.* What a name," she muttered, rolling her eyes.

"What is it? Is the name Gaelic?" Isolda asked hesitantly.

Meredith turned warm eyes on her. "Aye. It means 'brown horse.'" She snorted again. "Ansel has always been a verra…straightforward man." She shook her head, a smile curving her lips.

Isolda blinked at the bay stallion. "Brown horse?"

The animal's brown coat shone dully in the overcast light. The ridiculousness of the name bubbled inside her. Suddenly, a wild giggle tore from her throat. She clapped a hand over her mouth at the nigh hysterical sound.

"Forgive me," she said behind her hand. "I am very tired, and—"

To her surprise, Meredith's own laugh chimed merrily through the air.

"No need to apologize," Meredith said when she could speak again, placing a soft hand on Isolda's arm. "My brother can be most…serious, as I'm sure ye've learned in the time ye've spent with him."

Meredith's unspoken question hung in the air for a long moment, her curious gaze resting on Isolda. Isolda twined her hands together in front of her, suddenly anxious over how she could possibly explain everything that had happened since Ansel had come into her life.

"But that's enough chatter for now," Meredith said quickly, relieving Isolda of the need to speak. "If ye dinnae mind stopping by the stables with me to see to the horse, I'll get ye settled in the tower."

At Isolda's nod, Meredith led the way to one of the handful of wooden outbuildings sitting around the tower's base. Isolda followed on wobbly legs, too exhausted now to fight against the tug of her thoughts back toward Ansel.

After spending so much time in Ansel's presence, his sudden absence left her hollow and aching.

Aye, she was still in danger, but not from Edward's men. It seemed the greatest threat of all lay beating in her chest.

Chapter Twenty-Eight

"And ye're sure ye werenae followed to Brora?"

Burke leaned forward, his elbows propped on the small wooden table and worry creasing his forehead.

Ansel rubbed a palm over the scruff on his jaw. Bloody hell, it could well nigh be called the start of a beard by now. The dunk in the cold loch had done wonders to wash away the smell of horseflesh and hard travel, but he still longed to shave, and his body was beyond fatigued.

The warm meal of meat pies and roasted vegetables that sat in his belly threatened to pull him into an exhausted sleep. In the corner of his eye, he noticed that Isolda was having a hard time keeping her lids up. She slumped next to him on the wooden bench they shared.

"I cannae be completely sure," Ansel said wearily. "But we've seen neither hide nor hair of anyone on our trail. And I doubt that no matter how badly Edward wants to reach Lancaster's son, he wouldnae dare send men this deep into the Highlands. The men at the inn outside of Stirling prove just how unwelcome Englishmen are in Scotland."

Burke shook his head slightly, then glanced at Meredith. Niall and Fiona had long ago been tucked into their beds, but even still, Burke's gaze drifted to the spiraling stairs in the corner as if to reassure himself that his children were sleeping safely.

It wasn't so long ago that Ansel had tried to kill Burke for seducing Meredith. He'd found them in the barn behind Brora Tower, naked and entwined in each other's arms. Ansel had seen red—the red of the Sinclair plaid. Luckily, Meredith had stopped Ansel before he ended her chance for true happiness in marrying Burke.

Ansel almost chuckled tiredly at the memory. He couldn't ask for a better brother-in-law, though the fact that he came from the Sutherlands' rivals, the Sinclairs, was still a source of ribbing between them. But Burke was a good man—he was even more protective of Meredith and their children than Ansel was.

"I would never come here if I thought I was putting ye in the slightest danger," Ansel said quietly, holding Burke's gaze.

Burke nodded. "Aye, I ken ye wouldnae, Ansel. It is just…I havenae observed Kings to give up so easily when they want something."

Burke and Meredith's gaze shifted to Isolda. Ansel felt her stiffen beside him, her eyes no longer drooping and her spine suddenly straight.

"Perhaps if we kenned where yer son was, we

could ensure that Edward never finds him," Burke said gently.

Just as Isolda parted her lips to respond, Ansel spoke. "Isolda doesnae wish to divulge John's location. She fears—and mayhap rightly—that the more people learn where he is, the more danger both he and those who ken his whereabouts will be in."

Isolda's head jerked toward him, and those haunting green eyes pinned him. Surprise and gratitude flickered in her pale gaze.

Meredith reached across the table and placed her hand over Isolda's. "We willnae push ye. If it were Niall or Fiona..." She shuddered and squeezed Isolda's hand. "Ye are verra brave."

"Thank you," Isolda whispered, though her eyes still lingered on Ansel.

"Well, I believe ye were right to come here, Ansel," Burke said. "It is safe here, and we'll do our best to make ye both comfortable."

"Aye, and we are grateful," Ansel replied.

"But..." Meredith hesitated before going on. "What will ye do now?"

Ansel raked a hand through his hair. Burke and Meredith had listened, Burke with a grim frown on his normally kindly features and Meredith with wide eyes, as he and Isolda had explained all that had happened before they'd arrived at Brora. He'd told them of Garrick's visit to Dunrobin and the mission he'd given Ansel on the Bruce's behalf. He described the attack at

Dunstanburgh and their flight into Scotland. He left out the scorching passion he'd shared with Isolda but explained the unrest in Stirling and their hasty departure.

But now that they were finally safe at Brora, tucked deep into the Highlands, their next steps were unclear.

"To be honest, I dinnae ken," Ansel said, dropping his hands onto the table. "Bannockburn is still a fresh wound. Perhaps if we wait until things cool a bit, it will be safe for Isolda to return to England."

He glanced at Isolda. Her delicate features were drawn with worry and fatigue. His words clearly rang hollow to her. Hearing them himself, he had a hard time believing that it would ever be safe for her in England if Edward was determined to find her son.

"Ye don't have to decide now," Meredith said gently. "Take all the time ye need at Brora. As Burke said, ye're safe here."

Isolda nodded wearily, some of the tension finally easing from her body. Her shoulders slumped again as she let out a slow exhale.

Burke turned the conversation to how his cousin Garrick fared in the Bruce's camp in the Borderlands. As they spoke, Ansel caught sight of Isolda's head drifting down, then back up with a jerk. On the third droop of her head, he could no longer ignore her exhaustion.

He pulled her against his side and nestled her head on his shoulder.

"Rest, lass," he said gruffly.

She stiffened at the sudden contact for a moment, but her fatigue at last overcame her resistance and she relaxed against him. In a matter of moments, her even breathing against his neck told him that she'd slipped into sleep.

Ansel looked up to find both Burke and Meredith's perceptive gazes pinned on him.

"We shouldnae have kept ye up so late with our questions," Meredith said. Her eyes danced over Isolda as if she deduced a deeper implication to the moment she'd just witnessed. "I made up a chamber for ye two abovestairs."

"I'll need my own," Ansel said, his voice coming out harder than he'd intended.

Meredith cocked a dark eyebrow at him, and Ansel almost cursed to see that look on his sister's face.

"Dinnae be silly, Ansel. As ye well ken, there are only four chambers in this tower. Niall and Fiona are each in one, and Burke and I are in the third. That only leaves one for the two of ye."

"Then I'll sleep in the barn."

"The barn is full to the rafters with hay for the winter," Burke said. "There's no room, unless ye want to share a stall with yer horse."

This time, Ansel didn't bother suppressing the curse that rose to his tongue, though he was careful not to disturb Isolda's sleep. Burke and Meredith were looking at him far too knowingly.

"Ansel, ye dinnae need to be so stubborn all the time," Meredith chided. "It is obvious ye and Isolda share some sort of…connection. Why would ye insist on yer own chamber?"

Exhausted though he was, Ansel felt a surge of annoyance at his younger sister. She was clearly fishing for information. Worse, she was meddling with his carefully constructed plan to keep a safe distance between himself and Isolda.

Just then, Isolda shifted her head slightly, nuzzling into his neck. *Bloody hell.* So much for maintaining a safe distance.

"Keep yer nose to yerself, Sister," he said, leveling Meredith with a glower. "I'll be sleeping on the chamber's floor, then."

Meredith's other eyebrow rose to meet the first in amused surprise. "Have it yer way, ye old mule."

Ansel wrapped one arm around Isolda's shoulders and slid the other underneath her knees. It was a testament to just how exhausted she was that she hardly stirred as Ansel stood from the bench they'd been sharing.

Ansel's sudden movement startled a large orange cat that was warming itself in front of the kitchen fire. The cat stood and stretched, then lazily wound its way through Ansel's legs.

"And damn all yer bloody animals," Ansel muttered crossly as he strode toward the stairs with Isolda in his arms, narrowly avoiding tripping on the cat.

Meredith's muffled chuckle taunted him as he made his way up the spiraling stairs.

Without pause or thought, Ansel climbed past the three lower chambers. When he reached the top of the stairs, he found the fourth chamber's door slightly ajar. He eased the door open with one foot, the soft glow of the banked fire in the brazier spilling around him as he entered.

This had been his chamber as a lad. When he'd turned ten, he had moved to Dunrobin to begin training with Kenneth Sutherland in the duties and responsibilities of a Laird. Kenneth was of an age with Ansel, but he was Laird Sutherland's only son. As Kenneth's cousin, the responsibility of the Lairdship would have fallen to Ansel had anything happened to Kenneth.

Even though he'd spent much of his childhood and adult life at Dunrobin, Brora still felt like home. Or did the familiar warmth kindling in his chest have more to do with the woman in his arms?

He crossed the dimly lit chamber to the bed and slowly lowered Isolda down. Bent over her, the smell of lemons and lavender drifted to him. As he shifted the pillow under her head, his fingers came in contact with her silky braid. Her hair was still damp from her bath earlier that day.

His mind reeled back to the inn in Stirling—her dripping, dark hair, her heat-flushed skin, her breaths coming shallow as he drove into her.

Ansel's cock surged with unwelcome desire. Greedily, he inhaled her heady scent before dragging a blanket over her sleeping form with trembling hands.

Taking up another blanket, he forced himself to step away from Isolda. As he stretched out on the floor at the foot of the bed, her steady breathing filled the quiet chamber.

Shite.

His body wouldn't listen to all the reasons why he shouldn't—*couldn't*—want her, care for her, long for her. Yet the realization of a deeper problem stole over him as he lay on the hard wooden floor breathing in time with Isolda—his heart wouldn't listen either.

Chapter Twenty-Nine

"Ye might want to close yer mouth, lest ye drool all over yerself."

Ansel snapped his eyes from Isolda and pinned his sister with a narrowed gaze. She only smiled sweetly at him.

He and Meredith sat on a length of thick woolen Sutherland plaid, for though it was a dazzlingly bright fall day, the ground was still soft from the recent rains. In fact, the grass surrounding Brora Tower glistened in the yellow sunlight, sparkling to rival the crystal-clear skies overhead.

Yet despite the perfect autumn day, Ansel felt a familiar gray weight pressing in his chest.

"I wasnae drooling." Nay, he hadn't been, but he was staring. He couldn't seem to *stop* staring at Isolda these past five idyllic days at Brora Tower.

How she'd transformed in those few short days. Slowly, he'd watched the tension ease from around Isolda's mouth and eyes. Her shoulders straightened, but not with the cold rigidity she'd borne when he'd first met her. Nay, now she carried herself with an easy grace that entranced him.

It had taken all of Ansel's willpower of late not to reach out and stroke her glowing cheeks, or caress the dark, cascading tresses that she now left unbound from their confining plait. How he longed to kiss the woman blossoming to life before his eyes.

He somehow found the strength to remain sleeping on the floor at the foot of her bed every night despite the lure of her slow, steady breathing, which lifted her perfect breasts and parted her berry-ripe lips. He had to clench his fists as he sat by her side at Meredith and Burke's little wooden table for meals to avoid dragging her into his arms. And he never missed the gentle sway of her body whenever she busied herself with chores around the tower.

But far more perilous than the primal pull he felt toward Isolda was his knowledge of the source of her transformation.

She feels safe.

Even thinking it now sent his heart hammering against his ribcage. He'd finally earned her trust, and his reward was getting to witness her body relax, her mouth and eyes soften, and her laugh rise naturally in her throat.

Ansel felt Meredith's keen gaze studying him.

"Tell me, Brother," she said, far too casually for his liking. "Why is it ye've decided ye cannae own up to yer obvious feelings for Isolda?"

Obvious? He silently cursed himself. Aye, he must appear like a moon-eyed fool for all the ogling he'd been doing.

Unbidden, his eyes landed on Isolda once more. She stood a pebble's throw away, slightly farther down the hill upon which Ansel sat with Meredith. Isolda and Niall were working to train Meredith's most recent animal acquisition, a young deerhound. As Isolda bent to hand Niall a scrap to give to the wiry gray dog, her chestnut hair glinted in the sun.

Ansel let out a long exhale through his teeth.

"As I told ye before, Meredith, ye should mind yer own business."

She swatted his shoulder and shot him a scathing glare, though he almost smiled at her fierce little scowl. His sister had always been a soft-hearted, gentle creature—it explained the ever-growing menagerie of animals with which she surrounded herself.

"Ye *are* my business, ye old goat—and so is Isolda, for I find that we are fast friends," Meredith said, her eyes following Ansel's to where Niall and Isolda played with the deerhound. "Ye cannae be holding back because ye fear she doesnae return your affection," she prodded softly. "Her eyes are drawn to ye just as much as yers are to her."

As if beckoned by Meredith's words, Isolda lifted her head and locked eyes with Ansel. Before she could quickly avert her gaze, those pale green depths scalded him.

"It is no' so simple," he muttered under his breath.

Just then, the tower door opened off to their right

and Fiona's dark head poked out. She slid from the safety of the doorway, the large orange cat at her feet. The cat trotted toward where Meredith and Ansel sat in the sun, gingerly lifting its feet over the wet grass. Fiona, spying Niall and Isolda with the gangly deerhound, merrily scampered toward them.

In just a few days, Isolda had managed to capture the affections of all at Brora. Granted, Burke had an easy, friendly way with everyone. It was no great surprise that he quickly extended his kindness to Isolda. But Meredith, like Fiona, was normally shy and reserved. Yet both Ansel's sister and niece were clearly taken with Isolda, and Ansel reckoned that Isolda would be the first to break Niall's young heart.

The orange cat settled itself on Meredith's lap, and she stroked him absently as her gaze followed Fiona to where Niall and Isolda stood.

"And why is it no' so simple?" she said, shooting Ansel a glance out of the corner of her eye.

Ansel sighed again. Though his sister was sweet and warm-hearted, she was also a Sutherland, which meant that she was as stubborn and unyielding as the rocky soil in the Highlands. She would keep after him until she had her answers.

"King Robert has entrusted me with protecting her," he said, keeping his voice low. "I cannae be both her lover and her guardian. It would only lead to…distractions—which she could pay for with her life."

He turned to glance at Meredith and found her staring at him quizzically. "Ye are truly daft, arenae ye?"

Ansel frowned at her, but she went on. "Did ye ever consider the fact that yer feelings for Isolda make ye a *better* protector?"

"Ye dinnae understand," he muttered.

"Och, but I do. Ye are frightened for her, is that it?"

Ansel nodded curtly. Aye, he was frightened—he'd never felt so vulnerable knowing her safety depended on him. It was as if his heart beat outside of his body.

"Ye are frightened to lose her," Meredith went on, interpreting his silence. "Ye care so greatly for her that ye dinnae ken what ye would do with yerself if something happened to separate ye."

He swallowed but didn't answer. His gaze fixed on Isolda. The deerhound was playfully chasing a squealing Fiona in a circle around Isolda's legs, with Niall calling encouragement to the animal.

"Dinnae ye think that such a strong drive to keep her safe would be a good thing?"

Ansel's chest pinched painfully. He longed to believe Meredith's words, but he'd told himself over and over that he *couldn't* want her. He was a man of honor, of duty. Wouldn't he be turning his back on the mission his King gave him if he let himself care for Isolda?

Or might there be a sliver of hope that he could both honor his mission and claim what his heart wanted more than anything?

Before he could form a response to Meredith, the deerhound bumped into Isolda's legs as he made yet another loop around her. The young, ungainly animal was nigh full-sized, his head approaching Isolda's waist, but he clearly didn't have control over his limbs yet.

Isolda wobbled, then her foot slipped on the damp grass and she tumbled backward, landing hard on her bottom.

Like lightning, Ansel shot to his feet. Somehow he covered the dozen paces between them in a heartbeat. He dropped to her side, taking her gently in his arms.

She blinked up at him. Then to his utter surprise, chiming laughter erupted from her.

He couldn't help it. A deep chuckle rumbled through his chest, joining her merry laughter. He carefully helped her to her feet, his hands lingering on her waist.

"Oh drat," she said, batting at the mud on the side of her green gown where she'd slipped. When the mud wouldn't budge, she simply shrugged and shot him a grin.

The sun seemed dim compared to her radiant smile. His breath froze in his lungs as he continued to stare down at her. Her smile faltered as the air thickened with anticipation around them. The shrieking children, the overexcited deerhound, the tower, and Meredith's watchful gaze all seemed to fall away.

"Thank you," she said, blinking.

Ansel forced his hands to drop and stepped back.

"Of course." He cursed himself for a bloody fool as he quickly strode back to where Meredith sat and resumed his place on the plaid next to her.

"I think ye just proved my point, Brother," Meredith said. Though she kept her gaze casually on the orange cat in her lap, a mischievous smile curled her lips. "Yer love for Isolda makes ye all the better to protect her. It isnae a liability, but rather a strength."

"Love?" The word was out of his mouth before he could stop himself.

Meredith turned on him, her eyes wide with astonishment. "Ye are the greatest dolt I have ever known, Ansel Sutherland! Of course ye love the lass!"

It was as if a pit had opened up beneath him, threatening to suck him into the muddy ground. Yet at the same time, his heart seemed to have sprouted wings and taken flight in his chest.

He loved Isolda.

It was as clear as the sky overhead, as bright and pure as the sun bathing him in warmth.

He loved her. It was so simple, and yet so strong.

Suddenly he was on his feet again.

"I need to talk to her."

"Aye," Meredith said, her merry voice chasing him as he strode back toward Isolda. "Ye do."

Chapter Thirty

Isolda ruffled Niall's sandy hair as he darted past her and after the deerhound. She felt her lips curl as she watched the children chase the dog.

Niall was likely only a few months older than John. Her heart tugged at the thought. Would she recognize her own son when she saw him again after almost a year apart? She was so close to John now, closer than she'd ever let herself hope to be again.

A flicker of movement out of the corner of her eye caught her attention, pulling her gaze from the children and the deerhound. When she turned to find Ansel approaching again, her heart lurched, but for an entirely different reason.

Ever since he'd bathed at the nearby lake—he called it a *loch*, his brogue caressing the word—on the day they'd arrived, he'd donned his green and blue plaid in the same fashion as Burke wore his. It was belted around his hips and fell in pleats to his knees, where his woolen hose and boots met the edge of the plaid. An extra length of the colorful material was thrown over his shoulder across his simple white linen shirt. He truly fit the part of a Highland rogue now.

His eyes held her as he approached, his dark brows lowered and his mouth set firmly. Even in the face of his gruff demeanor, butterflies fluttered through her stomach. He was the most handsome man she'd ever seen.

He halted before her, so close that she had to tilt her head back to maintain their eye contact.

Suddenly, though, his steady countenance faltered. He shifted on his feet, a muscle in his jaw ticking.

"It was just a little slip. No harm done," she said quickly. "I am well, I assure you." And she was, except for the painful contortion of her heart when he'd scooped her onto her feet a moment ago after the dog had tripped her.

"I...I wish to speak with ye," he said, his voice low and rough.

She blinked, her mouth all at once dry and her tongue wooden. Something clearly weighed on his mind.

They hadn't spoken of their lovemaking at the inn since they'd had to flee Stirling. Ansel had made it more than clear that he thought their lapse had been a mistake. Although such knowledge stung, it was for the best—it served as a reminder that she, too, had her reasons not to make such a dangerous error again.

Whore.

Harlot.

Wanton.

The memory of her parents hurling those words at

her still burned almost six years later. And though Lancaster had never said as much, his treatment of her, and of John, proved that he, too, recognized her for what she had become—a nobleman's mistake, to be swept out of sight with the right amount of coin.

The heat of shame—for the past and for the traitorous longing she still felt for Ansel—burned her cheeks. "What is it you wish to discuss?"

Ansel cocked his dark head toward where his sister sat unabashedly watching them. "It would be best if we were alone."

"Are…are you sure that is wise?"

They had both been studiously avoiding being alone together these past five days—except for the fact that they shared a small chamber every night. Ansel was always careful to wait long after she'd climbed into bed to take up his place on the floor, and he was always gone by the time she rose in the mornings. Still, sometimes she woke in the middle of the night and listened to him breathing, deep and slow. His mere drawing of breath sent a searing knot into her stomach.

"Aye," he said. "Come. Walk with me."

He extended his forearm toward her, his eyes dark and unreadable as they scanned her face.

Slowly, she looped her arm in his. The cords of muscle in his arm jumped under her fingertips. It was as if a bolt of lightning passed between them at the contact. Heat coiled deep in her belly and rose into her cheeks.

"What is it?" she croaked as they drew away from where the others played on the grass surrounding the tower.

His arm stiffened once more beneath the thin linen of his shirt. Isolda dared a glance at him. For the first time since she'd known him, he seemed...tentative.

Ansel cleared his throat. "Ye...ye certainly have a way with Niall and Fiona," he said at last.

Surely this wasn't why he wished to speak with her alone. Yet his discomfort radiated off his large frame like heat from a fire as they strolled side by side down the grassy slope away from the tower.

Isolda felt her brows collide. What was Ansel about? He seemed to be struggling mightily with something. It would be cruel of her to push him, so she decided to go along with his line of conversation.

"Thank you. Fiona truly is sweet behind her shy exterior. She will grow into a great beauty like Meredith someday, I'm certain. And Niall..." Her throat tightened. "He reminds me a great deal of John—or how I imagine John is now."

"Ye miss him terribly."

It wasn't a question, but Isolda nodded at Ansel's gently spoken words.

"I...I suppose ye long to return to Dunstanburgh with John someday, then," he said carefully. "When it is safe for ye to retrieve John and return to England, that is."

Not long ago, Isolda would have bristled at the subtle undertone in Ansel's voice. It made it seem as though he was angling for information. She would have clamped her mouth shut at even the faintest impression that he was pressuring her to tell him John's location.

But she knew Ansel now. She trusted that he would never try to coerce or cajole the information from her. Instead, Ansel's line of conversation appeared to be probing her desire for her old life at Dunstanburgh.

"Nay, I think not," she said softly. "Dunstanburgh holds naught for John and me anymore."

Ansel's step faltered, and he turned surprised eyes on her. He recovered quickly and continued to guide them toward the sparkling lake beyond the tower.

"I ken that living in the middle of the castle's construction would be…uncomfortable," he said slowly. "But that willnae go on forever. Soon enough, the castle will be completed and ye and John could live in peace there."

Even as he spoke, though, a cloud crossed over his eyes. Her own heart squeezed at his words.

"I am no longer certain that peace will ever exist so close to the Borderlands," she murmured. "Or that John and I will ever truly be safe in England."

"But what of yer title and all the finery that comes with it?" he pressed. "Surely ye will miss the life ye had there."

Isolda would have laughed if her heart hadn't suddenly jumped into her throat, nigh choking her with emotion. Realization dawned on her. With a flashing clarity, she knew she had to tell Ansel the truth at last.

"Ansel...you must know something."

She swallowed, but her throat remained thick. She had hidden her secret for so long. Yet she trusted Ansel like a flower trusts the sun to warm it and draw it back to life after a long, cold winter.

"I...I am not a lady. Not truly."

He drew her to a halt again, this time at the lake's rocky edge. To her relief, he did not gasp in shock or level her with a sharp, questioning gaze. Instead, he kept his eyes on the lake's shining surface, saving her from the embarrassment of having him see her blush of shame.

"What do ye mean?" he asked at last, still pointed more toward the shimmering water than to her.

Isolda dragged in a fortifying breath. Something about gazing at the lake, gilded in sunshine and lightly ruffled by a soft breeze, helped her find the strength to speak.

"I am the daughter of a cloth merchant. My parents and siblings and I traveled between festivals and markets to sell our wares. We visited Clitheroe almost six years ago for the fair in honor of the Earl of Lancaster inheriting Clitheroe Castle from his father-in-law. Thomas..."

She had to swallow hard and forced her tongue onward despite the thick shame rising in her throat.

"Lancaster, that is," she went on, "saw me at the front of my father's stall during the fair. I was selling cloth to the ladies of the castle. He approached and…"

The bands of muscle under her fingertips bunched and twisted as Ansel clenched his fists.

"Did he force ye?" His voice was raw and rough, but he continued to stare at the lake.

"Nay," she whispered. "He wooed me, silly girl that I was. I had only just turned seventeen. Though we saw all manner of people in our travels, my parents kept me sheltered from the roving eyes and hands of men. I wasn't even supposed to work the front of our booth, for my father forbade it, but both he and my mother had been pulled into a dispute with one of the neighboring merchants."

A puff of air escaped her lungs to think back on her folly. How little she'd known of the consequences of her ignorance.

"Lancaster spoke to me at the booth. He begged me to meet him in secret. Of course I had never been the recipient of such attentions, especially not from such a powerful man. He told me that I was special, different. He made promises that I learned only later he had no intention of keeping."

She fell silent for a long moment, her heart twisting at the memories she so often tried to forget. Ansel remained quiet, letting her gather her words in her own time.

"Lancaster lost interest in me once he had taken

my innocence. When I realized I was pregnant, my family was preparing to depart to southern England for another festival. They denounced me, saying I had shamed them. They told me to seek Lancaster's protection, so I went to the castle to plead my case to him. They left while I was there. I've not seen them again."

"And Lancaster," Ansel said, gravel in his voice. "He sent ye to Dunstanburgh."

Isolda nodded, blinking back the tears that blurred the dazzling lake before her eyes. "He did me the honor of granting me a title, and he provided a guard and a maid for my comfort—Bertram and Mary. But the truth is, he bought my silence and my invisibility. He hid me and our son at Dunstanburgh, with no one else but an aging guard and maid the wiser."

She shook her head, pushing down her tears. She would not allow herself to indulge in such self-pity. She had made her choices, foolish girl that she had been, and she had lived with them alone for all these years, never allowing the shame to break her.

"It was actually a relief to be at Dunstanburgh, for there were no prying eyes—there was not much of anything at all when we arrived. I had the chance to remake myself as a lady. And I am thankful, too, that I got to study the ladies who purchased cloth from my family. By watching them, I learned how to dress, how to carry myself as a noble would."

Ansel let out a long, slow breath. "That is why ye clung to yer fine clothes and yer cold demeanor, isnae it? They were a mask behind which ye hid yer past."

Isolda's heart lurched. How had he seen through all of her defenses? And how was it that even as she laid herself bare before him, she still felt safe?

"Aye," she breathed.

The sun glinting off the lake was suddenly too bright, too harsh against the burning tears brimming in her eyes. She dropped her gaze to her feet, but her eyes landed on her mud-stained, simple gown of green wool instead.

A wild giggle rose in her throat, followed by a burst of full laughter.

Ansel looked at her fully for the first time since he'd guided her away from the tower. Concern was written clearly in his brown eyes as he stared at her. He likely thought her mad for laughing even as tears filled her eyes. The thought only made her laugh harder.

"What is it?" he asked, his brows colliding.

"My dress," she said between giggles.

His already concerned features darkened further. "I ken it isnae what ye are used to, nor what ye'd prefer, but—"

"Nay," she gasped, finally reining in her laughter. "That is just it—this is exactly what I prefer. I would trade all of Lancaster's titles and money and brocades and silks for…this."

She swept her hand down her dress, then let the gesture continue over the sparkling lake and the sun-bathed grassy hills toward the tower.

"I dinnae understand," Ansel said, though his eyes softened on her. Liquid warmth swelled inside her with only his look.

"I don't want Dunstanburgh or fine dresses or a title. This is what I want—family and a home and a simple but happy life," she said.

A life with you.

The words almost slipped out, but she swallowed them back just in time. Aye, she wanted Ansel, but he had made it clear that he was her protector, nothing more. "I...I have been so lonely all these years," she whispered instead.

Something flickered across his face—surprise, followed by hope, and then resolution.

"Isolda," he said, his voice a velvety caress. "Ye never have to feel lonely again, for ye carry my heart with ye wherever ye go."

Her lungs compressed in shock. "W-what?" she managed to breathe.

Ansel cupped her cheek in his warm, callused hand. She lost herself in the depths of his chestnut eyes, and the whole world seemed to fall away.

"I love ye."

The hard, handsome lines of his face blurred before her, but the tears that sprang to her eyes were nothing like the ones that had pricked there earlier. "You...you love me?"

"Aye," he said, his lips curling softly. "I have been trying to deny it, trying to keep distance between us.

But I cannae fight it anymore. I love ye. I want to be the one to bring ye the future ye long for. I want to be the one to share a family with ye, to keep ye safe, to live a simple life with ye."

Suddenly it felt as though the earth was tilting on its side. Isolda's legs wobbled precariously, her pulse hammering in her ears.

But just as suddenly, Ansel's strong arms were around her, steadying her and keeping her from tumbling to the ground.

"I love you, too," she whispered. Light and warmth surged through her, and she no longer needed his arms to keep her from falling. Nevertheless, she clung to him, for she feared that if she let go of him, she would go soaring right up to the heavens.

There was so much more to say, so much more she needed to share with him, but in that moment, her eyes landed on his mouth.

The air warmed between them, suddenly thick with anticipation. Ansel lowered his lips toward hers. Just before his mouth claimed hers completely, he froze. His lips hovered a hair's breadth from hers, his breath teasing her.

"I want ye—now and forever. Say ye'll be mine."

"Aye," she said, her voice tight with emotion. "Aye, Ansel Sutherland."

Before she knew what was happening, he had grabbed hold of her hand and darted toward a copse of trees in the distance. Her legs stretched to keep up with him, and her heart pounded in anticipation.

She was his—and he was going to prove it right now.

Chapter Thirty-One

Ansel had to force himself to slow down, for he was practically dragging Isolda toward the patch of woods ahead. His heart beat frantically in his chest, but it wasn't from the speed of their flight toward the copse—nay, it was the knowledge that he loved her, and she loved him, too.

They both skidded to a halt when they crossed into the woods. The air was cool under the shade of the boughs overhead. Though the pine trees stood as thick and green as ever, the leaves had fallen from the oaks, allowing sunlight to dapple the forest floor all around them.

Isolda panted from their wild dash from the loch's edge. She turned that pale green gaze on him. Her eyes were bright with emotion, her cheeks flushed and her hair windswept. The breath caught in Ansel's lungs. Never had he seen anything more beautiful.

"What are you about?" she asked, but the excited curve of her lips told him she knew very well what he intended.

"I have wasted so much time trying no' to touch ye," he breathed. "I intend to put an end to that now."

He stepped toward her, closing the distance between them. She held her ground even as she had to tilt head back to maintain their gaze. Her lips parted on an anticipatory gasp, and he saw his own desire, raw and hot, mirrored back to him in her delicate features.

This was not the time for teasing, or for gentleness. He needed to claim her and for her to claim him in return.

With a low growl reverberating in his throat, he captured her lips in a fierce kiss. The strength of his desire did not cause her to draw back, though. Instead, she met him, her fingers sinking into his shoulders and pinning them together.

Need surged into Ansel's cock. His tongue invaded her mouth, and he almost groaned at her velvet heat. He would soon be inside her, feeling her clench around him with the pleasure he would give her.

But nay, he had to do this right, not rush things. One hand slid into her hair, luxuriating in its thick silk. The other he used to cup her bottom, pulling their hips flush so that she could feel the hard length of his desire for her.

Isolda whimpered into his mouth, arching so that her breasts rubbed against his chest. By God, she wanted him as desperately as he wanted her. Her unbridled desire sent a nigh overwhelming lick of hungry flames through his veins.

Bloody hell.

There would be other times to go slow, a distant

voice said in the back of his mind. *Not now.* He couldn't delay any longer.

With the last shred of his willpower, he pulled away, breaking their kiss and his hold on her. He quickly unlooped the length of plaid from his shoulder and tugged his shirt over his head. Isolda stood watching him, her lips swollen and parted from his kiss and her breaths shallow and ragged.

Ansel's mind reeled as he thought of what those lips could do. *Later,* the voice whispered. *There will be time to explore our love in every possible way later.* For now, the need to be inside her, to join their bodies as well as their hearts, overrode all.

He made quick work removing his boots and hose. His fingers fumbled with the buckle on his belt like a green lad, so eager was he to be rid of it. At last, the buckle popped free and the pleated plaid slid from his hips. He caught it before it could land at his feet and spread it out over the leaf-strewn forest floor.

As he straightened, he realized that Isolda still hadn't moved. Her eyes were riveted on him, devouring his body.

"You are so beautiful," she whispered.

He would have chuckled, for calling a brawny Highland warrior beautiful was cause to shed blood in some taverns and inns. But on Isolda's lips, the word was spoken with reverence and longing. The knowledge of her unfettered desire sent his cock surging even more rigidly away from his body.

"Undo yer laces," he ground out.

Her hands flew behind her, where the simple ties ran down her back. As she loosened her gown's laces, he knelt on the plaid before her.

Ansel took hold of one of her ankles and lifted it slowly, giving her time to balance. He shucked off her boot, then peeled down her stocking. His fingers brushed the silken flesh behind her knee, and they both inhaled sharply at the same time.

He drew off her other boot and stocking in the same fashion, then slowly slid both hands up her legs.

Her skin was all warm cream and silk. He shuddered as he moved past her knees to the supple flesh of her thighs. His hands dragged her gown and chemise upward with them, baring her legs to his hungry gaze.

"Remove these," he said, his voice a low rasp as he pushed her garments higher.

As Isolda pulled her gown and chemise over her head as one, Ansel could no longer resist the longing to feast on her body. He rocked forward until his lips brushed the dark curls over her womanhood. She gasped at the intimate contact but was still caught in her garments.

With a slowly darting tongue, he parted her, tasting her desire. A moan erupted from her as he found that bud of a woman's pleasure. She at last freed herself from her clothes and carelessly tossed them aside. Her whole body went taut and little quivers rippled through her, originating where his tongue lapped and swirled.

Her knees trembled near his shoulders. Another breathy moan tumbled from her lips, sending a nigh painful throb into his bollocks. He would come undone with naught more than a warm breeze against his cock if he didn't claim her now.

Ansel pulled his mouth away and gripped Isolda's hips. He leaned backward onto the plaid, drawing her down with him until he lay on his back and she straddled him.

No words were needed now, for he recognized the liquid glint in her eyes. She understood his fierce need, for she felt it too. Her flushed skin, like berries and cream, and the way her teeth sank into her lip told him that she was just as hungry as he.

She positioned herself over him until his cock nudged her entrance. His fingers dug into her hips, letting her ease down onto his length. Inch by torturous inch, she lowered herself. She threw back her head, her dark hair cascading over her shoulders as he filled her.

By the time they were fully joined, he was panting through gritted teeth, his grasp on his self-control shredded to a mere thread. And when she moved, he feared he wouldn't last for her.

His eyes feasted on her perfect breasts, round and pink tipped and bobbing gently with her motion. One of his hands lifted to cup her. He brushed her nipple and drew another moan from her.

Ansel's other hand guided her in her rocking motion. He clenched his jaw against the urge to drive harder and faster.

But when he dropped his hand from her breast and his thumb found that nub of pleasure, Isolda's rocking turned to trembling, her rhythm faltering. He surged into her, driven on by her cries of ecstasy.

A heartbeat later, the scorching heat that had coiled so tightly within him exploded into pure pleasure. His voice rumbled over hers as they both hung suspended in blinding release.

Isolda slumped over him, spent. Gently, he rolled her to the plaid under him and nestled her head against his chest. They both breathed the loamy forest air for several long moments as they drifted back down from the heights of pleasure.

"You didn't seem surprised," Isolda breathed at last against his chest.

He eased her onto her back and propped himself on one elbow so that he could gaze down at her soft features.

"That ye love me in return? I was indeed surprised," he said, slanting his mouth in a playful smile. "I havenae done nearly enough good in my life to deserve the love of an angel."

"Nay," she said, a smile to match his curling her lips. "That is not what I meant. I mean...you didn't seem surprised about my past...that I am not truly a lady."

Her lips faltered and her dark brows drew together slightly as she gazed up at him.

He twined one of her dark locks around his finger. "I suspected as much," he replied softly. "What with Embleton being recently constructed alongside Dunstanburgh, and the fact that Lancaster had sent ye there alone, it seemed likely that yer title was…well…"

He fumbled for the words to avoid injuring her, for it was clear in the depths of her green eyes that Lancaster's callous treatment of her and John still hurt.

But she surprised him by nodding and letting his words fade. "But if you knew, why didn't you question me on it? Why did you still call me *Lady* Isolda?"

He smiled faintly as he let his eyes trace her furrowed brows, her cheeks pinkened with pleasure, and her mouth, which, while still soft, had turned down slightly.

"I wanted ye to tell me when ye were ready," he replied at last. "I wanted ye to trust me."

The slight tension in her face eased and she looked up at him with vulnerable eyes. By God, he loved this woman.

Her gaze slipped to his chest, and her fingers grazed his skin, raising a ripple of awareness though he'd only just spent himself within her.

"Does this still pain you?" she asked, her fingertips brushing lightly over the place where she'd stitched him together. That night at Dunstanburgh seemed ages ago.

"Nay," he said. "It is just one of many old scars now."

He let his hand skim down her body to rest low on her stomach. "And what of these?" he asked. He gently swept his fingers over the fine white lines that faintly marked her skin between her hip bones.

"Old scars as well," she said with a soft smile. "John gave me those while I carried him inside me."

Something familiar yet foreign tugged in Ansel's chest. It was similar to the love he now realized he bore for Isolda, but newer.

"I want ye to know," he said, pausing to clear his throat of thick emotion. "That I will love John. He is a part of ye, and I love ye. I will protect and care for him as I do ye, Isolda."

Isolda's green eyes filled with tears. "Thank you," she whispered. "I believe you. I…I trust you."

She blinked back the tears, her eyes suddenly locking on his with an urgent intensity.

"John is here, Ansel. In Scotland."

Chapter Thirty-Two

"What?"

Isolda flinched at the sharpness in Ansel's voice. His hand stilled on her belly, his body suddenly rigid.

Her heart rose in her throat, but she was not afraid. Nay, she was finally brave enough to speak what had been eating away at her for nigh a year. And she was brave enough to love Ansel.

"John is here," she repeated. "I am not sure exactly how far, but he is close."

"Isolda," he said, eyeing her cautiously, "I didnae tell ye I would love and protect John just to get his location out of ye—"

"Nay, I know," she said quickly. "You wouldn't do that. But...I *want* to tell you."

Emotion, warm and powerful, once again surged through her. The words tumbled from her mouth in a rush as sudden clarity urged her on.

"I trust you. And I don't want to run and hide anymore. I don't want to return to England. I want to live here in the Highlands with you and John, to live as we have at Brora."

Surprise followed quickly by tenderness flickered in Ansel's dark eyes. The look he gave her stole her breath.

"I want that, too, lass," he rasped, his eyes depthless as they held her gaze.

"Am I foolish for thinking this dream can become reality?" Her chest tightened with longing as she gazed up at him.

"Nay," he said softly. He cupped her cheek in his hand. "No' foolish at all, lass."

Nevertheless, as he considered her question, his face hardened and his eyes drifted to the leaf-strewn forest floor beyond her head. It was as if he had transformed into a fierce, protective warrior before her eyes as he thought in silence for a long moment.

"Edward cannae touch us here in the Highlands—if he could, he would have already," he said at last. "Ye ken I wouldnae take the risk if I thought there was one, but I believe we are at last free to live our lives in peace."

Renewed hope flooded her. "Then I can see John again. And we can find some place to call our own. And—"

"Dinnae get ahead of yerself, lass," Ansel said gently. "Are ye sure ye wish to tell me where John is?"

She held his gaze so that he had no room to mistake her. "Aye," she said. "I want to tell you. And I want us to fetch him together."

He nodded slowly and waited, his strong body motionless over her.

"A monk came through Dunstanburgh almost a year ago," she began. "The accidents had just started, though I sensed it was worse than it appeared. I had thought that no one knew about John and my existence, but I feared that if someone found out that Lancaster had sired an illegitimate son, John would be targeted."

Ansel nodded again, so she went on.

"The monk was on his way to the Highlands to rejoin his church—kirk, he called it. I told him of my fears for John, and he offered to take John with him into Scotland. He said John would be safe and secluded, and could study and live with the monks as other children sometimes do when they are to join the monastic order."

"Where was the monk headed?"

"He said it was called Fearn Abbey," she said, pronouncing it carefully to ensure she got it right.

The muscles in Ansel's arms and shoulders suddenly bunched. "Fearn Abbey in Cadboll?"

"Aye," she replied. "Do you know it?"

Ansel's eyebrows shot up and his mouth curved in astonishment. "We are only a day's ride from Cadboll, lass."

Her breath caught in her throat and her heart twisted. She had been even closer to John than she could have possibly imagined these past several days.

She knew it was the work of her imagination, but suddenly she felt as though John was nearly in her arms at last. His excited heartbeat would pound against hers when she wrapped him in a fierce embrace. His fluttering breath would rustle her hair. A tide of happiness would break over them both when she saw him again.

"Can we go there now?" Isolda said, sitting up suddenly. She felt no shame in her nakedness before Ansel. Instead of fearing exposure, she felt freer than ever before. Her whole life was about to begin anew—with John and Ansel.

"We will have to get a few things in order first," Ansel said. His normally hard features were relaxed, and his dark eyes twinkled with a joy that mirrored her own. "We'll need to pack, for we will have to stay the night at the abbey. And Meredith will demand an explanation."

As he mentioned his sister, Ansel rolled his eyes. Isolda couldn't help the merry laugh that bubbled up to her throat.

"I know you too well, Ansel Sutherland. You will relish every second of telling your sister that you have finally captured my heart."

"Finally?" Ansel's smile turned wolfish, a predatory glint in his eyes. "I'll get ye to admit that ye wanted me from the start—one way or another."

With that, he dove on top of her, setting dancing fingers to her ribs. She squealed and squirmed against his tickles, but to no avail. Her laughter chimed through the sun-warmed forest until he finally took mercy on her and claimed her mouth once again.

Chapter Thirty-Three

"Farewell!"

Isolda's hair tickled Ansel's neck as she twisted around in the saddle before him. She waved furiously behind them where Meredith, Burke, Niall, and Fiona stood at the base of Brora Tower.

Yesterday's perfect weather had broken overnight, and now they headed out into a dreary, misting rain. Yet Ansel hardly noticed, for spring had bloomed in his heart at the knowledge of Isolda's love. He was not a man given to flowery thoughts and soft emotion, but he couldn't deny the happiness soaring within him.

They had eventually returned to the tower to find Meredith's knowing eyes dancing with joy. Over a simple meal, they had told Burke and Meredith that they were going to retrieve John. Isolda had entrusted him and him alone with John's location, so Ansel had said only that John was in the Highlands.

At Meredith's pointed question, Ansel had proclaimed that he and Isolda would wed once they had retrieved John. Then they would return to Sutherland land and Ansel would petition Laird Kenneth Sutherland for a plot of land on which to settle.

Meredith had nigh tackled Isolda to the ground in a fierce hug. Burke had removed a treasured bottle of whisky from the back of one of the wooden cabinets in the tower's little kitchen so that they could all toast the happy news.

Now Ansel kept Eachann at a slow walk so that Isolda could twist backward to wave and look her fill upon her new family, who stood gathered around the tower despite the damp weather.

Niall bolted from Meredith's side and ran alongside Eachann, waving frantically at Isolda. She blew a kiss to him and the boy stopped in his tracks, staring after them with a stunned expression on his face.

"Ye'll ruin the lad for a lass of his own," Ansel said, the reproach in his voice softened by mirth.

At last, they slipped behind a gently rolling hill and the tower was lost to sight. Isolda turned face-forward in the saddle once more and leaned back against Ansel's chest.

"I can hardly believe that I will gain a sister, brother, niece, and nephew along with a husband," she breathed. "I don't want to wait a moment longer than necessary to be wed."

"Perhaps one of the holy men at Fearn Abbey can see to it," he replied, nuzzling his nose against her hair.

"Aye," she said contentedly, but then hesitancy returned to her voice as she went on. "Do you imagine that Laird Sutherland will grant you a plot of land? I must confess, I do not fully understand how such clan dealings work."

She craned her neck so that she could gaze up at him, her brows swooping together in consternation. "From the way you presented it last night, you seem confident that your Laird will acquiesce, but asking for land is no small matter. Do you truly believe we can start a life together in the Highlands so easily?"

"Naught in the Highlands is easy, lass," he said, cocking a smile. "But in this case, aye, I am confident the Laird will grant me what I ask."

"How can you be so sure?"

"I havenae told ye, have I?" He felt his smile widen as her pale green eyes narrowed on him.

"Told me what?"

"That I am the Laird's cousin, and that until he produces an heir of his own, I am next in line for the Lairdship."

To Ansel's satisfaction, Isolda's mouth fell open. "You...you are Laird Sutherland's cousin? And you would be Laird if—"

"Aye, but God willing, I never will be, for Kenneth is more than worthy, and some day—soon, if the clan has aught to say about it—he will have his own heirs."

Isolda continued to stare up at him, her eyes wide with disbelief. "At first I thought you were little more than a hired guard, just some Highland rogue paid to watch over John. Then I came to learn that you are in King Robert the Bruce's elite inner circle of warriors and that you were sent to me by the King himself. And now you tell me that you are the cousin of a Laird and in line for the Lairdship?"

"Aye," he said simply, enjoying her bewilderment.

Her brow crinkled again, and he had to bite back a bark of laughter that rose in his throat.

"You let me call you a barbarian! How could you?"

Horror at the memory washed over her features, and this time he couldn't stop a snort of amusement from slipping out.

"Are ye pleased to learn that ye are to marry more than just some Highland barbarian? Are ye glad that I am a man of consequence after all?" he teased.

"Nay, I am not pleased at all," she said, swatting his shoulder in mock indignation. "For I had hoped that you were born a commoner, as I was."

Her smile slipped as she held his gaze, her green eyes drawing him in.

"Truly, Ansel," she said softly, "you could not please me more, whether you were a King or a pauper. I love you."

His chest swelled with pride at her words.

As they rode, Ansel told her of moving from Brora to Dunrobin Castle at the age of ten to begin his training alongside Kenneth. He spoke of his largely happy childhood getting to spar and learn with his cousin, though he also confessed a longing to have a true home, a place he could call his own.

The rain picked up from a gentle mist to a drizzle as he guided them south toward Cadboll. Isolda slipped her hood up, and Ansel dragged the plaid that draped across his shoulder over his head.

Just as Isolda settled herself once more against his chest, Ansel's eye snagged on a dark flicker of movement in the distance.

He must have stiffened, for Isolda looked up at him.

"What is it?"

Ansel squinted through the hazy gray sheets of rain. "Likely naught," he said, his eyes taking in the lone figure standing next to a cart with a single horse hitched to it. "Just another traveler caught in this blasted rain."

As they drew nearer, Ansel realized that the cart was stuck in a patch of mud made worse by the increasing downpour. The old man standing next to the cart was covered in mud, likely from his efforts to free the cart's wheel.

When they were nearly to the man, Ansel pulled Eachann to a halt.

"Wait here," he said to Isolda, keeping his voice low. "There is no point in all of us getting muddy." He flashed her a smile before turning toward the man.

Gray-white hair stuck out from under the man's simple cap. His clothes, along with the large but aging draft horse, indicated the man was likely a simple farmer or laborer.

"Greetings, friend," Ansel said as he approached. "Ye look to be in a wee bit of trouble."

"Och," the old man grunted. "Wee my foot. The heavens cannae decide if it is summer or winter, it seems." He swept a hand through the rain, his mouth turned down as he looked accusatorily at the clouds overhead. "I was to fetch a new plow from my brother-in-law in Cadboll, but I cannae verra well do that in this cursed bog."

"We are headed to Cadboll as well—or rather, the abbey near there," Isolda said cheerily behind Ansel. Though she still sat atop Eachann, she'd drawn the horse closer to catch the old man's words. "Perhaps you could unhitch your horse as we could help you there."

The old man shook his head. "No good. I cannae fetch the plow without my cart." He crossed his arms with a sigh, glaring at the cart's wheel, which was sunk halfway into the mud.

"Then perhaps I can help. Ye drive the horse. I'll push."

The man eyed Ansel for a moment, assessing him. "Och," he muttered again. "Verra well. Much obliged."

He moved to where the old draft horse stood as Ansel took up position behind the cart. At Ansel's nod, the man slapped the horse's flank and urged the aged animal on. Ansel drove his shoulder into the back of the cart, his feet sinking into the mud as they sought purchase.

The wooden cart groaned and the mud sucked at the wheel, but they only gained a few inches.

"Again!" Ansel gritted through his teeth, redoubling his efforts against the cart as the old man tried to spark some fire in the draft horse.

At last, the cart creaked and the wheel sucked out of the mud. Ansel almost lost his footing and would have landed face-first in the muck if he hadn't managed to pull his boots free just in time to catch himself.

With his crisis averted, the old man was suddenly nigh leaping with merriment.

"Thank ye, my lad," he said to Ansel. "A good, stout Sutherland back was all I needed." He looked approvingly over Ansel's plaid, then bobbed his head to Isolda. "A good man, that is what ye are. I wish ye safe travels to the abbey. God will surely smile on such kind folk."

Long after Ansel remounted Eachann behind Isolda and nudged the animal southward, the old man waved and shouted his thanks.

Isolda giggled. "You are covered in mud nigh to your knees."

Ansel tightened his arm around Isolda's waist. "I see a stream tucked in that copse of trees ahead—care to help me wash?"

She giggled again, but the sound was huskier this time. Lust surged through him, cutting through the cold and dampness seeping into his bones.

"Aye," she whispered. "Though I may have to remove all your clothes to ensure that you are thoroughly clean."

✦ ✦ ✦

By the time they had regained Eachann's saddle and continued south, the rain had eased but the sky was the dark purple of a stormy evening.

Aye, that little romp in the woods had cost them a bit of time, but Ansel wouldn't trade it for the world. It seemed as though now that they had confessed their love, the passion that had crackled between them from the beginning raged like a wildfire.

Isolda nestled herself once more against his chest with a contented sigh. He would never grow tired of those gasps and moans of pleasure that he could draw from her. As he inhaled against her hair, he tucked away a reminder to himself to make sure she always had a supply of her intoxicating lemon and lavender soap.

Though her body was limp and languid against his at first as they rode, by the time the sky had darkened further into an overcast dusk, she must have sensed that they were near the abbey. She straightened, her body taut with anticipation as he slowed Eachann.

Ahead of them, the pointed roof of the abbey loomed out of the gray-black night sky.

"Is that Fearn?" Isolda breathed, her voice trembling.

"Aye."

Since they had approached from the back side of the abbey, they had to cross through the cemetery to reach the abbey's doors. Marker stones began to emerge from the darkness around them, lurking like ghosts in the moonless night.

She glanced back at him, and he caught a flash of white as she gave him a wobbly smile. "John is so close."

He opened his mouth to respond, but for some reason, unease crept up his spine.

The abbey was quiet up ahead, though that shouldn't have raised his suspicion. Since it was well after sunset, the monks would have retired already.

He could not place his finger on what was causing the hairs on his nape to stir. Though his gaze darted around the cemetery as they rode toward the abbey, his eyes landed on naught but shadows and stillness. Perhaps it was the mere fact of crossing holy ground that made him uneasy.

As he drew Eachann to a halt, Isolda threw her leg over the horse's neck and slid to the ground before Ansel could stop her.

"Isolda, nay," he said, his voice coming out sharper than he intended.

"What is—"

All around them, the grave markers sprang to life. It was as if the stone itself leapt toward them.

Nay, the stone grave markers weren't coming to life—men were emerging from behind them, weapons drawn.

They were under attack.

Chapter Thirty-Four

Ansel's body lurched into motion even as his mind lagged behind.

He flung himself from Eachann's back as he dragged the sword on his hip from its scabbard. With his free hand, he yanked Isolda back by the arm, putting her between him and Eachann. The horse snorted and sidestepped, but with a click of Ansel's tongue, he stilled, well trained war steed that he was.

Ansel's gaze skittered around the graveyard, his sword raised in front of him. He counted ten men closing in on them and sensed more than saw at least two more approaching behind Eachann. They moved like shadows and ghosts among the grave markers, their swords dull in the moonless night. Yet to Ansel's shock, they did not attack.

"I made sure that this time, the men I selected would be well-trained warriors rather than green village lads."

The flat voice floated over Ansel's shoulder from the abbey. He pressed his back against Isolda, squeezing her between his body and Eachann's, forcing the animal to pivot. Alert lest the men in the graveyard decided to strike, Ansel shot a glance toward the abbey.

A dark-headed man emerged from the shadows. His gait was lazy, though he moved with a fighter's languid lethality.

Familiarity crashed through Ansel's brain, followed by a swell of sickening dread.

"Ye are the man from Dunstanburgh," he said slowly, his gut turning to lead. "The one who attacked Isolda in her chamber. The one I should have killed."

Isolda gasped behind him. He didn't dare shift his eyes to her, but he could feel her trembling against his back.

"Aye," the man said calmly. "My name is Clemont, though that will mean naught to you."

"I bested ye and a dozen of yer men already," Ansel ground out through his teeth. "If ye wish to try yer luck again, ken that this time there are no windows for ye to jump out of, no place for ye to flee like a coward from my blade."

Annoyance flickered in Clemont's dark eyes, but instead of goading his ire, Ansel's words seemed to disappoint him. "You have already lost and you don't even know it," he said flatly.

He stepped aside and swept his hand back toward the abbey.

Ansel squinted into the dimness. A crumpled pile of cloth lay in the abbey's doorway.

The gears in Ansel's mind finally clicked into place. It was not a heap of cloth he was staring at, but the body of a monk.

"What have you done with John?" Ansel breathed, a knife of fear twisting in his belly.

A wordless, strangled cry rose from Isolda behind him.

"Do not concern yourself with the boy," Clemont said levelly. "You and I have more pressing matters at the moment." His dark eyes flicking past Ansel to Isolda. "The man paying my employer requires that I shear all the loose ends in the little mess he made. Collecting the woman for…disposal is the second of two threads to be collected and trimmed."

"Nay!" Isolda shrieked.

Ansel tightened his grip on his sword.

"Ye and your men will have to go through me before I let ye harm a hair on Isolda's head," he said through clenched teeth.

"Hence the pressing matters we must attend to—if you will not hand over the woman, I will most certainly go through you."

Clemont's voice was eerily smooth. Fear stabbed deeper in Ansel's stomach. The man had clearly ceased to care about taking life long ago. What horrors had he committed to make him so calm at a moment like this?

"Nay!" Isolda cried again, her voice cracking with panic. "Do not hurt John. He is an innocent child!"

Clemont waved away her words. "It doesn't matter. I have been paid, and I must see to my task. That is all. Now hand over the woman."

"How did you know?" Isolda hissed desperately. "How did you know where to find John? I only told—"

Then she gasped. Ansel realized with burning clarity what direction her thoughts had taken.

"I only told *you*, Ansel."

✧ ✧ ✧

The terror that pounded through Isolda's veins was suddenly spiked with something far darker—betrayal.

She pressed against Eachann's flank, trying to peel her body away from Ansel's as fear and disgust twisted in her belly.

"You promised you'd never betray me," she whispered, her throat ragged.

"I didnae!" Ansel shot a glance over his shoulder at her, his eyes pleading.

Her heart splintered into shards. John had been found. And Ansel had deceived her. She had trusted again like a fool, and now she and John would pay for it.

Even still, a sliver of her longed to believe him. The hard, warm planes of his body crushed against her protectively. His eyes were harried as he shot her another glance before returning his gaze to Clemont. Confusion cluttered her mind.

"I told no one, Isolda, I swear it," he said, his voice edged with desperation.

Before he could say more, Clemont spoke again.

"I have no interest in your lovers' quarrel," he said

levelly. "But your bickering wastes my time." He fixed Isolda with a hard, flat stare. "The old farmer you helped not far from here was quick to tell me where you were headed when a little pain was applied."

Isolda dragged in a ragged breath. "The man…you…you hurt him."

"I killed him, aye," Clemont replied, his voice soft and low. "It was a small price to pay for the information I needed."

It was as if the world tilted on its side. She had been so quick to question Ansel, to lose all faith and trust in him, when in fact *she* had been the one to tell the kind old farmer that they were headed to Fearn Abbey.

And that meant she'd cost the innocent man his life.

Sickness roiled in her stomach. She swallowed hard against the burn of bile rising in her throat.

"Enough talk," Clemont said levelly, turning his gaze on Ansel once more. "I won't bother telling you that you have a choice to hand over the woman. You don't—just as I don't have a choice in killing the woman and the boy. So let us get on with it."

Isolda felt Ansel stiffen even more in front of her. Then it felt as though everything ground to a halt and hung suspended and frozen for a long, terrible moment. The cold night air hung thick with anticipation. The men surrounding them stood poised to attack. Every muscle in Ansel's body was wound tight.

And then all Hell broke loose.

The four men closest to them launched forward,

blades whirring in the otherwise dead-quiet cemetery.

"Mount Eachann!" Ansel bellowed to her as he struck like an uncoiling snake at the first of his attackers.

The clang of metal on metal shattered the night. Isolda threw herself onto Eachann's back. The animal pranced with nervous eagerness as a battle erupted around them.

A scream of agony tore through the air. Isolda's heart lurched in terror, but her gaze found Ansel in the middle of the fray, still upright and swinging his sword.

He moved like Death himself. Every curve of his blade, every pivot, every block blurred into a lethal dance. Two more men quickly fell at Ansel's feet, but he didn't slow even as more attackers launched themselves at him.

Eachann's snort and sidestep jerked Isolda's attention away from Ansel. Two more men loomed out of the shadows surrounding the abbey, though Ansel was completely absorbed in fending off the four new opponents who closed in.

"Ansel!" she cried, unable to form any other word.

He spun and impaled one of his attackers with a mighty thrust. His gaze flickered to her before he pivoted once more to block a blade aimed to decapitate him. But just as he deflected the attack, he let out a sharp whistle unlike any she'd heard before.

Eachann tensed beneath her, his ears quivering for a heartbeat. Then suddenly the war horse reared, and Isolda had to cling to his mane to avoid being thrown to the ground.

Startled by the horse's sudden lurch, the two men charging from the abbey faltered in front of Eachann. The war horse's hooves darted out, catching one of the men square in the head and clipping the other's shoulder.

Isolda clung tight as Eachann's hooves once again connected with the ground, sending a jolt of impact through her bones. Before she could squeeze her eyes shut against the sight of two lumps on the ground, she glimpsed one lying motionless and the other moaning and crawling away, his arm dragging limply alongside him.

Ansel still fought with deadly grace, though now only two men surrounded him and no more emerged from the shadows. Blood darkened his shirt, though Isolda could not tell if it was his or his enemies', who lay unmoving around the graveyard.

He dove out of the way of an arcing blade and rolled, popping up on his feet a moment later. With not a hair's breadth to spare, he blocked a blow meant to hamstring him, then rammed his sword along his attacker's until his blade sank into the man's leg.

Before he could withdraw his sword, the other man launched a renewed attack. Ansel ducked under the swiping blade, then drove his shoulder into the second man, sending him toppling backward. Jerking his blade free, he ended the first man's life with a clean slice across the throat and turned to the other. Still lurching backward, the second man took Ansel's sword in the belly. He slumped to the ground, the last breath of air he'd ever take leaving him in a whoosh.

"I shouldn't be impressed, but I am."

Isolda's head whipped around to where Clemont stood. He'd moved to the abbey's doors, where the body of the monk still lay in a heap.

"My men should have handled you, but yet again you have bested them." Admiration tinged Clemont's voice, sending tendrils of disquiet twining up Isolda's spine.

Ansel straightened and staggered toward where Isolda still clung to Eachann's mane. He laid a bloodied hand against the horse's neck to soothe him.

"There is nowhere for ye to run, Clemont," Ansel panted. "Ye're finished."

"Nay," Clemont said, his voice once again flat. "Not quite."

His hand darted behind the abbey's doors and a second later, he dragged out a small, huddled figure.

The whole world fell away—the graveyard, the abbey, the bodies strewn on the ground, even Eachann's warm, strong body beneath her and Ansel's comforting nearness.

John trembled in Clemont's grasp.

Clemont flicked his wrist, and suddenly a dagger appeared in his hand. He raised the blade to John's throat.

Her sweet son blinked through the darkness, his pale eyes landing squarely on her.

"Mama?"

Chapter Thirty-Five

"I hadn't thought to kill him here," Clemont said, his voice as smooth and calm as ever. "It would be too much of a mess, you see. Too many questions that could be tied back to the man who hired me. But I'll do it if you do not lay down your sword."

Clemont's words sliced through the fog of battle clouding Ansel's mind.

Isolda cried out wordlessly, but Ansel could not tear his gaze away from the little boy in Clemont's grasp.

"Mama!" the lad cried again, this time recognition brightening his tone.

"John, don't…don't move," Isolda whispered.

"Drop your sword," Clemont said, his voice harder now.

Ansel needed more time. He needed to think, but blank darkness descended on his mind. How could he save both John and Isolda? And if he failed either one of them, how could he ever hope to live with himself?

Clemont's wrist twitched and John inhaled sharply. "Do I need to repeat myself?" Clemont asked coolly.

Ansel was out of options. Slowly, he bent and lowered his sword to the ground, then shoved it toward Clemont.

Clemont nodded curtly. "The blade slipped into your boot as well."

Ansel hadn't had time to draw the dagger he kept strapped to his boot in the fray earlier. Reluctantly, he withdrew the blade and tossed it to where his sword lay halfway between him and Clemont.

"Now, the woman. Have her come here."

He looked up at Isolda. Her hands were entwined in Eachann's mane, her eyes wide and shimmering with fear. He turned back to Clemont.

"Take me instead."

"Ansel, nay." Isolda's voice trembled, but he refused to look at her.

Clemont's teeth flashed briefly in the darkness. "You are full of surprises," he said. "You would offer yourself in the woman's place?"

"And the boy's."

Clemont shook his head slowly, never removing his gaze from Ansel. "I have underestimated you twice now. You would do anything to complete your mission to protect the boy and the woman, wouldn't you? Perhaps you and I are not so different," he said, that edge of respect returning to his voice. It made Ansel want to grind his molars.

"Nay, we are nothing alike."

"Oh no?" Clemont jutted his chin to the ground surrounding Ansel—the ground littered with dead bodies. "Aren't we? We are killers, merely hired men," Clemont went on softly. "Our own lives do not matter. All that matters is the mission—the lives we are sent to take, or save, as the case may be."

Keep him talking. The voice echoed in the dark recesses of Ansel's mind. No plan had formed there yet, but if nothing more, Ansel could stall.

"Ye are nothing like me. Ye have no honor," Ansel said, his brain skittering over all that Clemont had hinted at. "Ye kill for coin. Ye are a bounty hunter, are ye no'?"

"Aye." Clemont tilted his head in acknowledgement, his eyes emotionless.

"Who hired ye? King Edward? Or perhaps one of his lackeys?"

"It doesn't matter, does it?" Clemont's voice was once again flat.

Ansel was running out of time to think, yet he stood weaponless before Clemont, John's life balancing along the edge of the knife at his throat.

Something tugged at Ansel's scattered thoughts, something Clemont had said earlier.

"How did ye ken that I was hired to protect the woman and the boy?"

One of Clemont's dark brows rose as he considered Ansel's question. "I suppose it makes no difference now," he murmured at last. He cocked his head, his gaze flicking curiously between Ansel and Isolda. "The Earl of Lancaster told me."

Ansel's stomach dropped to his feet.

Lancaster.

Could the bastard have truly hired a bounty hunter to kill his own son?

"Although he paid my employer handsomely for my skills, he also saw fit to hire a bodyguard—you. Something about giving your Scottish King the impression of an alliance and ensuring that the woman would feel safe enough to lead me to the boy." Clemont shrugged as if it were all naught but a meaningless chore.

A new realization washed over Ansel, causing sickness to rise in the back of his throat. Lancaster had hired *him*, too. Just as Clemont had said, they were both just pawns, rented out for Lancaster's schemes.

Suddenly Isolda moaned and slumped over Eachann's neck. Ansel leapt forward, catching her before she tumbled to the ground in a swoon.

"Why?" Ansel growled, clutching Isolda to his chest. "Why would Lancaster pay to have his own son and the boy's mother killed?"

"Who knows why rich noblemen hire men like me?" Clemont said with another shrug. "I didn't ask."

But even as Clemont spoke, the gears in Ansel's mind ground into place. It was just as Garrick had said almost a month ago when he'd arrived at Dunrobin with this mission. Lancaster was planning to make a play for the English throne. An illegitimate son could be used against him to call his line of succession into question. But they had all assumed that Lancaster would want to protect his son from an attack, not be rid of him to eradicate such a vulnerability.

"And...and Lancaster had ye track us into Scotland?" Ansel rasped, looking down at Isolda. Her eyelids fluttered as she regained consciousness. His chest burned as if his very heart were being branded.

"Aye, and again, I must compliment you," Clemont said evenly. "Lancaster was sure you'd lead me directly to the boy once my men and I had driven you from Dunstanburgh. But you made it almost impossible for me to track you. *Almost*. I had nearly lost faith that you would ever seek the boy out, but then..." Clemont tilted his head at the shadowy graveyard and the bodies on the ground. "Here we are."

"And what did Lancaster order ye to do next?" Ansel ground out.

"As I said, the woman and the boy are loose ends to be shorn off. So you see, your offer that I take you instead of them is no good. You are naught to Lancaster."

Isolda stirred once again in Ansel's arms. Her eyes popped open and her gaze darted to Clemont and John. She strained against Ansel's hold as if she would dash to her son's side. Carefully, Ansel eased her down onto her feet, but he held fast to her hand.

"John is just a child," Isolda said, her voice quaking. "He will not remember any of this. Please, let him live. He never has to know who his father is."

"Enough," Clemont cut in, his eyes sliding from Ansel to Isolda and back again. "You have tried to stall me, and I granted you the information you sought—out of respect, that is all. There is naught left to discuss. Give me the woman."

"I'd rather die," Ansel growled.

Clemont shook his head slightly. "I am offering you a gift, Highlander. Hand the woman over and I won't kill them in front of you. They will die either way—there are no choices in that. But you do not have to watch."

John began whimpering softly, his eyes brimming with tears. Clemont gave the boy a hard shake, though instead of silencing him, John moaned louder.

Panic, hot and jagged, tore through Ansel's veins. He could sense the last of his options slipping away like sand through his fingers.

"What can I offer Lancaster instead?" he said, desperately raking his mind. "The Scottish army's movements? The location of the Bruce's camp?"

"Ansel, nay!"

To his shock, Isolda yanked her hand free of his and turned to him, her eyes wide and glistening.

"I was wrong to doubt you, even for a moment," she breathed. "You are a man of honor. You cannot betray your King and countrymen."

"Isolda." Ansel's voice was a ragged rasp. "Ye would rather I betray ye and John?"

"It matters naught," Clemont interjected. "I have

been sent for the boy and the woman. Naught you say or do will stop me."

Isolda took a slow step backward, toward Clemont, though her eyes remained fixed on Ansel.

"And if I go with you, Ansel will live?" she said over her shoulder, her voice trembling.

Ansel's gaze shot to Clemont. The man tilted his head in thought for a brief moment.

"I was paid for two lives, and his was not one of them. I have no business with him beyond this."

"Isolda, what are ye doing?" Ansel hissed. She took another step backward, broadening the space between them.

"Lancaster will never stop," she whispered. The tears brimming in her pale eyes finally began flowing down her cheeks. "John and I will never be free of him. But you still can be."

Clemont shifted restlessly behind Isolda. His hand tightened around the dagger at John's throat until his knuckles stood out whitely in the darkness.

Soft as an owl's wing, something brushed the back of Ansel's mind.

Clemont's dagger.

The blade was short and almost oval. Even in the low light, the sharp edge gleamed.

It was the same kind of dagger that Clemont had sunk into Ansel's arm and shoulder.

The same kind of dagger that Ansel had examined closely for clues…

And that he had tucked into his saddlebags.

Isolda took another step backward. She stood between him and Clemont, blocking Clemont's view. Slowly, Ansel shifted so that his arm brushed against Eachann's flank. He darted his elbow into the horse's side to make him start, then lifted a hand to Eachann's back just above the saddlebag as if to soothe him.

"Come along," Clemont said to Isolda, his voice suddenly sharp.

Ansel eased his hand into the saddlebag. Under cover of another of Isolda's steps, he moved ever so slightly to dig deeper into the bag. He held his breath, expecting Clemont to notice what he was about, but Isolda stood between them, hindering Clemont's line of sight. At last his fingers brushed cool metal.

Isolda's gaze shifted to the saddlebag. Her eyes jolted up to him, a question in their pale depths.

"I told ye that I made ye a promise, and I dinnae break my word," Ansel said, holding Isolda's frightened gaze as he slipped the dagger partway out of the saddlebag.

Isolda shook her head ever so slightly. "Think of John," she whispered, her gaze flickering to the dagger and back again.

"I am," he murmured. "Ye said ye wouldnae doubt me again. Do ye trust me?"

Isolda swallowed hard, but she nodded slowly at him, her eyes round.

"I trust you."

"Enough," Clemont bit out. "You have had your time to say goodbye. This ends—"

Ansel's heart leapt into his throat as he yanked the dagger free of the saddlebag.

"Now!" he bellowed.

Chapter Thirty-Six

Time seemed to slow.

Ansel's arm blurred in the corner of his vision as he threw the dagger as hard as he could.

Isolda flung herself to the ground, the dagger whizzing where her head had been a fraction of a second before.

The dagger cut through the night like a beam of light.

The air reverberated with a soft thunk as the dagger found its home in Clemont's neck. He jerked backward at the impact, dragging John to the ground with him.

John screamed in panic as he toppled onto Clemont. Isolda's cry of fear joined the lad's. Even before Ansel could uproot himself from where he stood, Isolda had scrambled to John's side.

"Mama!" the boy wailed.

At last, Ansel managed to drag in a raw breath of cold, fresh air. He rushed to where Isolda pulled at John to extract him from Clemont's grasp.

"Are you hurt, my dove?" Isolda cried, her voice still tight with fear.

"Nay, Mama!" John burst into tears as he launched himself into his mother's arms, free of Clemont's hold at last.

Ansel crouched next to their huddled forms. Unbidden, his arms caught them both up and he dragged them against his chest.

"Ye're all right, lad," he breathed. "Ye're safe now."

His eyes locked with Isolda's over John's dark head. Tears streamed down her cheeks as she gave him a wordless nod.

He gently released his hold on them and eased Isolda to her feet. She clung to John, pulling him up in her arms as she stood. Ansel guided them to where Eachann stood and moved the horse so that he blocked their view of Clemont.

When he trusted that they would not have to see their attacker again, he turned and let his gaze fall on Clemont's form.

The man lay wide-eyed on his back, the dagger protruding from his throat. He was still alive. His body lurched as he struggled to drag in a breath, but dark blood was already pooling around his head. Each ragged inhale made a rasping, wet sound that told of fast-approaching death.

To Ansel's shock, Clemont's dark eyes locked on him as he crouched by the bounty hunter's side.

"Perhaps…in another life…you would have been like me," Clemont wheezed, his words almost indiscernible. "If a man like my employer…had found you."

"Nay," Ansel said, though all the heat of anger suddenly drained from him.

"Then perhaps," Clemont whispered, "I would have been…like you."

Clemont lifted a shaking hand toward the dagger in his throat.

"Free me."

Ansel nodded slowly, holding Clemont's half-lidded gaze. His hand closed around the dagger and in one swift jerk, he yanked it free. Blood coursed eagerly out of the wound. On one final shuddering exhale, the light went dim behind Clemont's eyes.

As he stood, Ansel dropped the dagger by Clemont's lifeless body. At last, he turned away, a murmured prayer for the dead man slipping from his lips.

He returned to Eachann's side to find Isolda rocking John gently in her arms, though the lad was big enough that she struggled to hold him. Even still, she clung tight, her face buried in John's hair as she murmured soothing words to him.

"It is over," Ansel said softly. "Let us leave this place."

Isolda nodded, a slow exhale escaping her lips.

"Where will we go?"

"To Brora."

His response didn't answer the underlying question that lurked in her voice, though.

"And then?"

He gritted his teeth against the churning emotions in his gut. Aye, he'd protected John and Isolda, as he'd promised. But he'd been willing to betray his King to do so.

"I'll seek out Robert the Bruce. He must be told that Lancaster is no' his ally after all. And he must hear of my betrayal."

"But Ansel…" Her pained eyes met his over John's head. "You didn't tell Clemont aught. Why can't we let it be over, as you said?"

"Because I would have told Clemont everything I kenned if it could have saved ye and John," he said quietly. "Clemont is dead. He cannae report back to Lancaster about yer whereabouts or mine. And I'll make sure Lancaster can never reach ye again. But I must face my King and tell him the truth."

"And then what?" she whispered. "What of our future? What of marriage and a simple life together?"

The fear in her voice cut him as surely as a sword. If he could have, Ansel would have swung Isolda and John onto Eachann's back and guided them deep into the Highlands—somewhere no one would find them. Some place where the outside world would never encroach on their dreamed-of life.

Ansel cupped her cheek in his hand. Bloodied though he was, she leaned into him as if she drew strength from his touch.

"I swore to ye that I would keep ye safe, and I will keep that promise," he vowed. "Lancaster and his men will never get near ye or John again."

His heart twisted painfully in his chest. "But I must live up to how ye see me—I must be a man of honor," he said, his throat tight. "Which means I must face the King."

Chapter Thirty-Seven

Ansel's gaze trailed over the herd of shaggy Highland cows as they ambled down from the rolling hillsides where they had grazed for the summer. Herdsmen and their dogs guided the great beasts toward lower ground for their winter pasture in observance of Samhain.

Aye, today was a fitting day to meet with the King of Scotland, for Samhain was the time when the living met the dead.

Dread tightened into a knot in Ansel's belly. He was little more than a dead man walking this day, like a ghost freed only briefly from its world.

"There it is!"

Niall's excited cry broke through Ansel's morbid thoughts. Ansel dragged his gaze away from the cows dotting the hillsides to follow Niall's pointing finger.

Roslin Castle emerged from behind a grass-covered crest. It sat at the end of a long strip of land that grew increasingly narrow until the terrain fell away on three sides. The castle perched majestically at the end of the narrow spit of land, with the North Sea crashing against the cliffs far below.

Isolda, who rode Eachann with John nestled before her in the saddle, gasped as her eyes fell on the castle. Though Ansel was always struck by Roslin's impressive location from a defensive standpoint—only the narrow band of land provided access to the castle, which was blocked by a thick stone curtain wall—he'd seen it enough to forget just how strikingly beautiful it was.

Low clouds clung to the top of the four towers within the castle's walls, and the Sinclair clan crest and colors flapped in a breeze rippling off the surrounding sea. Gulls swooped and glided around the tower, their cries mingling with the crash of the ocean on the beach below.

"It is…beautiful," Isolda breathed.

Ansel looked up at her from where he walked alongside Eachann. His eyes traced the delicate line of her jaw, her softly parted lips, and the wonder in her pale green gaze.

"Aye," he said, his heart pinching.

"Come on, Papa," Niall said, his young voice tight with excitement. "Let's race there."

Niall squirmed between Meredith and Fiona atop their horse, at last sliding down to where Burke walked next to the animal.

"And what of yer sister and yer cousin John, Niall?" Burke asked, a gentle reproof in his voice.

Niall blinked, his dark blue eyes considering for a moment. "Perhaps I should take them into the castle instead of race with ye, Papa."

"Good lad," Burke said, giving his son a warm smile.

"Mind yer sister, Niall," Meredith said, handing Fiona to Burke, who set the girl on her feet.

"Yes, Mama. Come on, John."

Niall looked expectantly at John where he sat tucked against Isolda.

"Do you wish to run along and play with the other children, John?" Isolda asked softly.

Since they had rescued John from Clemont a sennight ago, John had been quiet and had stayed close to either Isolda or Ansel. But in the last few days, he'd played shyly with Niall and Fiona, even venturing out onto the grass surrounding Brora Tower.

John nodded, a soft smile coming to his mouth.

"Aye, Mama," he said, though before he slipped from Eachann's back, he gave Isolda a fierce little hug.

As the children darted toward the castle, shrieking in excitement for the Samhain festivities that awaited them there, Burke turned to Ansel.

"Are ye sure ye dinnae wish to tell me what is so clearly weighing on yer shoulders before ye speak to the Bruce?"

As it had for the last sennight, shame carved into Ansel's chest.

When Ansel, Isolda, and John had returned to Brora Tower from the abbey, they'd been bloodied, shocked, and exhausted. Ansel had explained a simplified version of the course of events to put Meredith and

Burke at ease, but he hadn't spoken of his betrayal of the King.

"Nay," Ansel said, resignation dampening the heat of dishonor in his veins.

"Ye ken I'll have yer back no matter what ye have to say to the Bruce, dinnae ye?"

Ansel's throat tightened with emotion. "Thank ye, Burke," he said. "Ye are a better brother-in-law than a man could ever hope to gain."

Burke nodded his acceptance, but Ansel could feel Meredith's questioning eyes lingering on him. Blessedly, she didn't push him for more of an explanation for his solemn behavior over the last sennight.

It had been a stroke of luck—or fate—that only a day after they'd returned to Brora from the abbey, Burke had gotten word that a meeting between the Bruce's most senior warriors and advisors was to take place at Roslin Castle in a sennight. The Bruce himself was even making the trek from the Borderlands under the pretense of celebrating Samhain with Burke's cousin, Laird Robert Sinclair, one of the King's closest allies and supporters.

It was the perfect opportunity for Ansel to share all that he had learned about Lancaster's deception with the Bruce's inner circle—and to confess to the Bruce in private that he had been willing to betray him. Though Ansel hadn't expected to be handed the chance to speak to the King a mere sennight after killing Clemont, he was grateful, in a way, that the waiting would be over.

Now he was headed to his fate—whatever fate the Bruce deemed suitable for a man who would have betrayed him.

As they approached the castle wall, Sinclair guards eyed them carefully from the stone parapets. Ansel took hold of Eachann's bridle and halted him just before the gates. Burke did the same with Meredith's horse as they waited for approval from the guards.

The gates and portcullis stood open, and the sounds of merriment poured forth from the castle's yard, but Roslin was still a formidable stronghold. It was Laird Sinclair's clan seat. Even for a merry fall festival, the guards had to be ever vigilant—especially with the King in attendance.

Though the guards' gazes snagged on Ansel's Sutherland plaid, they quickly recognized Burke as Laird Robert's cousin. Once they were waved through, they crossed under the raised portcullis and into the crowded yard.

Since dusk was fast approaching, a great bonfire had already been lit in the middle of the yard. Children and young people from the nearby village stood eagerly around the fire. Some were carving their initials into chestnuts and placing them on the fire's outskirts. It was said that if a young lad and lass's chestnut shells burst at the same time, they were fated to be wed.

As they wended their way toward the stables, Ansel caught sight of a trough of water filled with apples.

Young and old alike bobbed their heads into the trough. One lucky woman came up with an apple between her teeth, which would grant her good luck for the long winter ahead. Ansel noticed John, Niall, and Fiona waiting excitedly next to the trough for their chance to capture a lucky apple of their own.

The merriment filling Roslin's yard only blackened Ansel's mood further, however. Aye, Samhain was a time to celebrate the end of summer and the start to the darker days of winter. It was meant to be a joyful festival, one of games and pranks.

Yet Ansel could not forget that it was also a time when the border between this world and the next blurred. It was painfully fitting, since the King could decide to go as far as hanging Ansel for treason for what he'd offered to Clemont.

He helped Isolda down from Eachann's back and handed the reins to a stable lad, his heart heavy. Her gaze lingered on him, an unspoken question in her pale green eyes, but he could not face it now.

"Ah, I see my cousin Robert," Burke said as he lifted Meredith from her horse. "He has likely already gathered the men. I'm sure they will be most eager to hear all ye've learned about Lancaster."

There would be no more waiting, no more worrying over his fate now. Ansel would tell the Bruce everything—and accept whatever consequence he had earned.

"Robert!" Burke called across the crowded yard.

The Samhain revelers parted as the Sinclair Laird, his lady wife on his arm and a girl a year or so older than John on his other side, strolled through the merriment.

Robert Sinclair's ice-blue gaze landed on Burke, and a broad smile spread across his face. When he reached them, Robert pounded Burke on the back.

"It is good to see ye, cousin!" he said, then offered Meredith a bow.

Lady Alwin, Robert's wife, set aside formalities and embraced Meredith in a tight hug.

"Where are Niall and Fiona?" Alwin asked as she pulled back from Meredith.

Isolda inhaled sharply at Ansel's side. Ansel had known Alwin long enough to forget how strange it was to hear an English accent on the tongue of a Highland Laird's wife. It was likely all the more shocking to Isolda, whose own accent had been a source of trouble on their journey northward.

Alwin's gaze shifted at Isolda's gasp. Her blue-gray eyes widened slightly as she took in Isolda standing close to Ansel's side, but then they began to dance with mischief.

"How good it is to see you again, Ansel," she said smoothly. "And who is this lovely young woman with you?"

"Laird Robert, Lady Alwin," Ansel said stiffly, "May I present Lady Isolda of Embleton."

Isolda bobbed a curtsy, though Ansel didn't miss the fact that her eyes remained rounded, presumably over the realization that Alwin was English.

"Embleton?" Alwin said. "I'm not familiar with the place."

"It is a small town in Northumbria," Isolda said quickly. That drew a raised eyebrow from Robert and a curious smile from Alwin.

"Perhaps ye can explain things to Lady Alwin," Ansel said to Isolda. "Robert, I have a most pressing issue to share with the King and the rest of the men."

Meredith linked arms with Isolda, patting her reassuringly. "Come, Isolda," she said. "Jossalyn and Rona will be so eager to meet ye."

"My sisters-in-law," Alwin said by way of explanation, motioning toward the young girl at Robert's side. "Go along with the other children, Jane," she prompted her daughter.

Jane darted off toward the trough of apples, and Alwin took Isolda's other arm, giving her a warm smile.

"I cannot wait to learn more about the woman who is clearly so…special to our dear Ansel," Alwin said kindly, guiding the other two women away.

"She'll be well looked after," Robert said, turning to Ansel. "I must admit, ye've tickled my curiosity."

"Are the men already gathered?" Ansel asked, dodging Robert's unspoken question about Isolda.

"Aye," Robert said, lifting a dark brow at him. "They are all in the solar. We shouldnae keep them waiting."

"Good," Ansel said through clenched teeth.

Again, Robert shot him a curious look, but only nodded his acquiescence. He motioned for Burke and Ansel to follow him as he strode toward the castle's northwest tower.

By the time Ansel had reached the top of the winding stairs that led to the solar, dread sat like iron in his belly.

He dragged in a fortifying breath as Robert and Burke stepped into the solar. It was time to face the men inside—men to whom he would trust his life, men whom he respected, men with whom he'd fought for Scotland's freedom. Men he'd been willing to betray.

Clenching his fists at his side, he stepped into the room, ready to meet his fate.

Chapter Thirty-Eight

The well-appointed solar was nigh bursting with towering Highland warriors.

Laird Robert and Burke approached Angus MacLeod, the aging red-headed giant who was never far from the Bruce's side. Garrick Sinclair was locked in conversation with his younger brother, Daniel, their dark heads close together.

Ansel's gaze landed on his closest companions in the Bruce's army. Finn Sutherland, a distant clan relation of Ansel's, and Colin McKay, their compatriot despite clan rivalries, were talking quietly with Will Sinclair, Laird Robert's youngest cousin and Daniel Sinclair's former ward.

And seated behind Laird Robert's large wooden desk was the King of Scotland himself, Robert the Bruce.

"Ansel!" The King boomed, standing from his chair. "It is good to see ye."

Ansel swallowed the tightness in his throat and strode across the room. Several of the others nodded to him and smiled, but Ansel kept his gaze focused on the King. He delivered a stiff bow, though when he straightened, the Bruce extended an arm to him with a smile.

"I am glad to have the opportunity to speak with ye in person about the mission Garrick delivered to ye last month," the Bruce said. "Yer service goes a long way in these uncertain times."

"I'd ask ye to hold back yer praise until ye hear what I have to say, sire," Ansel said.

The Bruce's russet brows drew together at Ansel's clipped tone. Though the King of Scotland was a powerful and awe-inspiring leader, among this most trusted circle of men, he preferred to be more informal. Yet Ansel couldn't find the nerve to be casual as he delivered the information he bore.

"Verra well," the Bruce said, still eyeing Ansel. "What news, man?"

"Ye all may wish to sit for this," Ansel began, turning to the others in the room.

The eight warriors pulled heavy wooden chairs away from the tapestry-hung walls and formed a little circle in front of Ansel and the Bruce.

As the Bruce took his seat behind the large desk once more, Ansel cleared his throat.

"As most of ye likely ken, the King has been in contact with the Earl of Lancaster," Ansel began.

He quickly explained the Bruce's mission, for Garrick and the others who worked closely with the King already knew of his assignment. But when he told them that the man he'd been sent to protect was in fact a mere lad, and that Isolda was the lad's mother, the eyes fixed on him sharpened.

Ansel explained that Isolda had sent John into hiding, fearing that Edward sought to harm him. He told of the attack by Clemont and his men on Dunstanburgh, and their flight into the Scottish Lowlands, and eventually the Highlands.

When he reached the point in his tale when Clemont struck at the abbey, several chairs creaked as the men leaned forward.

"Clemont told me who hired him to kill John and Isolda," Ansel said. He dragged in a breath. "It was Lancaster."

"What?" The Bruce jerked to his feet, sending his chair scraping loudly across the stone floor.

"It makes sense if ye consider it," Ansel said. "Lancaster is angling for the English throne. How many times has an inconvenient bastard thrown an entire line of succession into question—or led a revolution against those in power?"

"And ye believe the word of a bounty hunter?" Laird Robert said sharply, his brows lowered.

"Aye, for Clemont had no reason to lie. He was naught more than a hired hand. If he had any loyalty at all, it didnae lie with Lancaster—it was with the man he said employed him, the man Lancaster likely contacted to arrange for an assassin."

Muttered curses filled the room.

"Lancaster thought to position himself as an ally to

the Scottish cause for freedom," Ansel said when the solar fell quiet once more. "But he used ye, Robert." He turned to the Bruce, holding his gaze. "The alliance was a façade, at least in part to rid himself of his son—and he sought to conveniently deprive ye of a trusted man in the process."

The Bruce dragged a hand through his red-brown hair, which had long ago turned gray at the temples.

"And though Clemont gave me no indication of who his real employer was, or how large an organization he was part of, Clemont was undeniably skilled. He claimed to have access to trained warriors as well," Ansel went on grimly. "This organization of bounty hunters could be just as dangerous as Lancaster, for any Englishman with enough coin could hire an assassin of his own to hunt down Scots involved in the cause."

Ansel's gaze locked with Garrick's. "That is likely what happened to Sir William of Airth, God rest his soul."

The room fell into a somber silence for a long moment. The Lowland lord's dismembered remains had been enough to motivate Ansel's mission a month ago. Now it was clear that they all stood against even larger and more powerful forces than they'd first suspected.

"So ye are saying that no' only is Lancaster a wolf in sheep's wool, but that he is in league with some unknown force of trained assassins who can be bought to target anyone if the price is right?" Garrick asked, leaning forward intently.

The Bruce slowly lowered himself into his chair, his mouth tight.

"Aye," Ansel replied at last.

"This is what the war for freedom has become," the King said quietly. "The English willnae likely meet us on the open battlefield again. Yet that doesnae mean we have won."

Daniel, the youngest of the Sinclair brothers, had remained silent, but now he spoke up. "How are we to face such warfare? How shall we defeat an unknown enemy, one who will strike in the night at soft targets—individual men, and even women and children—rather than wage war soldier against soldier?"

Garrick rose slowly to his feet. He had targeted countless enemies of Scotland for nearly a decade, his bow known to be among the deadliest in all of England or Scotland.

"We'll meet this new war as we always have, Brother," he said, though his gaze brushed across all those gathered in the solar. "Our own way."

"And what is that way, lad?" Angus, the old red bear, said, crossing his arms over his barrel chest.

Garrick swung around to face Ansel once again.

"Ansel managed to keep Lancaster's son alive and kill Lancaster's hired man," Garrick said. "Even no' kenning what he was up against."

Ansel swallowed the denial that rose in his throat.

Aye, he'd saved Isolda and John and defeated Clemont, but at the cost of his honor. He would tell his King the truth, but he would wait until they were alone to do so.

"What are ye saying, Garrick?" the Bruce interjected.

"That if the English wish to carry on this war behind closed doors and under cover of night, perhaps we should do the same," Garrick said. "We've never been afraid to set our own rules of battle."

Several of the men nodded slowly. Other than Will Sinclair, who had been too young to fight in the early years of the rebellion, they'd all learned the Bruce's unusual tactics of striking the English when they least expected it and avoiding battlefields where the Scots had been outnumbered and out-supplied. In that way, they had chipped away at the seemingly undefeatable English army until Bannockburn had seemed to turn the tide in the Scots' favor at last.

"If the English want to strike at individual marks and hire assassins rather than soldiers," Garrick went on, "then perhaps we should form a group of our own—a force of men who can protect those targeted by the English."

Murmurs once again broke out among the men, but this time the tinge of excitement was unmistakable in their voices. Ansel, too, felt an unbidden swell of hope at Garrick's suggestion. This new kind of warfare—of slinking and lurking, never striking in broad daylight—was infuriating to the men of action who filled the solar. But perhaps what Garrick spoke of was a way to take charge of the secret war that still raged between the English and the Scottish.

"Ye mean a corps of bodyguards?" Angus asked, raising a shaggy red brow.

"Aye, why not?" Burke replied, nodding to Garrick.

Angus huffed. "I dinnae ken about ye lads, but I am too old for all that."

"I hate to throw cold water on ye all," Laird Robert added. "But most of us are family men now, with responsibilities to our own people and clans in addition to our duty to Scotland and our King." To soften his words, Robert lowered his head to the Bruce.

"Are ye saying ye're too old as well? Ye havenae even cracked two score yet, *elder* brother," Daniel shot back at Robert, drawing chuckles from the others.

Yet Daniel sobered with the others as they considered Garrick's words. As Laird Robert had said, many of the men present, including Daniel, were married and fiercely devoted to their families. Like the Bruce, some had gray hair dusting their temples.

Finn, whose features were darkened with his usual stormy scowl, stood slowly. "I dinnae have a family beyond the one I have found in the Bruce's camp," he said slowly. "I would like to be a part of such a corps if it means thwarting the English and protecting the innocent in the name of the King and freedom."

The room suddenly grew sober at Finn's words.

"As would I," Colin said, standing alongside Finn. Colin crossed his arms over his broad chest, bobbing his sandy head to the Bruce.

"And I," Will Sinclair added, rising to his feet with the other two. Will was barely more than a score in years, yet he'd earned respect among the Bruce's men for fighting valiantly at Bannockburn.

"Ye lads will require training," Laird Robert said, eyeing them. "This is a threat ye've never faced before."

"I can help with that," Garrick said.

Daniel stood and clapped Burke on the back. "We all will."

Once again, the Bruce rose to his feet behind the large wooden desk. The gathered men fell silent as all eyes locked on the Bruce.

"Ye all make me proud to call myself yer King," he said, his voice low. "A corps of bodyguards to thwart England's attempts to conduct covert war through targeted hits, eh?" He rubbed his reddish beard, a little smile coming to his mouth. "Aye," he said at last. "That will do."

"We'll need more men, of course," Laird Robert said. "A few well-chosen warriors we can trust. But that shouldnae stop us from going forward with training for ye." He nodded to the three who had volunteered.

"Let us reconvene tomorrow to hammer out the details," the Bruce said. "For now, the Samhain bonfire awaits. This is a night to celebrate, indeed."

As the men began filing out of the solar, Ansel turned to the Bruce.

"There is one more thing, sire," he said, keeping his voice low. "Something I must tell ye—in private."

The Bruce motioned for Ansel to sit again, but he declined. Nay, he would meet his fate on his feet.

Ansel swallowed hard. The time had come to confess the truth.

Chapter Thirty-Nine

"I betrayed ye, sire."

The Bruce's eyes narrowed on Ansel. "What do ye mean?"

Ansel dragged in a breath. "When Clemont held John at knifepoint and was about to take Isolda, I…" Shame burned in his throat, but he forced the words out. "I offered him information on ye and the Scottish army."

"What?" The Bruce's voice was suddenly sharp, his eyes piercing Ansel.

Ansel refused to shrink back under his King's strident stare.

"I was desperate. I was attempting to stall Clemont, to find a way to save Isolda and John. I offered to tell him aught that would appease Lancaster in the stead of Isolda and John's lives."

The Bruce scrubbed a hand over his eyes and dropped down into his chair.

"Let me guess—ye are in love with the woman."

Surprise crashed through Ansel. "I—we…" He took another deep breath. "Aye, sire. How did ye ken?"

"Hell, man, it's in yer voice when ye say her name.

It's in yer eyes when ye speak of her." The Bruce dropped his hand from over his eyes and looked hard at Ansel. "Tell me all of it. What did ye reveal to Clemont?"

"Naught," Ansel replied. "I only offered."

"What stopped ye?"

Pride for the woman he loved mingled with his own shameful behavior in his chest.

"Isolda. She reminded me that I am a man of honor, that I couldnae betray ye." Ansel shook his head as if to clear the swell of love even the mere thought of Isolda prompted in him. "But I offered, nonetheless."

"I cannae fault ye for falling in love with such a woman," the Bruce said, his eyes flashing with something akin to respect. "From all ye've said of her, she sounds truly remarkable."

The King's gaze grew hard once again, though. "What would ye have done if ye had told Clemont my secrets? Would ye have let him report back to Lancaster?"

"Nay, sire!" Ansel blurted before he could rein in his tone.

"Would ye have let him live?"

"Nay. I would have torn him limb from limb—no' just for Isolda and John, but for working against Scotland. I'd do the same to Lancaster, too, if I ever thought I'd get close enough to the bastard."

"But ye willnae ever get close to him."

Dread stabbed Ansel's stomach. "Aye, sire. I accept

whatever consequence ye would give me—even if ye wish to take my life."

The Bruce leaned forward, placing his elbows on the wooden desk. "Nay, man. Ye willnae be getting close to Lancaster because Isolda and John still need ye—and because *I* still need ye."

A seed of hope budded in him, but Ansel refused to trust it just yet.

"What do ye mean, sire?"

The King exhaled slowly through his nose. "I gave ye a mission to protect Lancaster's son, Ansel. I thought such a task would help the cause of Scottish freedom by giving us an ally in Lancaster. As ye've discovered, I was wrong. But that doesnae change yer mission. Lancaster wanted Isolda and John dead, and by thwarting him, we are advancing Scotland's cause."

Ansel's mouth fell open, but he was too dumbstruck to care. "But, Robert, I betrayed ye. I put my heart ahead of my country and King."

"Hear me well, Ansel," the Bruce said, narrowing his eyes on him. "Ye are one of the most loyal men I've ever known. Aye, I am no' pleased to hear that ye offered Clemont information, but ye did so in the service of the mission I charged ye with—to protect Lancaster's son."

"What are ye saying?" Ansel breathed.

"That I still need ye. I wouldnae trust any other man to protect John and Isolda as well as ye will—call it the upshot of falling in love on yer mission. Ye will see to their safety, for as long as they are alive and well, we have a weapon to use against Lancaster."

Involuntarily, Ansel stiffened. "Ye would use them as pawns in this war? Ye would wield them against Lancaster in the future?"

The Bruce considered Ansel for a long moment. "Ye are lucky that ye are not the King of Scotland, Ansel," he said quietly. "For I dinnae believe ye would have the stomach for it. It is no' my aim to ever have to use an innocent woman and child thusly, however, I willnae deny that I am no' above using every advantage available to me to secure Scotland's freedom. And I expect ye no' to question me again."

The last was spoken with a subtle edge, reminding Ansel of just how precarious a line he had walked.

"I willnae," he vowed, dropping to one knee before the Bruce. "Ye'll never have reason to doubt my loyalty again."

The Bruce grunted. "Rise," he said, though the tension swiftly drained from his weathered face, to be replaced with an ease that Ansel had rarely seen in the years since the Bruce had crowned himself King of Scotland.

"I suppose ye wish to marry the lass," the Bruce said, a grin playing faintly behind his russet beard.

"Aye, sire," Ansel said, quickly straightening.

"Samhain is as good a time as any. What would ye say to having the King attend yer wedding?"

Ansel felt a smile break across his face even as his

heart leapt into his throat.

"I'll have to ask my bride, but I imagine she'll have no objections."

"Good." The Bruce leaned back in his chair, crossing his arms over his chest. "We'll get to that happy occasion shortly. But before then, I have another task for ye."

◆ ◆ ◆

Night had fallen in earnest several hours ago, yet still Ansel did not appear.

Isolda gnawed her thumbnail distractedly, her eyes tugging relentlessly toward the tower Ansel had entered earlier that evening. Several large Highlanders had emerged just as the ale was being passed around to the Samhain revelers, yet Ansel remained absent.

Meredith caught Isolda's hand and gently pulled the nail away from her teeth.

"Dinnae fash yerself, Isolda," she said softly. "The King likely just wanted to take extra time to thank Ansel for doing his duty and protecting ye and John."

Isolda sank her teeth into her lip. Meredith didn't know that Ansel thought himself disloyal, and that he was prepared to face the King's punishment. But Isolda did. No matter what she'd said, no matter how she'd tried to convince him over the last sennight that he was still a good man, he would only shake his dark head and turn away in shame.

"Come, enjoy the celebration with the others,"

Meredith said, though concern creased her brow.

Despite the merriment all around, Isolda simply couldn't put aside her worry. Even when Alwin, Rona, and Jossalyn had kindly tried alongside Meredith to draw her out of her dark mood, she had excused herself as politely as she could and stood in the shadows watching the northwest tower.

"Forgive me, Meredith, but—"

"Ah, there he is!" Meredith interrupted, her gaze fixing beyond Isolda on the tower.

Isolda whirled around to find Ansel striding toward her stiffly. His face was drawn taut and his eyes were fatigued as they locked onto her.

Dread coiled in her belly. She sent up a silent prayer, her heart hammering against her ribcage as she waited for him to reach her.

"It seems ye two would like yer privacy," Meredith said, her astute eyes shifting between Ansel and Isolda. "I'll be with the others." She slipped toward the bonfire, where Burke and several other towering Highland warriors stood with the women Isolda had met earlier.

"What did he say?" she breathed when Ansel at last halted before her. "What did he decide?"

Ansel cracked a wearied smile. "I'm sorry to have kept ye waiting and worrying," he said. "All is well. In fact, all is better than well."

Isolda let out a shaky breath as relief flooded her.

"All is forgiven," he went on. "The Bruce wishes for me to continue to watch over ye and John."

He might have had more to say, but Isolda launched herself into his arms and claimed his mouth in a kiss. When at last she released him, they were both breathless.

"Then it is truly over? We may live our lives in peace?"

"Aye, though we won't be receiving a plot of land from Kenneth Sutherland."

She felt her smile falter at that. "Where are we to live, then?"

"The Bruce thought it safer for us to remain closer to Roslin Castle. If Lancaster wishes to reach ye again, he'll have to go through all of Scotland to get to this remote corner of the Highlands. Laird Robert Sinclair has agreed and has a cottage in mind no' far from here."

A swell of gratitude and joy replaced the trickle of doubt from a moment before, nigh choking her. She hugged Ansel hard for another long moment, relishing in the feel of his strong, hard arms engulfing her.

But then uncertainty fluttered in the back of her mind again.

"You said if Lancaster wishes to reach us again. Do you think he will keep searching for us, hunting us?"

Ansel's hard features softened in the flickering light from the bonfire. "Nay, lass. I truly believe it is over."

"But…but how do you know?"

He gently tucked a strand of hair behind her ear. "The reason I am so late in joining ye for the festivities is because the Bruce wanted me to aid him in crafting a letter to Lancaster."

Surprise slashed through her. "King Robert is still willing to maintain their alliance?"

"Nay—or no' exactly. I think the Bruce is sore over the fact that he placed his trust in Lancaster and ended up getting played in the Earl's scheme like the rest of us. However, he is willing to let Lancaster think that he still has an ally in the Scots. If he ever seeks the Bruce's aid again, Lancaster will be sorely surprised to learn that he has been played in return."

Isolda shook her head slowly. She would be grateful to escape such political maneuverings shortly and slip into a simpler life. "And what of us? Will Lancaster know that we are still alive and hiding in Scotland?"

Ansel's lips curled into a roguish smile. "The missive informs Lancaster that the bodyguard he hired was found dead, but no signs remain of the boy he sought or his mother. Lancaster will surmise soon enough that Clemont has been lost as well, for his bounty hunter will never report back to him again."

The smile widened on Ansel's face as he went on. "The Bruce promised in the missive to continue the search for Lancaster's son, but the prospects arenae promising. This is the Highlands, after all. All manner of things can befall a man, and he is never seen again."

Tears of happiness brimmed in Isolda's eyes, blurring Ansel's handsome face. At last, it was over. She and John were safe.

"And speaking of losing oneself in the Highlands," Ansel said, "the King has instructed us to live a quiet life as man and wife to avoid notice. In fact, he insists that we wed as soon as possible. What say ye, my lady?"

The tears began streaming down her cheeks in earnest as she shook with laughter.

"I say aye."

Epilogue

"It's snowing!"

Isolda was jerked from a peaceful sleep by John's shrill cry.

"Come look, Mama, it's snowing!" he shouted again.

"Does it never snow in England?" Ansel groaned, rolling over and draping an arm around Isolda's waist.

"Not like this, it doesn't," she replied, allowing Ansel to pull her deeper into the warm cocoon of their bed.

But John would not be dissuaded. "Mama!" he shouted again. "When do you think it will stop?"

Ansel finally poked his head out of the blankets. He glanced at John, who stood in front of the window in the little private bedchamber attached to the back of their cottage. The shutters were thrown back and snow flurries swirled around John's dark head.

"Judging by the clouds coming in from the west, I doubt it will stop anytime soon, lad," Ansel said, winking at John. The boy squealed with glee and clapped his hands.

"Close the shutters, please!" Isolda called, but John

had already dashed from the bedchamber and to the cottage's door, where his woolen cloak hung on a peg.

"May I go out, please, Mama? Ansel?"

"Wait for us, my dove," Isolda called through the bedchamber's half-closed door. From where she lay, she could see John swing his cloak over his slim shoulders. He practically pranced in front of the door as he waited for them to join him.

"I'll take him with me to Roslin Castle today, if ye like," Ansel said, throwing back the blankets and slipping from the bed. "He can play with the other children there."

Warmth surged in Isolda's heart. How she loved this man, who had embraced her son as his own.

"Aye, if you are sure he will not be in your way."

"Nay, of course no'," Ansel replied, quickly clicking the shutters closed against the cold and donning a linen shirt. "I'll just be training the Bruce's corps."

That was how he spent most of his days—training the small, elite handful of men who would serve the King of Scotland as Ansel had: as a bodyguard for those most at risk from an English attack.

To facilitate his new role alongside Laird Robert Sinclair, Burke, and the other warriors who occasionally visited Roslin to train the Bruce's men, most days he took Eachann on a short ride from their little cottage to the castle. Ansel grumbled almost daily about how absurd it was for a Sutherland to make a home on Sinclair land, but Isolda saw in the sparkle of his chestnut eyes how happy he was with their simple life together.

She watched idly as he pleated his Sutherland plaid around his hips, tossing the extra length of wool over his shoulder.

"You don't think that the weather will hamper the messenger, do you?" she asked as he pulled on his thick winter hose and boots.

Once they'd gotten settled in their new home, Isolda had requested to get word to Mary and Bertram letting them know that they were safe. Ansel had insisted on carefully sending Isolda's letter through several routes to avoid even the slightest chance it could be traced back to them.

The letter she'd sent to York had taken over a month to reach them, according to Mary's responding missive. And of course Mary had followed Isolda's example, using code names and no identifying information. But Isolda was relieved to learn, almost three months after their emotional farewell, that Bertram was recovering nicely and that both he and Mary were safe and well in York.

Only a few days ago, she'd sent another missive through Ansel's elaborate channels, but from the glimpse she'd had out the window, the snow already lay thick, with the promise of more on the way, which would undoubtedly hamper the messenger.

"Nay, I think no'." Ansel said. "The messenger willnae mind a wee bit of this white stuff. He's a Highlander after all."

She snorted and he shot her a roguish grin, but then he let his lips fall. "The snow will keep ye indoors all day, though. Will ye be all right here by yerself?" he asked softly.

She lifted an eyebrow at him. "Mayhap I will join you in venturing to the castle as well. Lady Alwin told me on our last visit that she has recently purchased some fabrics and wants my opinion on them."

"Och, but if ye go to the castle, I cannae imagine ye lying in our bed as ye are now, hair tousled and cheeks glowing from the loving I gave ye last night." Ansel's voice dropped to barely more than a whisper, but even still heat crept up her neck at his words.

"I suppose ye'll just have to find a way to lure me back to bed this evening," she shot back, her saucy words undercut by the blush she felt rising to her cheeks.

Ansel's rich chuckle reverberated through their bedchamber. "Is that a challenge, my lady wife?" he asked, cocking a dark brow at her.

"Aye, husband," she said, her own husky laugh joining his. "A challenge I'm sure you'll gladly meet."

The End

Author's Note

Although this is a work of fiction, one of the great joys of writing historical romance is weaving a fictional love story into the rich tapestry of people, places, and events that the historical record gives us. As with every book I write, I got to learn so much through research, and I just can't help but share some of it with you!

Perhaps the most fascinating aspect of research for this story came from a character whom we hardly saw—Thomas, Earl of Lancaster. Lancaster was the first cousin of King Edward II. He boasted numerous titles, including the Earldoms of Lancaster, Leicester, Derby, Lincoln, and Salisbury, as well as a collection of Baronies and Lordships. At the height of his power, he was thought to be the second richest man in all of England, second only to his cousin, the King.

Although Lancaster fought alongside King Edward I ("Longshanks") against Scotland, when Edward II came to power, a deep rift opened between the two cousins. Lancaster wasn't pleased with how much money, resources, and time Edward was spending battling the Scottish, especially after the Battle of Bannockburn in June of 1314, which was an utter disaster from an English point of view.

Leading up to Bannockburn, Lancaster formed a group of nobles who attempted to restrict the King's power. Called the Ordinances of 1311, the rules it laid out attempted to establish a parliament of nobles who would have the power to circumvent Edward and restrict his ability to make decisions and spend money.

The English army's loss at Bannockburn was seen as Edward's ultimate failure. Although many historians estimate that the English outnumbered the Scots two to one, King Robert the Bruce led the Scots to what would become a decisive and pivotal victory over Edward, who had to flee from the battlefield to save his own life. (And a quick side-note on Sir William of Airth, who dies a terrible death in my story a few months after Bannockburn—he was actually killed on the first night of fighting at Bannockburn while guarding the baggage train, so at least he didn't have quite as bad an end as I fictionalized for him here.)

After Bannockburn, Lancaster all but became the King, coercing Edward to cede power and allow Lancaster to rule in his stead. Without spoiling too much of the historical details (because Lancaster may make appearances in later books in my Highland Bodyguards series!), Lancaster was no more effective than Edward in quelling the Scottish rebellion, and he met a decidedly unhappy end in 1322.

Lancaster did indeed hold many powerful fortresses throughout England, including Clitheroe Castle, where he meets (the fictional) Isolda in my story. Interestingly, Clitheroe Castle dates back to the era of the Norman conquest, and it is the second-smallest stone-built keep in all of England. Because it was so small, Lancaster and others likely added other buildings, such as a great hall, outside the curtain wall to keep up to date with all the modern conveniences and accoutrement of fourteenth-century castle living.

Lancaster is also responsible for the creation of Dunstanburgh Castle. He commissioned the construction of Dunstanburgh, which sits on the North Sea coast in Northumberland, in 1313.

Part display of Lancaster's power and wealth, part defensive stronghold against Edward II's reach, Dunstanburgh is situated on a promontory that juts into the North Sea, thus giving it only one side as a point of entry. That side boasts three artificial lakes to protect the castle and a curtain wall which encloses almost ten acres of land, making it the largest castle in Northumberland. Several towers were built to provide lookout points and protection for the castle, including the formidable three-story gatehouse tower.

Although the town of Embleton existed before the castle was built, Lancaster may have had plans to relocate the town's population to have Embleton serve as the castle's nearest village. Some of Embleton's villagers likely helped dig the artificial lakes and erect the curtain wall as part of their feudal duties to Lancaster. Master Elias, the Master Mason of the project, was possibly Elias de Burton, a mason who had been previously involved in the construction of Conwy Castle in North Wales.

Lancaster may have only ever visited the castle once or twice in his lifetime. It was the work of my imagination to have Lancaster send his former mistress and their illegitimate son there to keep them out of sight in the remote, unfinished castle. However, Lancaster did have one and possibly two bastard children. He was bound in an unhappy and childless marriage, which ended in divorce. Several years after Lancaster's death, though, accounts of an illegitimate son named John began appearing. John became a scholar of theology (which is why I placed him in the care of monks in my fictional representation of his childhood).

As if the existence of an illegitimate son named John who became a scholar of theology isn't enough of a juicy historical tidbit, here's another: Lancaster was indeed in communication with Robert the Bruce and other Scottish freedom fighters. He even gave himself his own code name: King Arthur. He fancied himself to be building a glorious kingdom, with Dunstanburgh as Camelot. All he had to do was play the Scots against Edward to claim the English throne for himself. Unfortunately for him, those treasonous letters to the Scots in which he called himself Arthur were used against him when his fate took a turn in 1322.

But let us set aside our dear old Earl of Lancaster for now. There are several other historical (and nonhistorical) notes worth pointing out.

Though I mentioned Sir Philip Mowbray and Stirling Castle only obliquely in this story, the history of both is fascinating. Stirling changed hands between the Scottish and the English several times during the Wars of Independence. Mowbray was a Scottish-born gentleman, but he held Stirling Castle as its Governor on behalf of the English before the Battle of Bannockburn. Mowbray switched his allegiance from the English to the Scottish side, and after the battle, he was placed in charge of the castle briefly once more. However, Robert the Bruce ordered Stirling to be slighted, meaning several of its defenses were torn down or destroyed so that it could never be recaptured by the English and used against the Scottish in warfare again.

As I explained in my note after Highlander's Return (The Sinclair Brothers Trilogy, Book 2.5), which is Burke and Meredith's love story, Brora Tower is an invention of my imagination, though Brora is a real place. As I have cast it, the fictitious Brora Tower is about ten miles inland of the (very real) Dunrobin Castle, which served as the Sutherland clan seat for centuries. Roslin Castle is also fictitious, though the Sinclair clan did make their home in the farthest northeast corner of the Highlands.

Fearn Abbey, where Ansel and Isolda travelled to recover John, still stands today. It is located near Cadboll, not far from Dunrobin and Brora (and for those of you who read Desire's Hostage (Viking Lore, Book 3), you may remember that Cadboll was the site where one of the most famous Pictish carved stones was found around 800 AD). The abbey was originally built in the 1220s about fifteen miles from its current location. It was relocated in the 1230s onto more fertile land so that the monks who lived there could farm.

I took the opportunity to showcase the celebration of Samhain at the end of my story. Samhain was one of four seasonal Celtic festivals, with its particular focus on the end of harvest season and the beginning of darker, colder days. Traditionally, Samhain was celebrated from sunset on October 31 to sunset on November 1, one full day. Festivities included bonfires, apple bobbing, chestnut roasting, pranks, and several other merry activities.

But Samhain was also a reminder of the coming of death. It was thought to be a time of liminality, when the border between the living and the dead blurred. As such, young men would sometimes go door to door, with their faces covered in masks or smeared with ash, asking for offerings to appease the underworldlings they were impersonating. If you haven't guessed yet, this is where the modern celebration of Halloween comes from!

A quick note about my portrayal of Scottish clan plaids worn as kilts. Although scraps of multicolored wool tartan have been discovered in Scotland dating back as early as the third century AD, kilts as we think of them today weren't worn until several centuries after this story takes place. Nevertheless, Scots did wear plaids as shawls or blankets tossed over their shoulders. I decided to include plaid around my male Scottish characters' hips because nothing says Scottish historical romance quite like a man in a kilt!

Thank you for traveling back to Medieval Scotland with me, and I hope Ansel and Isolda's love story has made your heart sing, as it has mine!

Thank you!

Thank you for taking the time to read *The Lady's Protector*! Consider sharing your enjoyment of this book (or my other books) with fellow readers by leaving a review on sites like Amazon and Goodreads. Reviews are much appreciated by readers and authors alike!

I love connecting with readers! For book updates, news on future projects, inspirations, my newsletter sign-up, and more, visit my website at www.EmmaPrinceBooks.com.

You also can join me on Twitter at:
@EmmaPrinceBooks

Or keep up on Facebook at:
facebook.com/EmmaPrinceBooks

Teasers for Emma Prince's Books

THE SINCLAIR BROTHERS TRILOGY:

Go back to where it all began—with Robert and Alwin's story in *Highlander's Ransom*, Book One of the Sinclair Brothers Trilogy. Available now on Amazon!

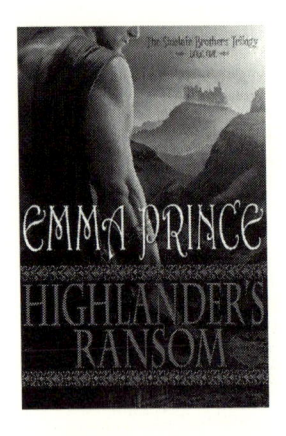

He was out for revenge…

Laird Robert Sinclair would stop at nothing to exact revenge on Lord Raef Warren, the English scoundrel who had brought war to his doorstep and razed his lands and people. Leaving his clan in the Highlands to conduct covert attacks in the Borderlands, Robert lives to be a thorn in Warren's side. So when he finds a beautiful English lass on her way to marry Warren, he whisks her away to the Highlands with a plan to ransom her back to her dastardly fiancé.

She would not be controlled…

Lady Alwin Hewett had no idea when she left her father's manor to marry a man she'd never met that she would instead be kidnapped by a Highland rogue out for vengeance. But she refuses to be a pawn in any man's game. So when she learns that Robert has had them secretly wed, she will stop at nothing to regain her freedom. But her heart may have other plans…

Garrick and Jossalyn's story unfolds in *Highlander's Redemption*, Book Two of the Sinclair Brothers Trilogy. Available now on Amazon!

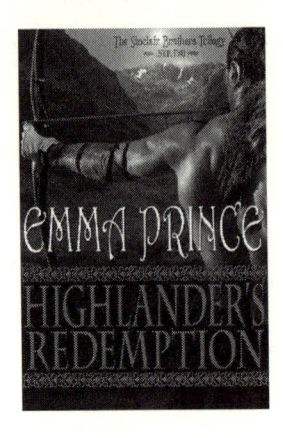

He is on a mission…

Garrick Sinclair, an expert archer and Robert the Bruce's best mercenary, is sent on a covert operation to the Borderlands by his older brother, Laird Robert Sinclair. He never expects to meet the most beautiful woman he's ever seen—who turns out to be the sister of Raef Warren, his family's mortal enemy. Though he knows he shouldn't want her—and doesn't deserve her—can he resist the passion that ignites between them?

She longs for freedom…

Jossalyn Warren is desperate to escape her cruel brother and put her healing skills to use, and perhaps the handsome stranger with a dangerous look about him will be her ticket to a new life. She never imagines that she will be spirited away to Robert the Bruce's secret camp in the Highlands, yet more shocking is the lust the dark warrior stirs in her. But can she heal the invisible scars of a man who believes that he's no hero?

Uncover Burke and Meredith's story in *Highlander's Return*, a Sinclair Brothers Trilogy BONUS novella (Book 2.5). Available now on Amazon!

First love's flame extinguished...

Burke Sinclair and Meredith Sutherland want nothing more than to be married, but ancient clan hostilities tear them apart. When Meredith is forced to marry another to appease her father and secure an alliance, the young lovers think all is lost.

Only to be reignited...

Ten long years of a stifling marriage nearly crush Meredith's spirit. But when her unfeeling husband dies and Burke, now a grown man and a hardened warrior, suddenly reappears in her life, the two may get a second chance at first love—if old blood feuds don't rip them apart once and for all.

Follow the thrilling conclusion of the Sinclair Brothers Trilogy with *Highlander's Reckoning*. Available now on Amazon!

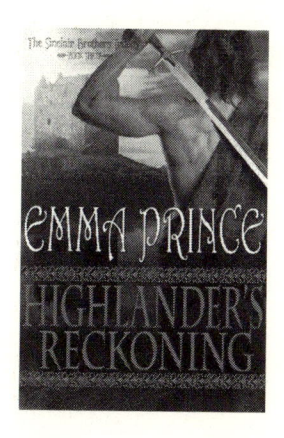

He is forced to marry…

Daniel Sinclair is charged by Robert the Bruce to secure the King's ancestral holding in the Lowlands—and marry the daughter of the castle's keeper to secure a shaky alliance. But the lass's spirit matches her fiery hair, and Daniel quickly realizes that the King's "reward" is more than he bargained for.

She won't submit without a fight…

To protect her secret—and illegal—love of falconry, Rona Kennedy must keep her new husband at arm's length, no matter how much his commanding presence and sinfully handsome face make her knees tremble. But when an all-out war with Raef Warren, the Sinclair clan's greatest enemy, finally erupts, will their growing love be destroyed forever?

VIKING LORE SERIES:

Love brave, bold Vikings as much as Highlanders? Step into the lush, daring world of the Vikings with *Enthralled (Viking Lore, Book 1)*!

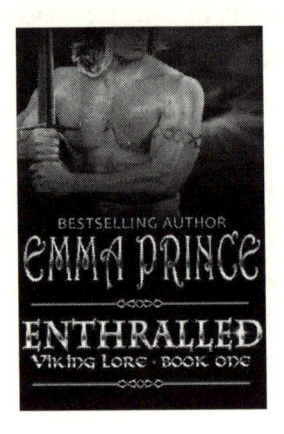

He is bound by honor…

Eirik is eager to plunder the treasures of the fabled lands to the west in order to secure the future of his village. The one thing he swears never to do is claim possession over another human being. But when he journeys across the North Sea to raid the holy houses of Northumbria, he encounters a dark-haired beauty, Laurel, who stirs him like no other. When his cruel cousin tries to take Laurel for himself, Eirik breaks his oath in an attempt to protect her. He claims her as his thrall. But can he claim her heart, or will Laurel fall prey to the devious schemes of his enemies?

She has the heart of a warrior...

Life as an orphan at Whitby Abbey hasn't been easy, but Laurel refuses to be bested by the backbreaking work and lecherous advances she must endure. When Viking raiders storm the abbey and take her captive, her strength may finally fail her—especially when she must face her fear of water at every turn. But under Eirik's gentle protection, she discovers a deeper bravery within herself—and a yearning for her golden-haired captor that she shouldn't harbor. Torn between securing her freedom or giving herself to her Viking master, will fate decide for her—and rip them apart forever?

About the Author

Emma Prince is the Bestselling and Amazon All-Star Author of steamy historical romances jam-packed with adventure, conflict, and of course love!

Emma grew up in drizzly Seattle, but traded her rain boots for sunglasses when she and her husband moved to the eastern slopes of the Sierra Nevada. Emma spent several years in academia, both as a graduate student and an instructor of college-level English and Humanities courses. She always savored her "fun books"—normally historical romances—on breaks or vacations. But as she began looking for the next chapter in her life, she wondered if perhaps her passion could turn into a career. Ever since then, she's been reading and writing books that celebrate happily ever afters!

Visit Emma's website, www.EmmaPrinceBooks.com, for updates on new books, future projects, her newsletter sign-up, book extras, and more!

You can follow Emma on Twitter at:
@EmmaPrinceBooks

Or join her on Facebook at:
www.facebook.com/EmmaPrinceBooks

Made in the USA
Lexington, KY
23 December 2018